Praise for OWN GOALS

'You don't have to be a football fan to enjoy Phil Andrews's racy first novel' *Sunday Telegraph*

'Witty insights into modern football' *Mirror*

'It's the Year of the Bloke – at least in crime fiction – and rookie private investigator Steve Strong is as blokeish as they come. What's New Bloke interested in? Football, sex and money – and strictly in that order ... a modern racy, pacy feel; blokes, jokes and a decent plot ... a smashing debut' *Yorkshire Post*

'A sardonic, witty debut novel ... highly enjoyable, cunningly plotted with an amiable, witty PI and an authentic behind-the-scenes Premier League backdrop for footie fans' *Publishing News*

About the author

Phil Andrews is an award-winning sports journalist. *Own Goals* is his first novel and he is currently writing his second, *Goodnight Vienna*.

Own Goals

Phil Andrews

FLAME
Hodder & Stoughton

The right of Phil Andrews to be identified as the Author of
the Work has been asserted by him in accordance with the
Copyright, Designs and Patents Act 1988.

First published in Great Britain in 1999
by Hodder and Stoughton
First published in paperback in 2000
by Hodder and Stoughton
A division of Hodder Headline

A Flame Paperback

10 9 8 7 6 5 4 3 2 1

A CIP catalogue record for this title is available
from the British Library.

ISBN 0 340 74822 2

Printed and bound in Great Britain by
Mackays of Chatham PLC, Chatham, Kent

Hodder and Stoughton
A division of Hodder Headline
338 Euston Road
London NW1 3BH

For Jill,
without whom I would not have turned to crime.

Chapter One

'I'm a private eye,' I said.

She hadn't asked, but I thought I'd tell her anyway.

My charisma was in need of a makeover. I'd been in this nightclub for hours without getting lucky. I was being assaulted by epilepsy-inducing strobe lighting, a deafening backbeat like a tilt-hammer in overdrive and a constant succession of dope merchants offering me alphabet soup. I read somewhere the place was owned by a health insurance company, so it was all good for business.

I was sipping ice beer straight from the bottle, as you do when you're trying to look cool, and it was getting to that time of the morning when desperation starts to set in. Wherever I looked, naked female flesh pulsated before my eyes in time to the beat, and the miniskirts, boob tubes and hot pants that accessorised it left little to the imagination. My pal Nick was schmoozing with the redhead he picked up last night and wearing his *I'm on for it tonight* expression. God, I hate people who gloat. If I didn't strike oil soon I'd be switching to pints to dull the disappointment of a long and lonely walk home.

The babe on the bar stool couldn't hear me for the din, so I shouted.

'I said: "I'm a private eye."'

I knew I had to work fast before the friend she was bound to be with came back from the girls' room.

This time I did get lucky. The words fell into a hole of silence the DJ had carelessly left in his otherwise seamless mix of sound. Would *he* be embarrassed! It was probably a sacking offence.

It was a high bar stool. My eyes were almost on a level with her thighs. They were sheathed in sparkling silver latex and they went back a long, long way.

She looked up from her Bacardi and coke. I'd grabbed her attention, all right. It's not every day a girl meets a real, live private eye. It's the sort of job that sounds exciting, that sounds sexy. Not that I'd know. I'd only been a private eye for eight hours, but everybody has to start somewhere.

Wasn't Marilyn Monroe discovered working in a laundromat? Wasn't Shakespeare waiting tables at the Globe when somebody said: 'We need something with a Danish prince in it by Tuesday. Can you write?'

Maybe I made that up.

'Sounds a bit sleazy,' she said.

I had to lean really close to hear what she said above the frantic funk. They could use her perfume to put you under at the dentist. I was looking down on those sparkling thighs now, trying to work out whether it was a skirt or a belt she had on round her waist. One of the inconvenient things about going through a divorce is that you don't get sex regularly. And before the divorce you're not getting sex regularly, either, which is one of the reasons for the divorce. So I had twice as much to feel frustrated about as most men. Sleazy? You bet

I felt sleazy, but it had nothing to do with being a private eye.

But what did I know, after only eight hours in the job? Mind you, of all the jobs in all the towns in all the world, private eye is the one everybody knows how to do. Otherwise, what's the point of all those old films on cable TV?

I've seen all the Bogart movies and there's nothing to it. Act tough. Laconic smile. Short sentences. I could manage all that. Especially the short sentences.

'Wanna dance?' I said.

She shrugged. If I ever needed lessons in laconic, I would take them from her. But she slid down from the bar stool and we were swallowed up by the general buttock-swaying, pelvis-thrusting, breast-bouncing, arm-waving with which the floor was in motion, as a stream flowing into the sea is absorbed by the waves.

Dancing is a form of foreplay. I've never been any good at it: Beth was always saying so. But this lass was certainly turning me on. Some mover. The smaller the sack, the more the ferrets struggle to get out, I suppose. If this was all that women wore these days, no wonder there were so many abandoned cotton mills in this city.

I'm a pub man normally, but even nightclubs have closing time. You can always tell when it's approaching. Instead of shouting 'Last orders', the DJ plays his slow number. It's also the moment of truth, like the day your A-level results come in the post. If you've struck lucky, the girl you're dancing with puts her hand on your dick. If not, she starts rummaging among the deodorant-sprays and tampons in her handbag for cab fare. And they say romance is dead.

It seemed she didn't have a friend in the Ladies, and when she stepped across the gap between us and propped her body against mine I resisted the temptation to punch the air and pull my shirt up over my head like City's strikers do when they score. Not that they've been scoring any more often than I have recently.

It slowed the ferrets down a bit, but I could feel they were still in there. And I didn't need to be a private detective when she said, in the blessed silence when the music had finally stopped: 'My place?'

Afterwards, I lay awake. By the time we'd finished it was getting light anyway. Daybreak crept in through the window like a dirty old man and sniffed at the crumpled latex tights and the knickers, slightly sweaty, on the bedroom floor, right next to my chinos and boxers. What kind of self-delusion is it that makes me surprised that women's underwear gets soiled and left in a heap on the floor just like my own? Now the appetite of the night before had been satisfied, I felt bloated and a bit dirty. This must be what they mean when they talk about seeing things in the cold light of dawn.

Face-down beside me on the bed, the girl I had picked up might have been dead but for the almost imperceptible rise and fall of her shoulders. Without its clothes, her body was less well structured than it had seemed in the club. The suggestion of a spare tyre at the waist, an incipient double chin, the flattened breasts like those doughy rolls my mother used to make before she put them in the oven. One of life's constant disappointments, like England's performance in test matches, is that women always look less attractive the morning after.

But my mind was already drifting back to a different club where I'd got lucky in a different way twenty-four hours earlier. The Double Two had once been a shirt factory in the old garment district, a Victorian-Venetian redbrick sweatshop where the city's *beau monde* now sweated in time to the latest disco hits and the shirts were more likely to be monogrammed CK than C&A. The drinks-pricing policy was supposed to keep out the riffraff but I'd gone along anyway, even though I had just been made redundant for the third time in my brief flirtation with paid employment and the divorce would take care of most of the redundancy money. But if you're travelling on the *Titanic*, you may as well get some champagne down your neck while you can, that's what I say.

You could tell everybody knew they were City players by the way most people were pretending they didn't know them from Adam. I've lost touch with soccer a bit since I got married. Beth holds the perfectly defensible view that it's just a few men kicking a bag of wind around, although with hindsight that should have warned me that the passion I'd finally discovered inside her sensible M&S briefs did not run deep. I stopped going to games when they started making you sit down to watch even though you don't want to and charged you twice as much for the privilege. But I still listen for City's result on a Saturday afternoon, and I recognised some of their faces from *Match of the Day*. Once a fan, always a fan.

I didn't know the names of many of the players, though, and if I did I probably couldn't pronounce them. English clubs don't go scouting in the local park any more: they go to Italy or Brazil instead. The players sat in an exclusive little group, looking exactly like they do when they are interviewed fresh from the showers after a match, hair slicked back, Armani suits, shirts and ties just a little too loud – though what they wore most comfortably was the aura of celebrity that set them apart from all the other pathetic punters like me.

The price of fame was that every so often they had

to listen to some drunken Sunday League player telling them where they'd gone wrong against Chelsea last weekend. Dancing didn't seem to come naturally, either. Strange how a finely tuned body that can waltz round a fullback like poetry in motion can be as graceless as the rest of us when there's a dance-mix backbeat to be followed. Not that they needed to dance. The girls gravitated towards them, anyway, even though they'd got nothing the rest of us didn't have, apart from money, fame and good looks.

I recognised one of the girls in the fan club. We'd all had the hots for Karen Pearson in the fifth form at school. She was a stunning natural blonde who'd developed earlier than most of the girls in our year and even then had a reputation to match her looks. I never got close. She loved to be loved, even by acned kids like me, but she already had a taste for older men with flash cars and the disposable income to which her looks effortlessly entitled her. Now, it seemed, her career path had taken her into the Premier League. It was comforting to know that in a changing world some things stay the same.

I'm strictly a Vauxhall Conference man when it comes to sex, and I know better than to try to play beyond my ranking. So I ignored them for the rest of the evening and concentrated on the women who didn't appear to be blinded by muscular thighs in designer suits. That narrowed the field a fair bit and it wasn't a great success, but the ignoring went brilliantly until around midnight, when the usual fracas by the doors caught my attention. A midnight commotion is one of the things you expect at a club, like a cloakroom and having to pay two quid for a glass of water. What sort of job satisfaction would there be for the door staff unless they could compensate for the grievous wages they earned with a bit of grievous bodily harm? So I wouldn't have paid much attention had Karen Pearson's blonde tresses not caught my eye.

I couldn't hear a thing above the disco beat, so I did my impression of a credit card being inserted into a Yale lock and sidled through the heaving mass of bodies towards the disturbance.

Karen may look a million dollars, but when she opens her mouth it has the same effect as spotting a pair of furry dice hanging from the driver's mirror of a Ferrari. I was used to the Yorkshire accent, of course. It was what she was saying that surprised me.

'He's sexually assaulted me and I want the fucking police.'

No pun intended. Karen was always decorative rather than intellectual. And the subject of her complaint was one of the City players. I didn't recognise him, but by the look of him he was one of the manager's recent foreign signings. Superbly tanned, dark hair carefully gelled into that casual unkempt effect and, I had to grudgingly admit, better-looking than I am.

His language gave it away. Body language, that is. The shrug, the wide-eyed, flat-handed, fan-fingered gesture of supplication, the look of injured innocence. They were as Mediterranean as palm trees on a picture postcard. Oh – and the fact that he was a student at the Manuel School of English.

'I do nothing. Nothing!'

He wasn't the first bloke in that place to misinterpret the meaning of the word 'no', even when they spoke English like natives. Most of the women I know regard getting groped in a club as a supplement to the price of admission, and the usual response is a knee in the scrotum rather than a call to the boys in blue. So this must have been serious.

The management would talk her out of it, of course. When you've got a licence to think about, even bouncers can be cool and reasonable. But what do I know? When the penguin in charge of security came out of the office next to the Gents, he said: 'I'll have to ask you both to wait in the foyer until the police arrive. They're on their way.'

Cue Continental semaphore and verbals and a rush to the payphone by one of the other players. And in a flash somebody was taking photographs. With an impressive piece of kit, too. I wouldn't take an expensive camera into a den of thieves like this with any confidence that I'd still be attached to it when I left, but if he was a City fan he was getting some good shots of some of his idols having a stand-up row with the most photogenic girl in the place.

He must have used a roll of film before the door staff ushered them, still arguing about who had done what and to whom, into the foyer. Then a squad car arrived, its flashing blue lights making the wet cobbles outside look like an extension of the disco we were standing in.

The bobbies were still trying to spell the Italian striker's name when the bloke in the three-piece suit arrived. I'm hopeless at guessing people's ages, but it's a fair bet he hadn't put a pair of rollerblades on his Christmas present list. He looked about as comfortable among the pissed and stoned flower of youth as a hedgehog in the fast lane. But his face was familiar, and when the players gathered round him I realised he was Tom Tomlinson, who'd been club secretary at City since I was a kid. You wouldn't recognise him in the street, but his picture turned up in the papers and on the local news from time to time. Players and managers came and went, but Tom Tomlinson had been around for ever.

I'd already realised this wasn't the night I was going to meet the new woman in my life, and being a nosy bastard by inclination I decided I'd hang around the foyer to see how it all ended before picking up a kebab for the long walk home.

The bobbies left, taking Karen with them, presumably to protect her from any further advances by the Italian stallion.

'Just tell me what happened,' I heard Tomlinson ask his players.

'She came over to the bar and started talking. We had a few drinks, then Carlo went out for a slash. She said she was going to the Ladies. Next thing, she's screaming rape.'

'Did she tell you her name?'

'Can't remember. There was half a dozen women around.'

'She's Karen Pearson,' I said helpfully. It's funny how you feel compelled to be of service to the rich and famous because of the little glow of association it bestows on you. I'm not as immune to celebrity as I'd been pretending.

Tomlinson looked at me. 'You know her?'

'Went to school with her.'

'Are you free any time tomorrow?'

'I'm free all the time tomorrow.'

'Give me a ring on this number at ten.' He handed me a card on which his name and the City FC badge were just discernible among the logos of the club's sponsors. 'I'd like a chat. There might be a few bob in it for you.'

A few bob? The millennium is just around the corner, City can spend the gross national product of Upper Volta on a reserve team fullback, and the club secretary still talks in pre-decimal currency. Typical of this city, that. Trying to keep up with the technological revolution when its heart still belongs to the Industrial Revolution, antiseptic shopping malls cheek by jowl with filthy steelworks. But it's never dull living with a schizophrenic, and it could be worse. It could be Milton Keynes.

My little flashback dissolved to the present again. I could feel her leg against mine, but it wasn't an invitation to reprise the sexual activity of the night before. She was kicking me out of bed.

'You'd better piss off. I've got to go to work.'

I sorted my boxers from among the dirty linen and put them on.

'Where's the bathroom?'

'It's the door you didn't come in by.'

The self-satisfaction at having broken my sexual duck had already evaporated by the time I had wiped the condensation off the bathroom mirror. The stubble did nothing to disguise the incipient pudginess of my face, and my tongue told me I hadn't brushed my teeth for more than twelve hours. If I thought the woman I had been sleeping with was less attractive in the cold light of dawn, God knows what she was thinking about me. I hoped I'd left clammy bathrooms in poky flats behind me for ever when Beth and I got married. Now I realised that this was the sort of place I'd be living in again when our divorce came through. Post-coital depression? Nah! Just good old self-pity.

I splashed some cold water on my face and sat on the bog, thinking of the phone conversation I'd had with Tomlinson. Ten o'clock was a bit early for me since my latest job had been rationalised out from under me, but a few bob was, allowing for inflation, a few quid, and I needed it.

'I want to know anything you can tell me about Karen Pearson,' he'd said. 'Where she works, if she's single, married, divorced, where she lives, if she's got love-life problems or financial problems.'

I've never liked Karen Pearson since I realised she wasn't going to fulfil my adolescent fantasies behind the bike sheds, but I didn't like the sound of any of that.

But before I could say so, he said: 'Come to the ground on Saturday and there'll be two tickets for the match waiting for you. Ask for me in the directors' bar afterwards and we'll have a chat. Will two hundred compensate you for your trouble?'

'Two hundred pounds?'

'It'll be in notes. I don't suppose you enjoy a close relationship with the tax man.'

On the other hand there are two ways of looking at anything. If all he wanted was biographical information about Karen, there was no harm in that. The trouble was that I hadn't seen her for ages, and although I knew where she lived ten years ago, who her best friend was at school and which of my classmates claimed to have had more success with her than I did, that was about the extent of my information. I know City have paid ridiculous sums for some fairly duff players in recent years, but they wouldn't pay two hundred quid for that. I didn't even know where to find her. It was a fair bet she no longer lived on the council estate we grew up in, and there would be a couple of pages of Pearsons in the phone book. So where did I start?

'Are you gunna be in there all morning? I've got a job to go to.'

Lucky you, I thought. Then I remembered I hadn't even asked her name. Some detective.

'It's Jackie,' she said. 'But don't get attached to it. I'm not thinking of doing this again.'

She didn't ask mine.

It's Steve, by the way. Steve Strong: almost average height, only slightly overweight, modishly balding, but not unattractive. But I would say that, wouldn't I? My wife obviously doesn't share my opinion, but that's another story. I may as well give you my CV – I've sent it out to everybody else in this city.

Name: Strong, Steven.

Age: thirtysomething.

Place of birth: this city (of which I am soon to be a bachelor once more).

Education: honours degree in English (third class – although I don't normally mention this).

Employment history: 1 researcher, local television; 2 local government officer, rodent control; 3 sales representative, security cameras.

Reasons for leaving: 1 redundant – the company lost the franchise, although it wasn't entirely my fault; 2 redundant (voluntary) – I don't like rats; 3 redundant (involuntary) – I was the sort of salesman who couldn't sell rap records to Rastafarians.

Marital status: temporary – to Liz (who now prefers to be known as Beth), whom I met at university but who has since grown up and seen the error of her ways.

Current employment: letting myself out of Jackie's bedsit and wondering how I'm going to gather two hundred quids' worth of information about Karen Pearson before the final whistle blows on Saturday afternoon.

Chapter Two

Fortunately, there aren't two pages of Humpages in the phone book. (If your name was Humpage, you'd probably change it.) There is one Humpage at her parents' address and one just around the corner, which must be her.

Ann Humpage, known at school, in the cruel way that even extreme youth does not excuse, as Dumpy, was Karen Pearson's best friend – the fat ugly one who always seems to ride shotgun with the most stunning girls. It's a cliché, but it's true. There must be some psychological reason for this. Perhaps because anything beautiful is seen to best effect against a plain background. I didn't know if they were still friends, but if they only exchanged Christmas cards she would know Karen's address. I was overdue a visit to my parents, anyway, and I could buy a toothbrush on the way and borrow Dad's razor.

It was never the best address in town, but when I was a kid all we really lacked was money. Now, judging by the rubbish in the gardens, the graffiti on the walls and the houses with sheets of plywood where the windows should be, self-respect, ambition and moral values had all gone missing, too.

I remember the maisonettes where Ann lives being built on the waste land we used to kick about on. That was only twenty years ago, when social engineering still seemed possible. The architectural engineering left something to be desired, though – concrete slabs bolted together and painted charcoal grey. They have already become slums, worse than the Victorian terraces they replaced, and fit only for demolition. There was no bell, so I knocked. After a long time the door opened a crack and a face that might once have been Ann Humpage's appeared. But what struck me most forcibly was the smell that wafted out. It was like a Marseilles sewer. When you can't keep the drains in good repair, you really are reverting to Third World status.

I recognised her face only because I knew what had been there before, as the residents of Ypres must have recognised the battlefields after the Great War. She had grown fat in the way that comes not from eating too much, but too much of the wrong things because you can't be bothered to eat the right ones. Her features were pale and coarse, like the bleached-out grass when you lift a brick off the lawn. She was wearing one of those shell suits that were never fashionable even when they were in fashion. She didn't recognise me at all.

'Steve. Steve Strong. We were at school together.'

'Are you with the Social Services?'

'No. Can I come in?'

She removed the chain and left me to push open the door.

I followed her into the sitting-room. I could see why Social Services were on her mind. They had obviously provided her furniture – a charity-shop collection of mis-matched castoffs. She was living in the lack of luxury. The carpet had the tacky feel of drying mucus, and it tried to cling to my shoes. The Ann Humpage I remembered had basked in the glow of the golden Karen, but since then Dumpy Humpy had had a great fall.

I sat down carefully, hoping she wouldn't offer me a cup of tea. I had a mouth like a furnaceman's scrotum, but the thought of drinking anything in that place turned my stomach. So much for private eyes being tough. But she just lit a Silk Cut and looked at me, neither pleased to see me nor hostile. Normally, I object to smoking on the grounds that drinking and lack of exercise are doing enough to damage my health without any help from sidestream smoke, but on this occasion I was grateful. At least cancerous tars mask the smell of shit.

'I wondered if you knew where Karen Pearson lived. You were friends when we were at school.'

She looked at me for a long time before she answered, as though there were more important things going on in her head than the need to formulate a reply. 'She went to London, modelling. I've not seen much of her since.'

'Modelling?'

'Clothes. Fashion model.'

Yes, that would have suited Karen. She not only had a great body, but she knew it. She liked to show it off.

'You've not seen her recently?'

'I see her mam sometimes. She still lives round here.'

'She didn't say where Karen's living now?'

Ann got up and took an envelope from among the giro slips behind the clock. It was addressed to Mrs Joan Pearson, but the flap had been sealed with a small gold sticker which said:

Karen Pearson.
Flat 7,
Chatsworth Court,
Millfield.

An expensive address on the smart side of town.

'Didn't you get in touch?'

'I phoned and left a message once, but she's never phoned back.'

I wasn't surprised. I couldn't see the desirable and fragrant Karen coming here, and I couldn't blame her. Now I had what I had come for, I wanted to leave as quickly as possible. I was getting up to go when I heard screaming. It was coming from upstairs. Ann didn't even glance up.

'What's that?' I asked.

'That's Warren. My kid. I'm a single parent. He's disabled. He's got learning difficulties. And he's incontinent.'

She said it with no emotion at all. Six flat statements discharged as though she were emptying the chamber of a revolver: bang, bang, bang.

It was that sickening moment when someone tells you something awful about their life and you know there should be something you can do to help, but there isn't. It is the only time I ever feel guilty without having done anything to feel guilty about. I sat down again and searched the pockets of my mind for the right words of sympathy. For the first time that morning I didn't mind not having shaved or cleaned my teeth. Bristles and bad breath felt like an expression of solidarity with this woman who could surely never have been the child I went to school with.

'Shouldn't he be in a home?' I asked.

'He goes to day-care three times a week. That's all Social Services say I need. Which means that's all they can afford. What do you think we live in – a welfare state?'

'I'm sorry,' was all I could find among the bits of

string and soiled handkerchiefs in the pockets of my mind.

'People always are,' she said flatly.

The smell of shit was even more nauseous now I knew where it came from. But I could detect undertones of the disinfectant she used to clean him up, like some poncy wine buff discovering crushed strawberries beneath the gutsy blackcurrant in a Cabernet Sauvignon.

'Do you want to go up?' I said, looking in the direction of the stairs and seeing my way of escape.

'You've woken him up with knocking,' she said. 'I never wake him up, even if he's shit himself. I'll have that to listen to for the rest of the day, now.'

I couldn't have known, but I felt as though I'd deliberately kicked some limbless person's crutches away.

Ann offered no apology for him. Take it or leave it was her attitude, and who can blame her? She had to take it whether she liked it or not, so at least I had double her options.

She went to the foot of the stairs, and as I got up to leave she turned and said, as much to herself as to me: 'Sometimes I stand over him at night with a pillow in my hand, but he's as strong as I am and I don't know if I'd be able to hold it over his face long enough.'

I had never before come across the desperation that might drive somebody to kill. I didn't know what to say or what to do, so I didn't say or do anything.

She went off to clear up the shit. I just felt like one.

Mum and Dad lived just round the corner, a million miles away. Theirs was one of the better council houses in the area, and they had bought it for a song and announced it to the world by putting in leaded windows and a Georgian front door. I suspect Mum even voted Conservative until somebody told her it wasn't respectable any more.

Whenever I went back to the part of the city I grew up in I realised what the Big Bang theory of the creation of the universe was about. We had all started out in the same place, but Ann Humpage had been flung in one direction, my parents had moved in another, and I had flown even further into space by going to university. The gap between us was widening all the time and would never be bridged. We were now worlds apart without having gone anywhere at all.

At least feeling sorry for Dumpy put my problems with Beth and losing my job into perspective. It didn't make me feel any better, but it shifted the imbalance, like water slopping around in the hold of a ship before it sinks.

But I salved my conscience a little just by walking through the door. Mum was embarrassingly pleased to see me; Dad was watching Eurosport on TV.

'I've got a spare ticket for the City match tomorrow,' I told him. 'Want to come?'

'Where did *you* get City tickets?'

'Somebody at work,' I lied. They were still trying to come to terms with me splitting up with Beth. I could do without the earful I'd get if I told them I'd lost another job.

'Football's not the same,' he said. 'Executive boxes! All-seater! I'd rather stand. In my day, they had Englishmen playing for City. If you were Scotch or Welsh you were a foreigner. Now who have they got? Ravioli, Tagliatelle. That's not a forward line, it's an Italian takeaway.'

'I'll take that as a "no" then, shall I?'

But Dad knew the names of City's players better than I did. The real reason he no longer went to matches was that they'd priced him out of the market. He can get a month's satellite TV for the price of a seat in the stand. It doesn't come with the atmosphere or tribal sense of belonging he used to get when he went to the ground, but the end result is the same – usually 2–0 to the opposition.

'Can I borrow your razor?' I said, and they were too tactful to ask why. I shaved and brushed my teeth and swallowed the cup of tea I'd been gagging for.

They kept me talking for an hour, and when I finally made it to the door Mother said: 'You'll be getting sacked, going in to work at this time.'

'I doubt it, Mum,' I said, and caught the bus up to Chatsworth Court.

If I'd bought a newspaper instead of a toothbrush, finding Karen Pearson's address would have been a damned sight easier. It was on the front page of that morning's *Post*, which I read over the shoulder of the woman sitting next to me on the bus.

Karen's face stared out from beneath the headline: CITY STAR ON SEX CHARGE.

She was pictured standing next to Carlo Marconi in the foyer of the Double Two, and the same photograph was in most of the nationals. That enterprising punter-cum-paparazzo had more than covered the cost of his night out, and it wasn't a bad picture, either. Photogenic girl, our Karen. Economical with the truth, too.

The allegations of indecent assault have been made by 25-year-old model Karen Pearson.

Twenty-five? Come on, Karen, we're both quite a few years older than that.

Chatsworth Court is out where the steel barons and wool magnates built their mansions when this city still manufactured things. The company's more mixed these days – property developers, scrap-metal dealers, TV comedians, football managers, that kind of thing – but it's still the best address in town. They've got more of most things rest of us: more money, more trees, more cars in ~~eway~~, more acreage of neatly trimmed lawn. Still, t~~u~~ ~~air~~, in some ways they've got nothing. No graffiti, no rubbish in the streets, no dog shit on the verges. But down these clean streets a man must go.

I wasn't alone. Chatsworth Court turned out to be a modern block of service flats down a quiet side-road, except that this morning it was anything but quiet. Workmen were digging up half the street to lay cable television. The other half was occupied by a couple of TV crews, a radio car, a huddle of blokes with notebooks I deduced were newspapermen and the usual iron-filing onlookers that any crowd attracts.

I joined them, though it was soon obvious that none of us would get to talk to Karen that morning. The delegations of reporters which went into the building from time to time always emerged with the same story. Karen was not talking – at least, not then. And not for free. All she was giving away was the address of her agent and the information that if they wanted her side of the story, money would have to change hands. Big money.

But I learned a lot about the media in that half-hour. Scoops are not really the obsession the movies would have you believe. What reporters are primarily interested in is not being beaten by the opposition. If information is scarce, they work in packs and pool what little they have. So I hung around to see what I could pick up.

The word on the street was along the lines of: 'The *Sun* and the *Mirror* will be bidding five figures for this. It's got the lot. Football, sex and a cracking bird who'd probably get her kit off if the money was right. And Marconi's mega on the Continent. It'll syndicate world-wide.

'Meanwhile, it's *sub judice* and we need something for a

follow-up tomorrow that's not going to put us in contempt of court. Where does she work?'

It's one of my theories that if you eavesdrop long enough you'll hear something to your advantage. On this occasion it was the name of the model agency where Karen worked. I jumped on the first bus back to town. In the absence of anyone else to interview, the local TV channel was questioning the sports editor of the local paper about the effect all this would have on City's championship prospects. And I thought incest was illegal.

The agency is up a narrow flight of stairs down a side-street in the city centre. The waiting-room has been partitioned off from whatever is behind it by a piece of plasterboard. It feels more like a doctor's surgery than an arm of the fashion industry, though if the people reading the maga-zines in my health centre looked like the girl who had beaten me to the only chair in the place I could become a hypochondriac. She could only have been a model. She was overdressed and over-made-up for that time in the morning, yet still managed to look underdressed for any time of day. Perhaps it was the length of her legs and the height of her patent-leather boots that made her velour skirt look shorter. Or perhaps it was the shortness of the skirt that made everything else look long. Either way, the copy of *Vogue* she was reading had been published this decade, so this definitely wasn't my doctor's surgery.

She didn't give me a second glance when I walked in, so I thought I'd initiate a conversation.

'Who's in charge round here?'

'Estelle.' She said it without lifting her eyes from the emaciated famine victims in her magazine.

'Estelle who?'

'Just Estelle. She runs the agency.'

21

'Is she in?'

She inclined her head towards the door in the partition.

'And how do I communicate with her? Tie a note round a brick and chuck it through the window? Or is there a bell I can ring?'

'I've been waiting an hour. There's been reporters on the phone all morning. You'll have to wait.'

I expect she only told people how much she enjoyed travel, meeting interesting people and raising money for animal charities if she was wearing a swimsuit and a number round her neck.

The window looked out on the service yard of the Paris Brasserie, a still life with wine bottles, waste bins overflowing with last night's *plat du jour* and the chef smoking a fag and picking his nose. I preferred the interior with seated figure, and I didn't even mind standing up to look at it. She was as pretty as a picture. Too pretty to make it really big in the modelling business, where you need to be in the last stages of anorexia and a candidate for Oxfam emergency rations before they drape the really expensive clothes over you. I was admiring the brushwork where her legs crossed about half-way up her thighs when the door opened.

The woman who came through it might have been this girl's elder sister – about thirty years older and thirty times smarter. If this was Estelle, her well-preserved middle age was a ringing endorsement for the renovative products advertised in the glossies. Her hair colour came out of a bottle, and her figure probably owed something to the inventor of Lycra. Her appearance said 'smart woman' in every sense – a former model with the acumen to realise that, unless you are Kate Moss, getting rich at this game means getting a string of other beanpoles to do the work for you. Nobody paid her to wear designer clothes any more, but she could afford them anyway. So why did something about her also remind me of a madame at a brothel? There was a sharpness in her face that was not just the result of one tuck too many, and in her voice that suggested that if you messed her about she'd apply those long, painted fingernails to your balls and squeeze hard.

'Can I help you?'

'I'm an old friend of Karen Pearson's. I just wondered . . .'

'If it's pictures you're after, I've sold the topless shots to the *Sun* and the bikinis to the *Express*, both exclusive. And my interview is being syndicated by an agency we work with. Do you want their number?'

'I'm not a journalist,' I said as she handed me a business card with the agency's number on it. 'I went to school with Karen. All I wanted was . . .'

'Listen, I've had schoolfriends round this morning, old boyfriends, even her brother. He turned out to be from the *Inquirer*. If you want pictures or background, see my agent. But you'll have to be prepared to talk serious money. Come on through, Debbie.'

Debbie uncrossed her legs and went on through, and I knew I wouldn't be seeing either of them again. Somehow, I didn't think the two hundred pounds Tom Tomlinson had promised me would constitute serious money. This was out of my league.

I was almost at the bottom of the narrow stairs when someone appeared in the doorway, blocking my way and shutting out the light from the street, like an eclipse of the sun.

'Sorry,' I said, as you do when something isn't your fault. We did that little dance in which we both tried to get out of each other's way. It wasn't easy, given the size of her, and we ended up bumping into each other and laughing. Her face was familiar, though I couldn't think why.

'Don't I know you from somewhere?' I said. It would have been the corniest line in the world if she had been remotely attractive, but she was even bigger than Dumpy Humpage.

'The telly,' she said. 'The tea adverts.'

Of course. The tea adverts on the telly. The ones with the fat housewife with the unfeasibly broad Yorkshire accent. This was her. I know you shouldn't be impressed at meeting a minor celebrity in an age when we know we'll all be famous for fifteen minutes, but if your fifteen minutes have yet to come it's still a strange feeling standing face to face with somebody who turns up half-way through *Coronation Street* and *Emmerdale* and *Brookside* every night. What's more, it was one of my favourite ads, cleverly delivered with an irony that had her target audience laughing at her and smug gits like me laughing at the sort of people who would buy tea on the strength of an awful ad like that. The best of both worlds. I was almost tempted to say, 'I admire your work,' but it would have been a bit pretentious even for me.

'Have you just come from the agency?' she asked.

'Yes.'

'Is there anybody in the waiting-room? I'm not climbing all those stairs if I'm going to have to hang about for hours.'

'Debbie's just gone in to see Estelle,' I said.

'Then I'm definitely coming back later,' she said. 'You're not Debbie's boyfriend or anything, are you?'

'I'm afraid not.'

'Yes, I suppose you would find her attractive, but teeth and tits don't have the same effect on me. She'll be in there an hour while Estelle massages her ego.'

'Are you a client?' I asked.

'Don't look so surprised, love. They don't just handle the

24

glamour stuff. They do the novelty end of the modelling market. The Big, the Fat and the Ugly, Estelle calls it. She got me the tea-bag job on TV.'

'There's hope for me, then.'

'I doubt it. I'm off for a coffee. Debbie will be in there for ages listening to Estelle tell her she's going to be the next Naomi.'

'Is she?'

'No, but Estelle tells all the girls that. If she didn't, they'd just keep changing agents until they found some-one who did.'

'I was just going for a cuppa myself,' I said. 'Can I tag along?'

'As long as you don't want me to put in a good word for you with Estelle.'

I followed her. It was a long shot, but as a client of the same agency she was the best hope I had yet come across of learning something about Karen that might get Carlo Marconi off a groping charge.

'I'm Steve Strong,' I said.

'Denise Talbot!'

There was no guarantee that she would tell me anything, of course. I'm not a policeman. Policemen can ask direct questions and expect to get answers. Private investigators, on the other hand, can just be told to go forth and multiply.

'What were you doing at Estelle's place?' she asked as we turned into the Grand Hotel. The Grand Hotel? For a cuppa? 'If you were after some work I can tell you now that you're not good-looking enough to be a male model and not ugly enough to do what I do.'

I decided not to put her on her guard by telling her I was making enquiries about Karen. If I was to get Denise to open up, subtlety would be needed, maybe even a bit

25

of subterfuge. So there was the question of morality to be considered. How did I feel about being underhanded with someone I'd only just met? Well, I wouldn't last long as a private eye unless I learned to be comfortable with it. And as I needed the money, I found that subterfuge fitted me like an old shoe, not to mention the rest of my favourite leisurewear, right down to the T-shirt, chinos and leather jacket.

'I'm a health inspector with the council. You can see into the yard of the Paris Brasserie from up there. We've had complaints about cockroaches. I was doing a bit of covert inspection.'

They say the best lies contain a grain of truth. I worked in the environmental health department until a year ago, when I became another of the council's cuts. Now I was recycling the experience, which was an environmentally friendly thing to do. And the bit about covert inspection was true.

The top-floor restaurant at the Grand wasn't the sort of place I normally chose for a coffee. Philip Marlowe would have foreseen this and negotiated himself fifty dollars a day to cover legitimate expenses. As a private eye I still had a lot to learn.

Denise wedged herself into one of the designer chairs and ordered Earl Grey and a slice of the sort of gateau that should carry a government health warning. To take my mind off the prices I said: 'Shouldn't you be drinking the tea you advertise?'

'I wouldn't go to the kind of café that would serve the tea I advertise.'

'As Groucho might have said,' I said, and her grin told me that picking up the allusion had earned me a couple of brownie points.

The waiter emerged with our orders from behind a sort

of space module built of chromium pipes and Day-Glo fibreboard.

'Aren't you having a bun?' Denise asked. 'The great thing about making a living out of being fat is that eating these things is a duty as well as a pleasure.'

I shook my head, and, using the presence of the waiter as cover, I mentioned that I knew a girl called Karen who had gone into modelling. 'She was in my class at school. I'm sure she was with the same agency as you.'

'Karen Pearson?' said Denise, spearing the gateau with her fork with more force than seemed strictly necessary. 'She's not a girlfriend of yours, is she?'

'I don't have as much luck with models as you seem to think I should.'

'The men who do only get grief from them, love,' she said. 'Either they get dumped for a bloke with more money or their wives find out.'

'I didn't have Karen down as that sort of girl,' I lied, although the longer Karen marinated in my memory, the more I suspected she was.

'It comes as standard in the modelling game. They're the centre of attention, God's gift to the camera, surrounded by men offering them all sorts to take their clothes off. It's the shortest route to becoming a bitch I know.'

'I didn't realise Karen was a supermodel,' I said, dangling a spoon in my espresso. I felt I was walking a tightrope, afraid to go too fast in case I fell off. No, there's a better analogy than that. It was like being pubescent again, sitting with a girl in the back row of the pictures. You start by sliding your arm along the back of her seat, and if she doesn't object you risk a kiss, and if she responds you let your hand slip down to her breast, and all the time there's the excitement of not knowing how far you'll get before she tells you to keep your hands to yourself.

'She did pretty well for herself for a while. Went down to London and got some high-profile work – Marks & Sparks knickers, C&A bras, that sort of thing. Then when her face got too well known it was mail-order catalogues and charity fashion shows. But she did all right. Made enough money to buy herself a nice flat.'

'So why did she come back?'

'Listen, unless you've got a figure like a well-used ironing board it's a short life and a merry one in this game. If you're young enough and pretty enough and lucky enough, you can make a decent living for a few years, but time and cellulite wait for no girl.'

'There's nothing more outdated than last year's model,' I said. Every private eye has a duty to come out with a snappy one-liner from time to time. Either she'd heard it before or she didn't find it funny, so I pressed on.

'She must still be doing all right if she can afford to live in Chatsworth Court.'

'I thought you hadn't seen her since you left school.'

'Read about her in the paper this morning,' I said, hoping a slight flush of the cheeks hadn't blown my cover. 'That's what brought her to mind.' Was this where my hand was politely removed from whatever part of her anatomy it had reached?

'You can buy a mansion in this city with what you'd get for a broom cupboard in London. But you've still got to pay the rates and the gas bill. And you can't earn that sort of money doing photo-shoots for the local paper.'

'So how does she pay the bills?'

She looked at me as though it was the most naive question in the world.

'Haven't you heard about the model's fall-back position? Flat on your back with a man between your legs.'

Bloody hell. I'd been worrying about slipping my hand

inside her blouse, so to speak, and she'd grabbed hold if it and thrust it under her skirt.

'Don't look so shocked, love,' she said. 'It must come with working for the council. You should get out more.'

'She's on the game?' I said. Now that *would* be worth two hundred quid to someone who was defending a charge of indecent assault.

'She doesn't stand on street corners or offer her services to sailors down the docks,' said Denise. 'But Estelle believes in getting the most out of her clients. She diversified into the escort business a long time ago. She gets her ten per cent from girls like Debbie when they're on their way up, and another ten per cent from their escort agency work on the way down, unless they've managed to catch themselves a bloke with money while they still have something to offer.'

So Estelle *was* a madame. Perceptive, or what?

'Karen's a call girl?'

'A high-class call girl, yes. Ironic, isn't it? I used to envy girls with her looks. You do when you're fat and frumpish. And now my body's in greater demand than hers, even if it is only selling tea bags.'

'And you get repeat fees, too,' I said.

'Estelle's escort girls get repeat fees, one way or another,' said Denise. 'If they're any good, their clients come back for second helpings. And even if they don't, there's more than one way to squeeze a second cup out of a tea bag . . .'

'Meaning what?' I said.

'You are naive, aren't you? Most of the clients are married men, and if funds run low there's bound to be one who'll pay a few quid extra to keep it from his wife.'

'That's blackmail,' I said.

'Girls like Karen prefer to call them charitable donations. They're tax free and she doesn't even have to pay ten per cent to Estelle.'

I called the waiter and paid the bill. Waiters have always frightened me. Must be my working-class upbringing. That's why I left him a tip instead of saying, 'Are you sure that's right? Ten quid for two hot drinks and a piece of cake?'

But then again it had been worth it to find out that Karen Pearson was both a call girl *and* a blackmailer.

There were showcases full of designer dresses in the hotel foyer, and Denise eyed them in the way a thinner woman would have looked at the slice of gateau she'd just eaten.

'But I'd still change places with her to be able to get into a size ten,' she said.

Chapter Three

City's ground looks like the starship *Enterprise* has gone through a time warp and crash-landed in the nineteenth century. It stands next to an abattoir among streets of redbrick terraces on the fringe of the city centre. But the old corrugated iron stands I remembered as a kid have been replaced by hi-tech concrete and tubular-steel jobs, and the cement terraces by plastic tip-up seats which pick out the word CITY in black on a sea of gold. It is the ephemerally expensive grafted on to the enduringly tatty, and it is as good a symbol as any of what this city has become.

Because there is no space around the ground, the car park is small, which makes it all the more satisfactorily exclusive for the few who have passes for it. They seem mainly to be people who think you need a Range Rover to get to Sainsbury's, and there is more than the national average of personalised numberplates. A lot of them involve tortuous permutations of CITY. But a personalised numberplate is probably not much more expensive than having the word 'prat' tattooed on your forehead if you want to announce to the world that you are an insecure, overpaid pillock.

The tickets Tom Tomlinson had left for me were for the directors' box, and I could tell from the look on the face of the security man who opened the plate-glass door that the jeans and leather jacket I was wearing were not *de rigueur*.

I was the first to take my seat in the exclusive little enclave just in front of the executive boxes, where corporate hospitality was being dispensed in glass-fronted cells with bars and buffet lunches and television sets for the guests who didn't like football.

Tottenham were today's opponents, so it wasn't exactly *Match of the Day*. The directors of both clubs drifted in just before kickoff, and the doorman's look became flesh. The ensemble of choice turned out to be an expensive camel-hair overcoat and alligator slip-on shoes with a gold chain across the instep, accessorised with a bottle-blonde with an expensive tuck where the bags under her eyes should have been. If you ever get asked at the pub quiz whether it is possible to be an aesthete with no taste, the answer is in the affirmative.

But once the game started I remembered how much I liked football.

I hadn't been to watch City for years. I had forgotten what a great occasion a big match can be, the pitch pure emerald under the floodlights in the autumn gloom, the rising excitement when the players come out. Apart from the little ghetto of visiting supporters behind the goal, the stands were a solid mass of black and gold from which the smell of money rose like steam. You didn't need to look at the balance sheet to see how City could afford so many expensive foreign players. You just had to count the replica shirts in the crowd, in all sizes from children's to extra-large with beer-belly extension, whole families arrayed in black and gold, and multiply that by the forty quid they cost in the club shop.

And I had forgotten how much it matters that City should win. The need to identify with your tribe that had persuaded most of the people around me to part with their hard-earned cash in exchange for an appallingly designed envelope of polyester swept over me the moment the players came out. Never mind that I had spent three years honing my critical and philosophical skills at the wheel of higher education. When the referee blows his whistle and the ball rolls forward from the centre spot, good and bad, right and wrong are reduced to a simple choice between shirts of different colours.

City were under-strength. Carlo Marconi wasn't playing for obvious reasons, but Pierre Bartola and Gary Allen were also out with injuries. Dad reckoned they were our three best players, and events supported his judgement.

City swarmed forward for the first ten minutes as the reserves who had been brought in tried to prove they were as good as the players they were replacing. We all knew it was just a matter of time before the first goal went in, and the optimism a crowd always brings with it to a soccer match rose like mercury on a hot day. The ball ricocheted around in the Tottenham penalty area. Shots cannoned back off defenders' bodies. The keeper turned a rising drive over the bar. But the first goal didn't go in, and gradually it became clear that key players can make all the difference to a side.

Without Marconi, City had no playmaker who could keep the attacks flowing, and without Bartola they had no midfield ball-winner who could break down the Spurs attacks and reverse the flow of the game. The fullback Vince Naylor made some surging overlapping runs down the flank, but the stand-in striker had neither the pace nor the anticipation of Gary Allen, and Naylor's crosses fell harmlessly into the holes where Allen would have been.

Spurs scored once in each half. I can't remember how. It's your own side's goals that stick in your memory. The opposition's are just a nuisance. The nearest City came was when the ball bounced down off the underside of the crossbar, but the linesman was from Redditch rather than Russia, and we lost 2–0.

The crowd had lost heart long before the final whistle. Towards the end they didn't even have the energy to respond to the taunts of the Tottenham fans. But they clapped City's depleted team politely off the pitch, and as the stadium emptied people were already beginning to talk about how things would be different next week, when the side was back to full strength. Despite all the evidence to the contrary, hope springs eternal in the human breast that wears a replica shirt.

Tomlinson had told me to meet him in the directors' bar after the game, and I followed the camel-hair coats and wrap-around furs like a nasty smell until some jobsworth stopped me at the door.

'Directors only in here, sir.'

'The club secretary asked me to meet him here,' I told the shoulders in the club blazer.

'Directors only in here, sir.'

He had the conversational skills of a speak-your-weight machine, but he was also built along the same solid lines, so I hung around in the foyer hoping Tomlinson would appear. It gave me time to admire the trophy cabinet. I would have admired it more if there had been anything in it other than the Yorkshire Senior Cup, the winning of which had involved beating such giants of the game as Doncaster Rovers and Halifax Town.

Ever since Jack Cox had taken over as club chairman and started throwing his money about, City had promised great things. They'd made it to the Premier League in his first full season, and last year they'd qualified for Europe, but there was still no proper silverware in the cabinet. They were prepared for it, though. The cabinet was wired up to an impressive burglar alarm.

Tomlinson finally appeared from somewhere under the stand and smuggled me into the directors' bar.

'Try and wear a collar and tie next time,' he said. It was usually Beth's job to tell me things like that, but as she was leaving me there was a vacancy in that department.

'Get yourself a drink. I'll be with you as soon as I've sorted out the attendance figures and the gate money.'

My shoes needed polishing anyway, so I waded through the shag-pile to the bar. The cabinet may have been short on trophies but there were plenty of them in here. Trophy wives, that is.

So this was where all those designer labels in the Grand's showcases ended up. The camel coats had come off to reveal the bespoke tailoring underneath. I've never seen so much worsted or so many pastel shirts with white collars and cuffs. The style police were obviously not allowed in here, either. They probably turned up improperly dressed.

I stood around and felt out of place while I tried to catch the barman's eye. It's not easy when you know he's deliberately avoiding you. In the end I went and stood right in front of his white waistcoat, stared straight into his bow tie in City colours and ordered a beer. When I fished some change from my pocket to pay he made 'the drinks are complimentary at this bar, sir' sound like a request not to piss on the sandwiches.

I leaned on the bar and looked around. They were the

sort of people who turned enjoying themselves into a series of little business meetings, but most of the action was at the far end of the room, where there was a lot of hovering around an oldish bloke who I realised I recognised as Jack Cox. I was too far away to hear what was being said, but, like watching TV with the sound turned down, the body language spoke louder than the dialogue. There was a lot of brown-nosing going on.

'At least there's one man not worshipping at the shrine.'

She was standing next to me and, although she hadn't asked, the barman was refilling her glass. Some bloke called Pavlov had a theory about it, as I recall: if you ring somebody's bell often enough, they start doing things automatically. The barman's automatic response was to pour a gin and tonic whenever he saw her.

She was well preserved, expensively dressed, middle-aged, slightly slewed. She might have been a trophy wife once, but she was now in need of buffing up. She clearly thought spirits would do the trick. She wasn't drunk, but she was at that stage of chirpy loquaciousness that has to be worked at. It seemed that the dressing-room was not the only place where half-time drinks had been served.

And she didn't like drinking alone. She'd never set eyes on me before, but she needed a listener and I would do.

'It's the wrong time and place to say this, I know,' she said, 'and no one likes to see healthy young men running about in shorts more than I do, but spending Saturday afternoons in the open air in the depths of an English winter has limited attractions. Not that any of them come for the football,' she added, indicating the group of men around Jack Cox. 'That's what they come for. To see if any of the gold leaf will rub off on them. Will you have another drink?'

'I'm OK,' I said, nursing my beer.

'You'd hardly believe this, but he dragged me back from the Greek islands for this. If that isn't grounds for divorce, I don't know what is. I mean, where can you get a decent moussaka with fresh béchamel sauce round here?'

I could see her point. You'd be struggling to find fresh béchamels, even on Barnsley market.

When Tom Tomlinson appeared and led me to a table, the look on his face said he was doing me a favour.

'Who is that lush?'

'That's Brenda Deakin. When we told her the drinks were complimentary in this bar she thought we said compulsory. She's the wife of Brian Deakin, our previous chairman.'

I followed his gaze to the table at which Deakin was in conversation with a thickset, red-haired man. I recalled seeing Deakin's face in the papers when he ran the club. They were the only figures in the room who seemed unaware of the golden presence of Jack Cox, to whom all sightlines seemed to lead, as in a Renaissance religious painting. But soccer was the new religion, and Jack Cox was City's Messiah.

'Now then,' said Tomlinson, 'what can you tell me about the girl?'

The club secretary was businesslike and to the point. He gave the impression he had a job of work to do even though everyone else in the place was enjoying themselves. He had been a player himself in the days when they still wore baggy shorts and cleaned their own boots and earned a maximum wage of twenty pounds a week. He probably knew more about football than anyone at the club, but he looked like the sort of bloke who still thought money ought to be worked for, rather than handed out in suitcases by sponsors and television companies.

He was short and stocky without being fat, and his thinning grey hair was pasted across his skull. Brylcreem had obviously been in mode in his youth, and though most of his hair had since disappeared he had carried on using it. His glasses had frames larger than were currently fashionable, and he wore a dark grey suit but seemed uncomfortable in it. He should have been wearing a tweed jacket and matching porkpie hat. He looked out of place among the expensive tailoring. The only person who looked more out of place was Jack Cox, but he could afford not to care. He owned the place.

I told him everything Denise Talbot had told me.

The bit about blackmail was what interested him. It was what had interested me.

When I had finished, he handed me two hundred quid in used notes across the table. 'Here. You've earned this.'

For the first time I felt like a real private eye. A pile of used notes is somehow more exciting, more dangerous, more conspiratorial than a cheque drawn on the Royal Bank of Scotland, even if a wad of two hundred in twenties is disappointingly thin.

'Do you want to earn some more?' Tomlinson asked.

Is there a market for umbrellas in Manchester?

'For doing what?'

'I'm telling you this in strict confidence. If the media get hold of it, you're off the case.'

The case! Now we really were talking private eye language. And it frightened me to death.

What I had learned about Karen Pearson would be useful to Tomlinson, but it was a stroke of luck I was not sure I could repeat.

'Yesterday, Vince Naylor was arrested. Very similar incident.'

'You what?'

Naylor's powerful runs down the wing had been the best things about City's performance that afternoon. If they lost him too, City really would be struggling. He was the sort of hard-tackling defender every side needs to complement the delicate skills of their ball-players. Naylor would never make the international side, but he was a solid, dependable defender with attacking flair and the kind of wholehearted, old-fashioned approach to the game Tomlinson would appreciate.

'The newspapers haven't picked it up yet,' Tomlinson continued, 'but when they do it will cause us a lot of harm, coming on top of the Marconi incident.'

'It'll blow over,' I said. 'Footballers are always getting themselves in the papers for thumping taxi-drivers and biting people's ears off in clubs. It comes from having too much money and free time when they're too young to handle them.'

Tomlinson nodded.

'I was a player here for ten years, and I've been club secretary for the last thirty. I've seen plenty of that. But this feels different.'

'What's he supposed to have done?'

'Very similar scenario to Carlo's – except the complainant in this case is a man, not a woman.'

'Vince's not . . . ?'

'No, he isn't. And I wouldn't let him hear you suggest it if you want to stay connected to your teeth. This wasn't a sexual assault. He's accused of causing grievous bodily harm to a man in a Blackpool pub. But the circumstances were the same. The players are not supposed to drink for forty-eight hours before a match, but you know what they're like. He was over there with some of the others, having a few beers. He got up to go to the Gents, and as he came out this feller staggered into him and then accused Vince of beating him up.'

'And what does Vince say?'

'All he did was push him away and he fell down.'

'Must have been a firm push to cause GBH.'

'That's just it. Vince says this bloke was bleeding when he came towards him. As though he'd already been in a fight with someone else.'

'What do the other players say?'

'None of them saw it. They were still in the bar.'

'Were there no witnesses?'

'Two. They both back up the victim's story. Vince is adamant that they're lying, and it's a very serious matter for him. He's been in trouble before.'

That *had* been in all the papers. Naylor had been in an argument with a taxi-driver, and the court had taken a dim view of his breaking the driver's nose and throwing him through a plate-glass window.

'He's got a suspended prison sentence hanging over him for that,' said Tomlinson. 'If he's convicted again he'll go down for six months.'

'Leopards and spots spring to mind, Mr Tomlinson,' I said.

'That's the obvious explanation, yes. But there is another one. Someone's got it in for our best players. First Marco, now Naylor.'

'With copycat crime it's usually the criminal who is the copycat, not the victim,' I said.

'I think our players may *be* the victims,' said Tomlinson. 'Someone could be setting them up. They're picking their targets carefully so that it looks as though they're behaving in character. Coming on top of all our injuries, this could have a disastrous effect on the club. We haven't won a game for a month.'

'Have you told the police this?' I asked.

'What can the police do? These incidents took place in different counties. There are two separate investigations going on, and as far as the police are concerned, if the incidents are proved in court, that's the end of it. And the evidence is overwhelming in each case. All I've got is a conspiracy theory based on nothing more than a gut feeling.'

'But who would want to set up City players? What's in it for them?'

'I don't know. That's what I want you to find out. From what you've told me about Karen Pearson, she doesn't sound like the sort of lass who'd start screaming if someone like Carlo made a pass at her. I think she might be the key to this. Go and see her. Find out what went on the other night. Find out whether she's lying and, if so, why.'

'Look, Mr Tomlinson, I'm not a professional investigator. There are agencies that specialise in this sort of thing.'

'I know. And they charge big fees. While Jack Cox is a tax exile in the Isle of Man, Brian Deakin is still in day-to-day control here. Brian thinks it's just coincidence. He won't let me spend a lot of money on what he says is just a conspiracy theory, so I'll have to make do with you for the time being. You went to school with the lass. You've got an excuse to go and see her.'

It was hardly a vote of confidence, but funnily enough it made me feel better about going on with the case. If I failed to turn up anything else, I'd only be living down to his expectations.

'All right,' I said. 'But I charge two hundred a day.'

I thought I was chancing my luck. Two hundred a day sounded to me like the sort of big money the club secretary had been told not to spend. I still had a lot to learn about the finances of a Premiership football club.

Tomlinson just smiled. 'Sounds reasonable. Most of the people we employ wouldn't sign an autograph for that.'

'Plus legitimate expenses.'

'The next legitimate expenses claim I see will be the first,' he said. 'But I think we can run to reasonable expenses.'

I was beginning to think I'd undersold myself, and when I heard the helicopter landing on the pitch I knew I had.

'Sounds like the chairman's transport,' said Tomlinson.

As a tax exile, Cox flew in every fortnight to watch City play, and then flew straight out again so that he wasn't in mainland Britain long enough to be classed as a resident.

Cox's entourage moved with him towards the door, minnows round a shark. And the shark looked a little snappy.

'Jack's not happy,' said Tomlinson. 'He put up the money to buy Marconi and Naylor himself, and if they're convicted they could both be out of the game for a long time.'

'And what else does he get for his money?' I asked.

'This city and this club mean a lot to Jack.'

'But not enough for him to want to live here and pay taxes.' Now I was a fully fledged private eye I had a duty to insult my employer. Philip Marlowe did it all the time. 'And he does all right out of it. Every kid in town with a City shirt is advertising Cox's Carriers across his chest, and their parents are paying him for the privilege.' I was starting to sound like my father.

'Jack's all right,' said Tomlinson. 'I've known worse chairmen.'

'I'll need to talk to Carlo Marconi,' I said.

'He's been told to make himself scarce. The media are in full cry. Come to the ground on Monday. I'll get his agent to make sure he's here.'

'Are you sure this is not just a coincidence? Maybe they have both been bad lads,' I said as I got up to go.

'When you've been around footballers as long as I have, lad, you get to know when they're lying. They might be wealthy and famous, but they're still kids, and you can always tell when children are lying. I believe Marconi. And, though I wouldn't usually trust him as far as the corner flag, I believe Vince Naylor.'

You get to know when people are shrewd as well. Tomlinson might be past his best-before date, but the little tamperproof seal was still intact.

Chapter Four

'Steven!' she said as she pushed open the door of the spare room I now slept in.

When she called me Steven rather than Steve I knew I was in trouble. I was in trouble anyway, of course, otherwise I wouldn't be sleeping in the spare room. What I mean here is more trouble than usual.

'Yes, Liz,' I mumbled from under the duvet.

'Don't-call-me-Liz.'

She bit the words as she released them, so that they would cause more damage on impact, like dumdum bullets. But it was my own fault. I had deliberately drawn her fire. I had called her Liz to annoy her. No, let's be accurate about this. I had called her Liz to get my own back. I didn't yet know what I would have to get my own back about, but there would be something. There always was. It had degenerated into that kind of relationship.

'Liz was your name when I met you,' I said. We were at college then. Since she had risen to the dizzy heights of chief buyer for a national chain store she preferred to be known as Beth. Which says it all, really.

Things were different when we were at college. I was

the one with the hard currency in those days. I was an English student. I knew which books to read, which films to see, which gigs to go to. My friends were amusing and unconventional. I even loosed off the odd shaft of wit myself. Liz, on the other hand, was doing business studies. Business students rarely had enough equity in Life and Charisma plc, so girls with Liz's looks tended to put in takeover bids for people like me.

The balance of power began to shift as soon as the results came out. She got a 2:1 and it was the fast track to a management trainee's job and a wardrobe full of tailored suits. I didn't, and it was the stopping-train to the realisation that the ability to deconstruct the works of a Ford Escort would have been more use than knowing how to deconstruct the works of Ford Madox Ford.

'I want you out of that bed,' she said.

I resisted the temptation to say that I wanted her in it, although it would have been true. Liz, Beth, Elizabeth (which was actually her name) was still an attractive woman, well preserved and well turned out, although in a way designed to frighten other women rather than to attract other men. As a student at the mercy of my testosterone levels, it had been her looks, rather than her personality, which attracted me. She had never been very sexy. Sexiness to her meant no more than a difference in her level of willingness, which was now running on empty. But as she stood in the doorway with the light shining through the latest range of nightwear she herself had chosen as the next thing Mrs Average would be snuggling up in, her silhouetted legs were still as good as ever, and I would have been prepared to put our differences behind us for half an hour or so. But I also knew how she would respond – like the girls you see on the prom at Blackpool wearing KISS ME QUICK hats and expressions that say: *Just try it and you'll be crawling round the pavement looking for your goolies!*

'What for?'

'I've got some friends coming round to spend some quality time, and I want you out of the flat and that car of yours off the drive so that they can park.'

Quality time! That was the sub-text behind our impending divorce. When I asked her what was wrong with our relationship, she said, 'The quality's not there, Steve,' as though she was rejecting a batch of knickers from one of her suppliers.

'Why should I shift my car from my own drive?'

'It may have escaped your notice, but I'm the one who's paying the mortgage. And, unlike you, they all drive respectable cars. They won't want to leave them in the street.'

She was already tossing my clothes on to the bedside chair and stuffing the CDs I had been listening to the night before back into the rack. What was going on? Had they agreed to come only on condition that they would be given a conducted tour of the spare room? *This is where I keep my Filofax, this is where I keep those floppy scarves I wear with my business suits, this is where I keep my husband!*

It could have been a scene from the sort of movie we went to see at university. My arty friends would construct entire philosophies based on scenes like this from whatever perspective was fashionable that week: Marxism or feminism or pessimism. And Liz would say: 'It was just a fat slob lying in bed while his wife picked up his underpants.'

It was certainly symbolic of what we had become: Jack Spratt and his wife. She was active and I was passive, she was tidy, I was a slob. For her, still being in bed at eleven o'clock on a Sunday morning was a sign of degeneracy. For me it was the thing you did before you decided what you were going to do. It was like the time before the creation of the universe: value-free, the status quo, a neutral position beyond criticism. With goodwill on both sides, we could have licked the platter clean. Instead, we were falling apart.

'I have always stayed in bed on Sunday mornings. That's what Sunday mornings are for. They allow you to time-shift Saturday night to a more convenient moment, like videoing *Coronation Street*. It's you who's changed, not me,' I said.

'That's just the point. We're thirty years old, Steven. It's time you did change. You could start by getting a job, then you could find a place of your own and we wouldn't have to have these conversations.'

I didn't like being reminded that I was in her house under sufferance, so I got out of bed. She handed me my boxer shorts. I had lost the right to be naked in her presence, even in my own room.

'I haven't got a permanent job because since we left university we have been through recessions and downsizings and rationalisations and a Conservative government.'

'You forgot to mention the plague of locusts.'

'I did not. I distinctly remember mentioning the Conservative government.'

'I voted for them as a matter of fact, Steven.'

'You always did like to stand out from the crowd.'

The other infallible clue that a woman has gone off you big time is that she stops laughing at your jokes. Liz didn't laugh, and I knew we were beyond the point where I would ever get her to laugh again. Which was a pity, because the things I had originally liked about Liz I still liked. Like most heterosexual men, what I wanted in a wife was a combination of mother-substitute and my own private whore. Liz was rather better at the former than the latter, but a fifty per cent success rate is good for me. She was dependable, level-headed and honest. I knew she would never leave me for someone else, which was comforting. She was leaving me, of course (or rather throwing me out), but it would have been much more damaging to my fragile self-esteem if there was another bloke involved. She was not like that. But as she had no craving for children and had settled into a fulfilling and rewarding career, she seemed to have no immediate need for a man. Especially one who exasperated her as often as I did.

'As a matter of fact I start work on Monday.'

'What? A permanent, paid job?' She said it incredulously, but also as though it was the last thing she wanted to hear. For if I got the job she claimed she wanted me to have, she would have to find something else to moan about. She had plenty of choice. There was my untidiness, my reluctance to part with my clapped-out MGB and the fact that I held Dylan Thomas and Cole Porter in higher esteem than the inventor of the mobile phone, to name but a few. But my inability to hold down gainful employment was the easiest excuse she had for striking me from the books, writing me off as a bad debt.

'Self-employed,' I said.

'Self-employed what?'

I was already ticking off the things Beth would expect of a job – monthly salary paid by direct debit, company pension, company car, paid holidays, bank holidays, sickness pay, health insurance, share options, staff canteen. As what I was about to tell her met none of these criteria, I began to compensate by making the bed.

'Private investigator,' I said as I smoothed out the

bottom sheet and threw the duvet flamboyantly over it. While we were still living together (as opposed to simply living in the same flat) she complained I didn't do enough around the house, so I started making the beds and hoovering. She followed me round the flat and did it again, her way.

'Get real, Steven,' she said. The shake of the head, the closed eyes, was the body language of contempt. 'How long are you going to live on Fantasy Island?'

'They're paying me two hundred pounds a day plus exp . . .'

'The bed needs to air before you make it,' she said, flinging the duvet off again and opening the window. 'Now get dressed and go out and take that car of yours with you.'

To have told her it wouldn't start would only have confirmed her view of me and my car, so I washed and shaved and released the handbrake and let the MG roll slowly back into the street.

I went to see Mum and Dad partly because I had nowhere else to go on a Sunday morning but mainly because they took the *News of the World*.

Big cities are like trees. Take any arterial road as a core sample and you can date their concentric rings. Mum and Dad live between the Victorian redbrick terraces that open into the street and the concrete high-rise flats that open into lifts that stink of piss. Theirs is a brick-built semi with its own garden in a cul-de-sac on a prewar council estate. There's a parade of shops just round the corner with a butcher and a baker, though the candlestick-making franchise has been replaced by a video store. They are respectable working class and therefore an endangered species, though maybe they wouldn't be if the council hadn't started tipping slums on their gable ends and poking them into the sky when they ran out of money to build proper houses like this.

Mum's pleasure at seeing me twice in one week almost made up for her disappointment that Beth and I were splitting up. She had always liked Beth because she was a nice, sensible girl. Now she felt she should dislike her but hadn't yet come up with a reason, apart from the divorce.

'You'll stay for your dinner,' she said.

As usual, I took the line of least resistance. It led straight to Yorkshire pudding and an afternoon in front of the movie channel.

'Did you see the game?'

'Just the highlights on telly,' said Dad.

'Short programme then, was it?'

'You can't expect City to play well with their three best players out of the side. What they need is strength in depth, but even with Jack Cox's money they can't afford the silly prices being paid for players these days. Now in the old days we would have been bringing kids through the youth team . . .'

And when you needed a centre forward you just shouted down the nearest pit-shaft. I'd heard it all before, so I let him ride his hobbyhorse off into the sunset while I flicked through the paper. There was a teaser on page one:

UNCOVERED – THE GIRL WHO BLEW THE WHISTLE ON MARCO – PAGE 7.

And there she was, Karen Pearson as I had never seen her before. I knew the picture was a few years old, and that photographers had airbrushes and other ways of touching these things up, and that she probably had her nipples in ice seconds before the shot was taken (is that how the chest freezer got its name?), but it reminded me why every lad in our school had wanted to take Karen behind the bike sheds.

And I was going to see her tomorrow.

I tried to imagine what Beth would make of the little rush of adrenaline I was getting at the thought of it. I was in a win-win situation. My theory was that either Karen would admit that she had set up Carlo Marconi and tell me who had put her up to it, or she would try to buy me off with sex.

Yes, I know Philip Marlowe always declined to have sex when gorgeous women offered it to him, but I'm new to this job, so it's too soon to expect perfection.

Before seeing Karen, however, I first needed to talk to Carlo Marconi.

Chapter Five

She had a long neck and an aquiline nose to match, deep blue eyes and a pale face surrounded by curly hair on the short side of outrageous and the forgivable side of ginger.

Not Carlo Marconi. Pay attention! I'm talking about the girl behind the reception desk at the football ground. Jack Cox hasn't got round to building a new stand yet, but the foyer has been given a makeover by someone whose day job is designing building-society interiors. The stainless steel and the matt-grey high-density fibreboard don't clash too fiercely with the rusting corrugated-iron roof.

I call her a girl because she is about my age and it makes me feel better.

'If you're press you can wait for Mr Farrell over there,' she said.

Jimmy Farrell was City's manager, and to prove it there was a sign that said MANAGER on his office door. A little group of hacks and a photographer were already hanging around outside it, waiting for their daily audience with the man responsible for City's playing activities.

I thought she was a bit offhand for a receptionist, but

at least she didn't say, 'My name is Carol King. How may I help you?', which more than made up for it. Her attitude seemed to stem from some inner hurt that made her care a little less what people thought of her than a receptionist should. But it wasn't far removed from sassiness. She wore a uniform in the club colours, and I knew her name was Carol King because it said so on the badge above her left breast. Lousy suit, so-so badge, nice breasts.

'I'm not Press,' I said.

'And you're not a player, are you?'

'Do I look that unfit?'

'Yes. And you're not an agent.'

'How do you know?'

'You'd be better dressed. And you'd be a slimy creep.'

I could have played guessing games with her all morning, but she was losing interest.

'So what do you want?' she asked.

'I'm here to see Carlo Marconi.'

'So you're Steve Strong, private eye.'

It was the first time someone else had said it, and it didn't sound bad.

'I've never met a private eye before,' she said.

'Neither have I.'

'What?'

'Never mind. I'll explain over a drink some time.' I don't normally flirt when I'm sober, but some women have that effect on you. Carol King was one of them. And she didn't tell me to get stuffed, which is always encouraging.

'Mr Tomlinson said you'd be here. Marco's in with Mr Farrell and his agent, Marty Weller. They'll be out in a minute. Then you'll see what I mean about agents.'

I saw what she meant about agents.

Carlo Marconi came out of the manager's office with Jimmy Farrell and a small man who smoked a big cigar and wore a suit that would have blended with the wall-paper if the wallpaper had been puce with a silver thread. His jewellery weighed more than he did. He looked like a bad caricature of a Hollywood movie mogul, but the effect his appearance had on the reporters made his cigar seem like a cattle prod. They had been waiting to see the City manager, but Weller and his client had the better story.

'Marty!'

'Any chance of a word with Marco?'

'What's he say to the girl's accusations?'

The photographer was shooting film like clay pigeons, though Weller and Marconi were sitting ducks. The agent put his arm round his client and grinned at the camera. The club had been keeping the Italian away from reporters since his arrest, but this was no media ambush. Weller must have known they would be there, and he seemed happy to play ball.

'Marco absolutely rejects these charges, and we are confident that they will never come to court,' he said in a London accent that would have made a pearly king blush. A vote of confidence in a football ground is usually worth less than the down payment on a box of matches, but Weller sounded confident enough. Like many small men, extroversion and a loud voice made up for his lack of stature. He could have coxed a rowing-club eight and saved them the expense of a megaphone.

'Can Marco tell us what happened in his own words?'

'His English ain't too good,' said Weller. 'But we'll be talking to the police about it. Nightclubs are crowded places. This young lady's obviously made a mistake. A case of mistaken identity.'

That didn't seem likely. There had been no one else in the corridor by the lavatories when the incident was alleged to have happened, and Mediterranean tans are as rare as virgins in Yorkshire nightclubs in the middle of November.

Carlo Marconi looked bemused and said nothing. Jimmy Farrell said nothing either, but he looked annoyed. Being ignored is not what Premier League managers expect at their own daily press call. Carol King came to his rescue.

'Mr Weller, Mr Strong's here to see you.'

'Steve!' Weller greeted me as though we were old business associates. Shaking hands was like grasping a bunch of ripe bananas. 'Mind if I use your office for five minutes, Jim?'

Jim looked as though he did, but the reporters realised they were not going to get any more from Weller or Marconi, and they turned to the manager. As we went into his office he was saying something about not having paid ten million pounds for Marconi to sit on the bench while the police made enquiries about his private life.

Weller swivelled in the high-backed chair behind Farrell's desk. The smile was still on full beam.

'Steve! Tom Tomlinson says you want to talk to Marco about the other night. But you heard what I said to the reptiles out there – there's nothing to talk about. Marco never laid a finger on the girl, and when she sees there's no money in it she'll back off. I've seen it before, Steve. It happens all the time in this game. Gold-diggers didn't die with Busby Berkeley. It's no secret that players like Marco earn big money, and there are plenty of little tarts out there who think they've got what it takes to get their hands on some of his dosh. When this Carol . . .'

'Karen!'

'Whatever. When dangling her tits in front of the boy didn't work, she tried the other approach. She's looking for a bit of payola.'

'Has she asked for money?' I said.

'Not yet, but she will. Compensation for shock and distress, they usually call it. For a financial consideration she won't press charges.'

'It's usually called blackmail,' I said.

Marty shrugged. So Denise Talbot had been telling me the truth about Karen, it seemed. If it was going to be this easy, I wouldn't be on two hundred pounds a day plus expenses for long.

'Tom Tomlinson thinks it might be part of something more sinister,' I said. 'Vince Naylor is facing an assault charge, and he says he didn't do it, either. The victim was a man, and nobody's said anything about blackmail there.'

Weller tipped the chair back and laughed. The decibel count probably contravened the regulations in a built-up area. Marconi looked at him and then at me, wondering what was going on.

'Vince Naylor! Listen, I've seen Vince Naylor chop Ryan Giggs's legs from under him two yards from the referee and then claim he never made contact. Vince Naylor is a thug and a pathological liar, and consequently a great player to have in your back four. But if somebody says Vince gave him a knuckle sandwich after closing time, suggesting that it was out of character is probably not going to impress the magistrates. I'd go for provocation or self-defence rather than the not-guilty plea.'

'He's got a suspended sentence hanging over him. If he's convicted of this, he goes down for six months,' I said.

'So he would deny it, wouldn't he?' said Weller. 'Want my advice? Slip the guy Vince thumped enough readies to persuade him not to press charges. It's a cost-effective alternative to buying a new right back at today's inflated prices.'

'Isn't that called perverting the course of justice?'

'Dear me, you have got a lot to learn. Personally, seeing Vince Naylor go down for a half-stretch would give me more pleasure than seeing Arsenal knocked out of the Cup by Leyton Orient, but it wouldn't be justice. Do you know how much it costs to keep someone in the slammer for six months? A lot of bunce, that's how much. And who pays for it? The taxpayer – the bloke who spilled Vince's beer and had his teeth rearranged for his trouble. So slip him a few quid, and everybody's better off. And if you want to punish Vince, stop it out of his wages. That'd send the price of brewery shares plunging.'

You can tell a lot about people from the language they use. Eskimos have fifty different words for snow, but Weller had even more for money. Yet it told you nothing about the man at all. Marty Weller was a living example of post-modernism, although he probably didn't know it. Novelists spend years cultivating the sense of irony that came to Marty Weller naturally.

The wide-boy persona served two purposes. It got him recognised, which was useful in his line of work, and it stopped people laughing at him. As the tabloids have realised, you can't laugh at someone who is sending himself up. The only way you could hurt someone like Marty Weller was by punching him on the nose. He might be an obnoxious little bastard, but I could see why the top players employed people like him. He took responsibility for their wage demands and their transfer fees, and by blaming them on market forces offered them a kind of religious absolution that was well worth whatever percentage he kept for himself.

'Listen, Steve, how long have you been at this job?'

'Not long.'

'I didn't think so. I know a few geezers in your game in London and, to be honest, if I thought there was any point in having this tart investigated, I'd bring one of them in and get the job done proper. No offence, of course. But if you take my tip you'll find yourself another racket. There's no lolly in it. It's a charity game, like cancer research. Once you find a cure, people stop giving you money.'

'But until the club stops giving me money I'm going to go on doing the job,' I said.

He took the cigar out of his mouth and looked at me over tented fingers. 'How much they paying you?'

'Two hundred a day,' I said.

'And there's, what . . . a week's work in this? A grand plus whatever you can fiddle on expenses. Listen, I'll do you a favour.' He took a chequebook and a Mont Blanc pen as thick as his cigar from his inside pocket and began to write. 'Two grand to compensate you for loss of earnings.'

He held the cheque across the desk to me.

'You're offering to buy me off?'

'I'm paying you not to go stamping all over toes that will get better sooner if we leave them alone. My client's been upset enough over this. Footballers are sensitive souls. They don't play well if they're upset. I don't want you doing anything to upset him more.'

The cheque hung there between us like an unanswered question. It was tempting to reach out and take it. Two thousand quid would keep me for a couple of months while I looked round for a proper job. Beth would think I was behaving like an adult. I could stay in bed in the mornings, get up late, tinker with the MG and get it back on the road.

But when I'd spent the money I would either have no

job, or a job I didn't want to do. I would still be living in Beth's flat on Beth's charity. And I wouldn't know if I could have made it as a private eye. Of course, it also made it easier to take the high moral ground because I knew it would annoy the hell out of Marty Weller.

'Like your client, I'm on the payroll of City FC, and I intend to do the job they're paying me to do.'

Weller held the cheque over Jimmy Farrell's wastebin and slowly tore it to pieces.

'When you're holding out for more,' he said, easing his frame out of the tilting chair, 'you need to know the strength of your negotiating position. What you've got doesn't stack up to more than two big ones.'

In a single gesture he stubbed out his cigar and switched off the bonhomie. 'You're a novice who's stumbled into a job that's too big for him. Don't compare yourself with Marco. He's a Premier League player. You're just out of your league. But don't get in my way, Stevie.'

Carlo Marconi got up too, smoothed down his Armani suit and followed Weller out of the room. I had no idea if he had understood a word of what we had been saying. It had not been the most successful client interview a private investigator has ever conducted, perhaps, but it hadn't been a complete waste of time. If ever I felt like giving up on this case, I'd think of Marty Weller and try a little bit harder to come up with something that would leave him with shit on his two-tone shoes.

'I thought you said he was a slimy little creep,' I said to Carol King on my way out. 'Is he bribing you to be nice about him?'

Weller and Marconi were standing by the smart new plate-glass doors that had CITY engraved on them in the way pubs used to have PUBLIC BAR frosted on to their windows but in a more self-consciously arty typeface.

Weller was talking to a man who was on his way in. He had lit a fresh cigar and the smile was alight again, too. The pair of them seemed on fairly intimate terms, like two members of the same tribe meeting by chance in the jungle.

'Morning, Mr Deakin,' said Carol King as City's former chairman passed her desk.

'Weller's obviously well connected round here,' I said.

'The agents know all the directors,' said Carol. 'They're the ones who control the purse strings. The manager can buy players only if they say so. Do you know Brian Deakin?'

'No, but I was once knocked over by his wife's breath.'

I followed Weller out and watched him drive away in a new and rather vulgar Rolls-Royce.

But Marco was still in the car park, standing under an advertising hoarding on which some supermodel whose name I couldn't remember was displaying to great advantage a particular make of brassiere. The same poster had been responsible for a spate of traffic accidents all over the city.

When he saw me he came over. He moved in a way that was languid and athletic, laid-back and purposeful at the same time. And his English turned out to be better than previously advertised.

'When I say I don't touch that woman I tell the truth,' he said. 'Why I want to mess with a . . . *donna di malaffare* . . . when I got *her* for my girl?'

He was referring to the model on the hoarding. And he wasn't joking.

'She's your girlfriend?' I said, looking – not for the first time – at the magnified and magnificent cleavage. My mind went back to the even more revealing pictures of Karen Pearson in the Sunday papers, and now I knew why some models made it to the top and some, like Karen, fell by the wayside. This didn't prove Marco hadn't groped her, of course. If superbosom was on a film shoot in the Bahamas, a bird in the hand, as they say . . . But as Tom Tomlinson had said, you can usually feel when someone is telling the truth.

'Yeah. And she don't like the bad publicity about this. You find out the truth about this and show I never touch that woman. OK?'

'OK,' I said.

Chapter Six

There was only one place to start, and that was with Karen Pearson.

The media posse had disappeared from outside her flat, although the cable company was still digging up the road. There was no reason why Karen should talk to me. We had never been particularly friendly at school. She might not even remember me, and if she showed me the door that would effectively be the end of my career as a private investigator. Either Weller would buy her off or it would be her word against Marco's in court.

I rehearsed my little speech as I walked up the stairs. My heart was pounding as I rang the bell, and not from the exertion of the climb. Now that it had come to the crunch I was as nervous as hell.

There was no reply, but the woman in the next flat opened her door.

'Are you from the cable company?'

It seemed a pity to disappoint her, so I said I was.

'Karen's out, but she left the key with me.'

Even Arsenal don't have many results as lucky as that. I thanked her and let myself in. It was a nice flat in a girlie sort of way – pink carpet, pink velvet suite, chintzy curtains. The bedroom door was open. More pink and fluffy things, which was disappointing. What had I expected to find – mirrors on the ceiling, bondage equipment on the bedhead? If she was on the game, perhaps she played on a neutral ground.

There was a bureau in the sitting-room, with a few papers and items of mail on the open flap. As I passed, a slip of curled paper fluttered to the floor. It would have been rude not to pick it up. It was one of those slips you get from a cash machine which tells you how much (or how little, in my case) is in your account. The last amount deposited was for five thousand pounds. No wonder Karen could afford to subscribe to cable TV.

At first I thought it was payment from a newspaper for her exclusive revelations. Then I noticed that the money had been deposited the day before she had accused Carlo Marconi of indecent assault.

I was still wondering about that when the front door opened and Karen walked in. 'What the fuck are you doing here?'

'Hi, Karen. The lady next door let me in.'

'Do I know you?'

'Steve Strong. We were in the same year at school.'

'And did I tell you then that you could break into my flat whenever you wanted and read my bank statement?'

'Sorry,' I said. I know: that sounds a bit feeble for a private eye. Perhaps when I've been beaten up a few times I'll start getting the hang of being tough about things like that.

'The football club wants me to talk to you about what happened in the Double Two the other night.'

'Why should they want *you* to talk to me?'

'I'm a private investigator,' I said.

Maybe I didn't say it with enough conviction, because it did not disturb her icy-cool for more than a nanosecond.

'I've said everything I've got to say to the police. Now, why don't I call them and have you arrested for breaking and entering?'

I used to think the University of Life was just a name on the T-shirts of those with inferiority complexes about people with degrees. I was wrong. Whatever Karen Pearson had been doing while I was at university learning that T.S. Eliot was an anagram of TOILETS, it had equipped her to handle situations like this better than I could. Life studies had made Karen a tough lady.

'Look, I have to talk to you. If I'd rung the bell, would you have let me in?'

'No, but I would have appreciated being asked. Now get out.'

As she held open the door I could see that she still had the high cheekbones, the almost platinum hair and the perfect legs that had us salivating in the fourth form. She was sexy in an obvious way, but without being too tarty. Although it was late autumn she was wearing a top that showed her bellybutton and an inch of midriff: the minimalist approach to turning men on.

But closer inspection revealed that some exterior decoration was already being done and a little building work would be needed before long. Make-up filled her pores like a thin skim of plaster, and the incipient flap of skin beneath her chin would sooner or later sag like paper peeling from a damp wall. But compared with the ruin that Ann Humpage had become, Karen Pearson was still in pretty good nick for her age.

'A friend of yours was asking after you the other day,' I said. It was a desperate throw, but she had to ask who it was, didn't she?

65

'Ann,' I said. 'The two of you were inseparable when you were at school.'

'You mean she was like a limpet,' said Karen. 'I couldn't shake her off.'

'You did when you left school.'

'She was never going to keep up, was she? Dumpy was always a loser. I suppose that's why I hung around with her for so long. I was doing her a favour. The minute I went off to London she got herself pregnant by the first bloke who was desperate enough to screw her. Poor cow.'

'She's still living on the estate,' I said. 'She's got a disabled kid. She asked to be remembered to you.'

'I'll bet,' she said. 'And little Steve Strong has become a private investigator, has he? You never seemed that interesting.'

She was holding those paper carrier bags with the cord handles that show you can afford not to shop in Marks & Spencer. She took them into the bedroom and dumped them on the bed. I closed the door from the inside.

'Look, Karen, all I need to know is what happened. For old time's sake.'

'I don't remember any old times with you, Steve. But all right. He came out of the Gents, where I suppose he'd been playing with his cock, walked towards me and put his hand just there.'

She placed her hand on the front of the ski pants she was wearing, at the point where the stretchy velvet material defined her mound of Venus. It stirred something in the trouser department for me, too, but for some bizarre reason it also made me think of Marty Weller. He had tried to buy me off with money, and there was something about the upfront way Karen offered this sexual confidence that made me feel she was trying to buy me off as well.

66

'And that was enough to make you send for the police?'

'Yes. It was. I don't like being treated like a tart.'

'That's not what I heard.'

The look she gave me said that if I ever entertained hopes of getting anything out of her, information or sex, I'd just blown it.

'What's that supposed to mean?'

'It means I've heard you'll sleep with men if the money is right, and that they don't necessarily stop paying when they put their trousers back on.'

'You what?'

'Prostitution and blackmail. Or is there some other reason why somebody's just paid five thousand quid into your bank account?'

For the first time since she had come home to find a strange man in her flat she looked rattled. For a moment she said nothing, as though computing the odds before placing a bet. But it didn't take her long to decide that if she were going to bet against someone, then it would be me.

'Now I *am* going to call the fucking police.'

I could have done a runner, but what was the point? Karen knew who I was. It wouldn't be difficult for the police to track me down, and the last thing I wanted was the constabulary turning up on Beth's doorstep. Besides, the reasons Karen would give the police for calling them might prove interesting.

As a council tax payer, I was impressed by the speed and efficiency with which they arrived. No histrionics, no blue lights or sirens: just a patrol car pulling up outside and a couple of bobbies appearing at the door with helmets under their arms.

But what Karen told them was the last thing I expected.

'I want this pervert arrested,' she said. 'He's a bloody

67

stalker. He was outside my flat the other day, and when I got back just now he'd tricked his way in pretending to be the cable TV man.'

'Is this true, sir?'

'Well, yes, but . . .'

'I'm frightened to go out because of blokes like him. My picture was in the papers the other day and ever since I've been plagued by dirty old wankers like him. Listen to this!'

There was an answering machine beside the phone, and she pressed the playback button. The tape babbled back on itself and then kicked in with some sad bastard telling Karen what he would like to do to her and what he was currently doing to himself. She sat on the sofa with her head in her hands. Tears would have been an understandable reaction from most women to the filth we had been listening to, but I knew Karen was tougher than that.

'I think we'd better discuss this down at the police station, sir.'

So much for police brutality. They just beat you about the head with an old sock stuffed with tightly packed politeness.

'We'll be in touch, madam, to get a statement. Do you want a WPC to come and sit with you?'

'I'll be OK,' she said. 'Just get him out of here.' When she lifted her head there was no sign of tears.

On the way to the station I told them my story. I think they believed me, but it didn't stop them giving me a hard time.

'Private investigators and security firms give us more grief than ordinary, decent criminals. They also make us feel redundant. In future, sunshine, stick to divorce stuff and leave criminal investigation to us.'

But when we reached the station they showed why private eyes can get things done quicker than the police. They had to do things by the book. Which meant I had to be released on police bail. Which meant Beth had to come down and stand surety for me.

Beth was level-headed and businesslike. I knew she wouldn't overreact. I could count on one hand the number of times I've heard Beth swear.

'Steve, you are a total fucking prick. If I have to fucking forfeit five fucking hundred quid, you are a dead man. Get in the fucking car.'

OK. Two hands. But at least I didn't have to answer a loving wife's standard question: 'How was your first day at the office, dear?'

Chapter Seven

When I got up the next morning, Beth had left last night's *Post* on the kitchen table open at the Situations Vacant column. There was no note, but she had ringed three of the ads in red felt-tip. They all looked so numbingly boring that if you had a vasectomy without anaesthetic while doing them you probably wouldn't feel a thing. But the way things were going I would be needing a proper job fairly soon. Sending off for the application forms would buy me some domestic peace for the price of three stamps, and I posted the letters on my way to the football ground.

The public areas of the stadium had all been given a makeover at Jack Cox's expense, but the furniture in Tom Tomlinson's office looked as though it had been there longer than he had. The oak desk was innocent of any of the trappings of a modern business executive: no computer screen, no Filofax, the telephone didn't look like the flight deck of Concorde and he didn't even have one of those naff executive toys made out of rubbery play-dough that you squeeze to relieve stress.

A glass-fronted oak cabinet filled one wall. It held

copies of all City's match-day programmes, bound in leather, a volume for each year. The walls were hung with framed photographs of teams of the past with their arms folded and their knees apart and the date painted on the football between the captain's feet. Most of them were in black and white. Because the players were all young men caught up in the fashion of the moment, they offered a cultural history of Britain since the war, from the short-back-and-sides and tight shorts of National Service days, through the long-haired rebels of the late 1960s and Afro-permed 1970s to the baggy shorts of the 1980s.

But the sequence of pictures stopped shortly after sponsors' names started to appear on the shirts, as if Tomlinson could not be bothered to frame the most recent ones. His office reminded me of the headmaster's study at a boys' school. And, like school history lessons, it stopped a few years ago, just short of the contemporary. It was as though Tomlinson hadn't quite come to terms with today's teams, with all their foreigner players and the way money was rewriting soccer history.

I told him about Marty Weller's attempt to buy me out and about Karen's call to the police. But Tomlinson didn't need any further confirmation of his gut feeling that something fishy was going on. He tossed that morning's edition of the *Post* across the desk. The page-one splash headline said:

CITY STAR

IN SEASIDE

RUMPUS

'I don't know how they got hold of the story. The police say they didn't release it, and we certainly didn't. And the players who were with him got him out of the pub before it blew up into a big issue, so it's not likely that another customer tipped off the papers. You'd better go and talk to Vince Naylor,' he said. 'He'll be up at the training ground. Carol on reception will give you a pass to get in. And go and see the bloke who says Vince thumped him.'

Tomlinson handed me a copy of the court summons. The complainant's name was Kevin Carter and the address was in Blackpool.

I hoped the MGB would get me over the Pennines. After I failed to get it started when Beth's friends were coming round, I phoned my mate Nick and he towed it round to his lock-up workshop under the railway arches. Nick pretended he dealt in classic cars – Morris Minors, that kind of thing – but what he really did was repair them, which was just as well because the kind of cars he sold needed repair fairly often. That made my MGB right up his street, though he'd spent most of the time I was there describing how the redhead he'd picked up was to sexual activity what Olga Korbut had been to gymnastics, so God knows what kind of job he'd do on my car.

'What I don't understand,' I told Tomlinson, 'is why two different people should bring false charges against City players. Is it one of the other big clubs trying to stop us winning the League?'

'It's not horseracing. We haven't got round to nobbling the opposition. Not off the field, anyway.'

'Then what's the angle?'

'That's what I want you to find out,' said Tomlinson. 'Do you know Tony Wilson – sports reporter with the *Post*?'

'I've seen his name in the paper.' It was Wilson who had written the Vince Naylor story.

'Go and talk to him. Tell him I sent you. He's covered City for twenty years. He knows more about what's happening at this club than anybody, me included. You can tell him you're making enquiries about Vince and Marco, but don't give him enough to write a story. Tony's a good friend of this club, but he's a journalist first and foremost.'

'What's a nice bloke like you want in a place like that?' said Carol King as she wrote out my pass for the training ground.

'I need to talk to one of the players.'

'Which one?'

'Vince Naylor.'

'Don't use any long words.'

'That bad, eh?'

'He's only here because the zoo wouldn't have him. He was frightening the gorillas.'

'You don't have a very good opinion of professional footballers, do you?'

'I was married to one,' she said.

'But not any more?'

'I still have the ring. I no longer have the player.'

'I'm sorry.'

She shrugged. 'Don't be. I knew it was a gamble. Footballers either end up running pubs in Heckmondwike or earning zillions of lire in Rome or Milan. The pub landlords need a woman to make the sandwiches, but a wife tends to cramp your style on the beach at Rimini.'

'And yours got the Italian job?'

'And a bimbo named Gina who makes a great bowl of pasta.'

You don't often come across a woman with a half-decent line in self-deprecating wit, and I liked that. I didn't even find the underlying rattle of bitterness that is the symptom of a malfunctioning love life particularly annoying, because I knew the feeling myself. Carol King

74

had the kind of personality I find attractive in a woman. All right, I liked some of her physical features, too, but it's important for a man to retain a healthy balance between the sensitive and sensual sides of his nature.

'Listen, I'd like to talk to you some time. Working in reception, you must know all the players pretty well.'

'Yes. But information will cost you the price of a drink.'

'Are you sure? A private investigator's an even lower form of life than a politician or a journalist.'

'I'll take a chance,' she said. 'You don't seem like one of those blokes who spends all night explaining why the 4–4–2 system is better than three central defenders and thinks his body's so wonderful I'll tear his clothes off the minute the pubs close.'

They weren't the most positive reasons for agreeing to come out with me, but there's no shame in being chosen because you're not as bad as the alternative. That's how most Prime Ministers are elected.

'Where shall I see you?' I asked.

'In the wine bar in the Victoria Arcade. After work tomorrow.'

And she had a point about the 4–4–2 system. Give me three central defenders and a couple of overlapping fullbacks every time.

City's training ground was on the edge of town – a brick pavilion and an all-weather pitch with a surface of raked sand like a parade ground. It was surrounded by a six-foot chain-link fence and floodlights. It could have been a prisoner-of-war camp except that the inmates were German and Italian as well as English and Scottish, and the wire was not to keep them in but to keep other people out.

When I arrived there were plenty of people outside the wire. Soccer groupies: young lads who should have been at school, teenage girls who confused damp knickers with a liking for football, and a few sad adults with autograph books and beer bellies that strained the credibility of their replica shirts. They peered through the mesh, watching the tracksuited players run backwards and sideways across the sand and dribble balls round traffic cones. It was the sort of training that would prove invaluable the next time the opposition selected a set of traffic cones instead of a back four.

The world's moved on since *Upstairs, Downstairs*. Now it's insiders and outsiders. The insiders drive the Mercs and BMWs with the sponsors' names on in the car park. The outsiders pay forty quid twice a season for the latest designer nightmare of a City shirt with a logo that turns them into unpaid sandwich boards for Cox's Carriers. Some of them pay a pound a letter to have the name of a player on their backs. The current name of choice was Marconi.

I showed my pass to the security man, and as he ushered me through the locked gate I learned what it was like to be an insider at the club. Maybe it was little more than a magnified sense of the reflected glory that made people fork out for shirts and car stickers and anoraks at the club shop. But privilege made the mirror seem more highly polished.

Jimmy Farrell was in his tracksuit, shouting instructions to the players, but when he saw me he left the little group and came across.

'You here to talk to Vince? I see he's got himself into the headlines again. I'll call him over when we've finished. Take him straight to the pavilion, will you? I don't want the vultures getting at him.'

I had noticed the little knot of reporters as I came in. They were watching the players in a different way from the fans, as professional gamblers watch the horses in training on Newmarket Heath.

I stood on the touchline until the training routine ended. Vince Naylor trained with the same barely restrained anger with which he played. He had none of the inbred empathy for the ball, or sense of balance or flowing grace of a born footballer, but looked instead like an animal bred to do a specific job. A pit bull terrier, perhaps. He was no taller than me, but his thighs were defined with the clarity of one of those textbook anatomical drawings in which the skin has been stripped away from the muscles.

Farrell blew a whistle to bring the session to an end and brought Vince over.

'Are you the detective?' he asked in his Glasgow accent. Before I could confirm it he jabbed a finger towards me and said: 'Then listen. I want this fuckin' sorted.'

He wore fading tattoos on his arms, and his close-cropped hair made him seem both ugly and menacing, which was presumably the effect intended. I don't know if he frightened opposing forwards, but he certainly worried me.

Vince Naylor was the antithesis of the beautiful, languid Carlo Marconi. If someone had set out to accuse one player of sexuality and the other of brutality, the choice would have been simple. Vince was not the sort of bloke you'd want to upset without a referee to protect you, and preferably not even then.

'Take him to the pavilion, Vince,' said Farrell, 'and keep your hair on. He's on our side.'

Farrell strode across to head off the sports writers who were being allowed through the gate, and I followed Naylor and the other players into the pavilion.

Most of them stripped off and went to the showers, but Naylor led me into a small back room used for weight training and perched himself astride a steel bench from which barbells were suspended.

'So what are ye gonna do aboot all this?' he said. 'I'm all over the fuckin' papers this mornin'.'

He began lifting and lowering the weights as we talked, as though the constant expansion and contraction of his muscles was as essential to life as breathing, something that even a conversation that could make the difference between freedom and imprisonment ought not to be allowed to interrupt.

'I need to know what happened before I can do anything,' I said. 'Talk me through what happened in Blackpool, Vince.'

'Nothin' fuckin' happened, did it? We went over there for a quiet drink – tae see the illuminations. After a wee while I went oot for a jimmy riddle and this dickhead walked up and started shovin' me. I just shoved him back. It was no' hard. He fell on his arse and started screamin' that I'd thumped him.'

'How hard did you shove him?'

Vince Naylor looked as though he could shove for Scotland if the mood took him. He pumped iron as rhythmically as a machine, and the sweat glistened on his taut skin.

'Look, it was nothin'. If I'd really wanted to thump him, he'd still be in hospital, no sweat.'

'How much had you had to drink?'

'Listen, son, I wasnae drunk. Two or three pints is all. We'd only just got there.'

The echoing voices of the other players drifted through from the showers. Like any group of young men, they fooled around when they got together. I wondered how much fooling around there had been in the Blackpool pub, and whether it had got out of hand.

'Did any of the other players see what happened?'

'No. I told ye. I'd gone for a jimmy. I don't need somebody to hold ma tackle for me, son.'

'The police report says he had a broken nose and blood all down his face and shirt.'

'Somebody else must have thumped him, then, 'cos I never touched him. I'd never set eyes on him afore.'

'So why should he pick on you? And why claim you'd broken his nose if you hadn't?'

'Listen. I play the game hard, and I upset the opposing fans sometimes. Some of them like to have a go back. Especially when they've had a few drinks.'

The voices were coming from the changing-room now, where the players were getting back into the designer leisurewear they had arrived in, their day's work over. I would have expected liniment and sweat, but the smell that wafted in could have come from a tart's handbag. If the players weren't being paid to use pungent personal hygiene products, they needed smarter agents.

'And was this Kevin Carter a hard man who'd been tanking up on Dutch courage?' I asked Naylor.

'No' really. He hardly touched me.' He let the weights he was lifting clatter to the concrete floor. 'Listen. The footba' club's payin' you to sort this out. So get it fuckin' sorted. OK?'

'I'm trying to,' I said.

'Aye, and while you fanny aboot I've got a six-month suspended hanging over me because some other pillock in a pub thought he was well-hard. I'm no gonna be spendin' Christmas in jail for sumthin' I didnae do. So sort it!'

One of the other players stuck a showered head round the door. 'You still tossing off in there, Nails?'

Vince picked up a can of deodorant and flung it at the closing door. 'Go fuck yoursel'.'

If this was his idea of playful banter, no wonder there was blood on the floor of the pubs he frequented.

'Don't worry,' I said. 'We'll sort it.'

'Listen,' said Naylor, setting the weights in motion again, 'if I'd thumped that guy I would have broken his bloody neck, not just his nose.'

It was probably unwise to believe much Vince Naylor said, but my instinct told me that Tomlinson was right again. I believed him.

The other players had begun drifting away to their sponsored cars, signing autographs as they struggled through the little knots of fans. But Naylor showed no sign of going. I left him working out his frustrations on two hundred pounds of Sheffield steel.

The trouble with being a Humphrey Bogart fan is that I expect things to be as they were in a 1930s Hollywood movie, but the modern world keeps letting me down.

Take the *Post*'s editorial floor. No clacking typewriters, no strident telephones, no forests of paper cascading from the desks, no Rosalind Russell crossing her legs on the edge of the news editor's desk. It was as if all these things had been sucked into the silent computer screens that held the journos so spellbound they didn't even seem capable of talking to each other.

Tony Wilson's face was familiar, and I realised he had been among the little group of reporters at the training ground. The *Post* billed him for years as 'The Voice of City'. He was middle-aged and balding and still dressed in the modern equivalent of what was in fashion in his formative years. Tony wore a navy-blue blazer with silver buttons, grey flannels, and a gold tie embossed with the

City crest. He looked more like a bank manager winding down for early retirement than a journalist who had broken the biggest sports story of the week. He was also the oldest man on a sports desk made up mainly of sharp-looking blokes in their twenties and the token woman.

But on his desk were the things that set him above the others – at least until tomorrow's paper came out. There was the page-one story about Naylor and yesterday's follow-up to Marconi's arrest, also beneath his byline and the headline:

CITY ACE
TO FIGHT
SEX CASE

'Thanks for seeing me, Tony,' I said. 'I know you're a busy man.'

'Yeah. It's been a busy week. But Tom Tomlinson's an old mate, so what can I do for you?'

When I told him he pulled on an old gabardine mac and buckled the belt at the front, which was something I thought had died with Robert Mitchum.

'I talk better over a liquid lunch,' he said.

The barman at the Dove and Rainbow began pulling him a pint of Stones as we walked through the door. Tony Wilson sucked down the first inch of his pint and leaned back against the bar – a man content in his comfort zone.

'It makes a change to have somebody to talk to over a pint,' he said. 'This place used to be full of journos at lunchtime. Now these young kids are scared to leave their desks in case someone younger and cheaper has been brought in to replace them when they get back.'

'I want to pick your brain about City,' I said.

'Fire away. I'll tell you what I can, but don't expect me to reveal sources.'

'Tom says your ear is as close to the ground as anyone's. Has anybody got a grudge against the club? Anybody who'd want to set up Marco and Vince Naylor?'

He gave me the look of a man who sniffed another good story.

'I'm not saying anybody *has* set them up,' I said quickly. 'It's just a line of enquiry.'

'I've got a grudge against the club,' said Wilson. 'Like all the other Premiership clubs, it's sold out to television. The satellite TV companies run football now. They pay the piper millions of pounds a year, so they call the tune.'

It was obviously a hobbyhorse he rode whenever he got the chance, but I was panning for gold here. I was willing to let any amount of dross sluice by if the odd grain of useful material came from it.

'Telly dictates when matches should be played, what time they should kick off, keep us waiting for bloody hours after a match to talk to the managers because they've got first call. I've been covering City for thirty years. Up in the office I've got notes of every match they've played in that time, who scored, what time, who was booked, who was sent off. And now I have to wait in line to talk to the manager until some lass with a clipboard says so.'

'You still seem to get the big stories first, though,' I said.

'Any fool fresh off a journalism course can interview a soccer manager, but the exclusives come from contacts. And you only build up contacts when you've been around a few years, and when you take time out from the office to talk to people in pubs. My editor wanted to put one of our youngsters on to covering City because he'd got more empathy with the younger fans who watch soccer on TV. He knows nothing about the club. He's only parking his arse here until a space becomes vacant at the BBC. But when I broke the Naylor and Marco stories he thought again.'

'Couldn't have come at a better time for you, then?' I said.

'You could say that.'

'And you got the stories through contacts?'

'Don't tell the editor, but both stories came from anonymous tip-offs I received at home. Are you ready for another?'

I covered my glass with my hand. I was out of training for this sort of lunchtime drinking, and when you've no idea what you're doing it's better to keep a clear head.

'Suit yourself,' he said. 'I'm having one.'

'Do you get many anonymous tips?'

'No. We get plenty from people who don't want to be named. But the fact that they were anonymous makes no difference. They came to me because I've been the Voice of City for thirty years.'

'City must have changed a bit in those years, especially since Jack Cox bought his way in,' I said.

'Jack Cox? Have you met him?'

'No.'

'Join the club,' said Wilson. 'He never gives interviews. He thinks journalists are beneath him. But where would soccer be if the media didn't keep the interest in the game going. I'm not saying he hasn't done a lot for the club and this city, mind. We'd still be languishing in the lower leagues if Jack hadn't taken over as chairman from Brian Deakin and started splashing his money about on new players. He spent ten million of his own brass to get us into the Premiership. He spent another twenty getting us into Europe.'

'So what's in it for him?'

Wilson thought a moment before he answered. 'I'm buggered if I know,' he said. 'When he first bought his shares in the club, the television money hadn't really started to flow. He said he just wanted to put some of his money back into the city that had earned it for him, and I believed him. Now? I don't know. Football used to be a bottomless well into which businessmen poured some of their money just for the publicity and prestige. Now there's so much cash floating about in the game that there's serious brass to be made. Players, agents, directors – they're all looking to jump on the gravy train.'

'Rumour has it that Cox has so much money he doesn't need any more.'

'Rumour may be right. Jack certainly hasn't gone as far down the road to commercialisation as some clubs. He's built the executive boxes and the club shop, but that was just to meet a demand. If he wanted to cash in on City plc he would have brought in a marketing manager and got rid of the club secretary. Tom Tomlinson's one of the old school. He was happier when players wore baggy shorts and were paid twenty pounds a week and were called Alf or Ron or Len. Golden guy, but he's more interested in football than in money. There aren't many of us left.'

He finished his second pint while I was still half-way down my first.

'Can I get you another?'

'I never have more than two. Come on back to the office. I'll introduce you to Mrs Mountfield. She'll let you trawl through the cuttings. And if you find out anything I can print, here's my home number. Any time, day or night. I don't mind when I get a story – as long as I get it first.'

There were more cuttings in the *Post* library on City than on any other subject.

'Football's what sells papers,' said Mrs Mountfield, who looked as though she had known Caxton personally. Computers had taken over the rest of the editorial floor, but the cuttings were still clipped with scissors, stuck on paper and filed in brown envelopes. They would have been yellowing if they weren't pasted on paper which was already yellow because it was offcuts from reels of newsprint.

They told me nothing I didn't already know about Marco, and confirmed that Naylor had broken the nose of a taxi-driver in a late-night row over a fare. Six months, suspended for two years. The Blackpool victim's nose had also been rearranged, so the *modus operandi* was the same.

The file on Jack Cox was thinner than I'd expected. No first-person interview, a lot of stuff about his reclusiveness, his tax exile in the Isle of Man, how he made his fortune in road haulage. But trying to piece together a picture of the man from the cuttings made me realise how superficial most newspaper coverage is. It tells you little more than the PR image people like Cox generate about themselves – and perhaps how tough British libel law is.

The biggest file was on Jimmy Farrell, who was brought in by Cox to get City into the Premiership and whose managership had been remarkably successful until the recent run of losses. There were also several envelopes on Brian Deakin, though most dated back several years to when he was City chairman. I skimmed quickly through them. He had been nothing like as publicity-shy as Cox, but his game seemed to have been Monopoly rather than football. He was a director of a string of small companies in the city, and some abroad. In a rare piece of investigative journalism, Tony Wilson had uncovered a Deakin company in Pakistan which made footballs using underpaid child labour.

None of the other directors took up much drawer space. As Tony Wilson said, they seemed to be there just for the business contacts and the prestige, a businessman's hobby one step up from the Rotary Club.

I put the cuttings carefully back into their envelopes and returned them to their cabinets.

'You can come again,' said Mrs Mountfield. 'I've been trying for years to get any of the reporters to do that.'

Chapter Eight

Pressing the little button on the gear lever to slip into overdrive on the M55, I realised why I had bought the MGB and pumped money into it at regular intervals as Jack Cox pours money into City. The kick in the back, the little surge of power, the sense the low-slung bucket seats give you of doing ninety when you are well inside the legal limit. And as I kept saying to Beth, I would get back what I paid for it if I ever decided to sell it. Not the monthly garage bills from Nick, of course, but what I paid for it.

The tower rose slowly out of the flat, green fields of the Fylde. I prefer Blackpool out of season. There are fewer drunks who think they are immortal and challenge you to run them over as they step out in front of your car, fewer streetwise kids from Manchester and Birmingham just passing through on their way to the House of Correction. But the wind comes in off the Irish Sea and sweeps the chip papers and beer cans down the Golden Mile just the same.

Kevin Carter's address was in a street of redbrick terraced houses behind the Pleasure Beach, but there was nobody in. I was getting back into the car when the landlady of the boarding-house next door came out and told me where to find him.

He ran a slot-machine arcade on the Golden Mile, next to a place that offers jugs of tea for the sands. He was easy enough to pick out. Everyone else there should have been in school. And he was the only one whose facial features had been scrambled into an anagram as painted by Francis Bacon. The colours were of raw meat – the claret of congealed blood across the bridge of his nose, his right eye a blue-black bruise, the flesh above his cheekbone a dirty impact-yellow. Whoever had done him over had done it well. I just hoped it wasn't Vince Naylor.

He was stacking piles of copper in the little glass change-booth in the middle of the arcade. He was about my age, my height, a bit paunchy, T-shirt and hair both in need of a wash. The kids on the arcade games were blasting hell out of whatever popped up on their screens. The atmosphere was tough, and it seemed sensible to conform. I turned up the collar of my leather jacket, put on my toughest face, went up to the booth and said: 'Kevin Carter?'

'Yeah.'

'We need to talk, Kevin.'

'What about?'

'I think you know.'

He thought he knew, too. But he didn't. He jumped to the wrong conclusion. The look that came over what was left of his face said he thought I was going to rearrange it some more. And I never thought I was that frightening, even when I try to look my toughest.

'If you've come for your money, it's sorted until January. The arrears are paid off. Everything. Didn't anybody tell you?'

'Tell me what?'

'I don't have to pay you any more until the new year. Look, I've had the thumping, I've done what you asked me to, I'm going to stick to the story when it comes to court – I don't owe you anything.'

If I'd been faster on my feet I would have tumbled to it straight away. Kevin Carter was paying protection money to somebody. He'd got behind with his payments and someone had given him a reminder wrapped round a crowbar. They'd then offered to wipe the slate clean until January if he picked a fight with Vince Naylor in the pub and blamed him for his injuries.

But I didn't work all this out until later. Instead, I said: 'Who gave you the thumping, Kevin?'

It was enough for him to realise he was making a mistake.

'Who the hell are you?'

'Steve Strong. I work for Vince Naylor's football club. I'd like your version of what happened in that pub.'

'I've got nothing to say. I've told it to the police.'

That line was beginning to get tedious.

'You didn't get those injuries in a little scuffle in a pub.'

'Fuck off out of it, or I'll have you for intimidating witnesses.'

I shrugged. Kevin Carter wasn't going to tell me any more, but he had already told me more than enough. He had confirmed that, against the odds, Vince Naylor was telling the truth.

If I was a private eye in a movie, I'd slip some loose change into a bandit, pull the lever and hear the tinkle of coins falling on the floor as I hit the jackpot. But I was out of change and, as I left, Carter was already feeding some of his into the payphone on the wall.

*   *   *

I mulled things over as I drove back over the Pennines. It was easy enough to work out that Kevin Carter was the victim of a protection racket. And that he was the sort of little creep who could be persuaded to tell lies in court. But who was behind it all? Whoever it was would need to know that Naylor and a few of the other players had gone to Blackpool for the day. They would also need to be in league with whoever was selling Carter his protection. But there seemed to be no connection between the two. I felt like one of those truants in the expensive trainers in Carter's arcade. I kept feeding my money in, but the three little lemons refused to line up in the window.

The second lemon came up when I swung into the service road behind our flat and found an oil drum in the middle of the road. I hit the brakes. The MG might be mechanically challenged, but the bodywork and chrome were pristine and I wanted them to stay that way.

I didn't notice the two men until they yanked the driver's door open, grabbed my arm and pulled me out. I was too surprised to offer any resistance, which is why my body kept on going, across the pavement and into the six-foot wall at the back of the flats. I twisted my head to try to see what was happening, which was why my nose didn't take the full force of the impact. Instead, I felt the flesh beneath my right eyebrow split, and blood streamed down my face.

Funny how the human brain works. It processes trivia when it should be panicking. For a couple of seconds I found myself wondering why we bleed more from the bits that have least flesh cover. It's the same when you nick your ear when shaving. By the time I focused on what was happening, they had spun me round and pinned my arms against the wall. They needn't have bothered. They both came in catering-size packets and were built for heavy-duty use. I wasn't about to argue with them.

I had no idea who they were. It was dark down that street. I'd been meaning to write to the council for ages about the streetlamp. But they had scarves across their faces anyway.

'This is just a little warning. Don't go poking your nose in, either with Karen Pearson or in Blackpool. Understand, pal?'

I nodded. I understood, all right.

'Because next time you might run into something sharper than a brick wall.'

One of them twisted my arm up my back and flung me across the bonnet of my car. I could hear the blood hitting the paintwork as regularly as a dripping tap. Just as well I'd gone for the oxblood paint job.

The next thing I heard was glass breaking and a car being driven away.

When I stopped shaking and pulled myself upright I realised they had kicked in my headlights so I couldn't follow them. Until then, I'd been frightened. Now I was mad.

I reached into the car, pulled out a wad of tissues from the box I keep in the glove compartment, tipped my head back over the seat and tried to stanch the flow. It took the white corpuscles ten minutes to win the battle.

In the meantime I tried to make sense of it. Two men. The one who spoke had a local accent. That narrowed it down to about half a million suspects. But it was also someone who knew I'd just come from talking to Kevin Carter in Blackpool, and who knew I'd been to see Karen Pearson. That narrowed the list of suspects down to zero, which was even less helpful.

I looked at my watch. I was supposed to be meeting Carol King for a drink, but I knew I should go inside and clean myself up. Beth would be there, and she would do everything you are supposed to do with cuts – antiseptic and cotton wool and plasters. And afterwards I would get a lecture on the stupidity of getting involved in something I couldn't handle and knew nothing about.

The alternative was to walk down one of the smartest shopping malls in the city to meet a woman I wanted to impress looking like something out of a butcher's skip. Yes, on balance that was preferable. I had no headlamps, but the main road was well lit and the rear lights were still working. Now the bleeding had stopped I didn't even mind being beaten up that much. It felt like that moment at the end of a visit to the dentist when your mouth feels as big as a football and the size of the cheque you are writing out feels even bigger, but everything's cool because the ordeal's over.

The ordeal was over. I had been beaten up. Steve Strong had been initiated into the fraternity of private eyes.

There are arcades and there are arcades. You can spend a lot of money in a Blackpool amusement arcade and come away with next to nothing. The Victoria Arcade is lined with jewellery stores and shops selling expensive knick-knacks from behind fake Georgian shopfronts. You can spend a lot of money there and . . . well, maybe there isn't that much difference, to be honest.

They've roofed over the street with glass, and now there's a fancy café where the traffic used to run. It has waiters with white aprons out of a French farce and tables with wire-mesh surfaces that look great until you try to balance a wine glass on them. Carol King was sitting at one of them, clinging to a glass of Chardonnay.

'My God,' she said when she saw me. 'Where have you been?'

'Something came up.'

'It looks as though it was a concrete floor.'

I told her what had happened.

'You ought to get that face cleaned up.'

'I'm all right,' I said bravely.

'*You* might be, but I'm not sitting here with you looking like that. People I know use this place. You look like the treatment room after we've played Wimbledon.'

That seemed like the end of a beautiful evening, but it was only the start. She took me back to her house, which was in a very respectable district. It had been left to her by the player she had been married to. He could afford it. He had been transferred to Lazio for a lorra, lorra lire. He would have been worth even more if he hadn't been unfortunate enough to be born in Wales, which meant it was unlikely that his talents would ever be displayed at the World Cup Finals.

'Bathroom's there,' she said.

I didn't look too bad when I'd cleaned myself up. There was an inch-long wound I had somehow managed to set off bleeding again, and a bit of swelling.

'Have you got any plasters?'

She threw a box of Elastoplast at me and almost took my other eye out, but the plaster stemmed the bleeding. By the time I had finished she was pouring sugo over two plates of spaghetti and had opened a very acceptable bottle of Cabernet Sauvignon from somewhere pretending to be the Australian outback.

'We'll eat this watching the telly,' she said.

'What's on?'

'Don't you read the sports pages?'

'Only for the scandal.'

'City are playing Ajax in Amsterdam tonight. UEFA Cup.'

During the pre-match hype, I said: 'I wouldn't have run off to Italy. Your pasta's not that bad.'

'Must be Gina's tits he prefers, then,' she said, but there was real bitterness behind the flippancy.

'Wasn't it someone called Carol King who wrote "It Might As Well Rain Until September"?' I said.

'Yeah. And she had a point.'

The talking heads eventually disappeared and the match began. Marco was still missing from the side, but Gary Allen was back from injury. Now I had a stake of sorts in the club, I found myself wanting City to win almost as much as I had when Dad took me to watch them as a kid. Carol was even more keyed up, and City played well until Ajax scored just before half-time.

Carol opened a second bottle of wine, but when Ajax scored again straight after the break we were drinking to drown our sorrows.

'There's always the return leg,' I said.

'Not from two goals down,' she said.

The clock on the screen had ticked past ninety minutes when Gary Allen got the ball on the right and the defenders backed off him, trying to funnel him out to the corner flag to waste a little more time. As he tried to cut inside, he seemed to have pushed the ball too far, but a divot in the turf teed the ball up for him and it fell perfectly into his stride. He thumped it with his right boot, and the moment he hit it you knew it would fly into the top corner of the net.

We rose as one person from the sofa and yelled: '*Yeeeeeeeeees!*'

It must have been the wine, unless she always turns and hugs the person next to her when City score. I bet she doesn't kiss them, though. Not with tongue, anyway.

The next thing I knew, Jimmy Farrell was being interviewed about the prospects for the return leg, but we weren't really listening. Carol was looking at me with that unmistakable expression, and then she said softly: 'Away goals count double.'

It was the plainest invitation to unbutton a girl's blouse I've ever heard.

A couple of hours later, in her bed, I said: 'Remember I wanted to pick your brain about some of the players?'

'You men are all the same,' she said. 'As soon as you've had sex, it's straight back to the only thing you're really interested in: football.'

Chapter Nine

I was in the hallway reading Nick's bill for the work he had done on the MGB when the phone rang in Beth's flat. My face felt like the Novocaine was wearing off after a visit to the dentist – battered and lumpy. My nose wasn't broken, but it was still sore. Not half as sore as I was at the bastards who had kicked in the headlamps on my car, though. Have you any idea how much replacement headlamps cost for an MGB? Nor have I, but whatever number comes to mind, Nick will be able to double it.

As I ran up the stairs to try to reach the phone before it stopped ringing, I wondered whether headlamps smashed in the line of duty qualified as legitimate expenses. I made a note to ask Tom Tomlinson next time I spoke to him.

It was Tom Tomlinson on the phone, but this didn't seem like a good time to ask.

'Have you seen today's *Post*?'

I hadn't, but it seemed to be the only reliable source of information in this case. Maybe I should place an order.

'Buy one and come straight to my office.'

I bought a copy at the corner shop.

The shit had hit the fans again.

Phil Andrews

It was all over page one under Tony Wilson's byline:

CITY STAR IN
DRUGS BUST

I read the story in snatches whenever I hit a red light on my way to the ground, although the headline said it all.

The star in question was Pierre Bartola, the French midfielder. He was City's best player when he could be bothered to perform to his potential. Moody and mercurial, he was the only player in the side, perhaps in Britain, maybe in Europe, with the ability to turn a match with one flash of inspiration. Now it looked as though his inspiration came in the form of white powder, cut with a credit card and sucked up through a twenty-pound note.

Bartola had been charged with possession of a restricted drug after Customs found a wrap of cocaine in his bag when the team returned from Amsterdam. How stupid can you get? Why take the risk of smuggling the stuff in from the drugs capital of Europe when any street-corner dealer in the city can supply you? They even throw in some hash as part of the deal, like those CDs they stick on the covers of music magazines. The football club had declined to comment, and when I got to the stadium I found out why.

Tomlinson was in the entrance lobby talking to Carol King. The curved brass nameplate of a steam locomotive, with City's name embossed on it over the club colours of black and gold, was screwed to the wall behind her desk. Tom looked more than ever as though he belonged to the same bygone era. He was drawn and tired, as though he had been up most of the night. He sounded weary as he invited me in to his office. I gave Carol what I hoped was a fond glance and followed him.

'You look knackered,' I said.

'If you'd spent most of the night trying to stop Pierre Bartola smashing up the airport, you'd be knackered,' said Tomlinson. 'He's got a nasty temper when something upsets him.'

It wasn't an original observation. The prospect of Bartola's Gallic flair turning into a Gallic flare-up was the main reason a number of people watched *Match of the Day*.

'What happened?'

'We arrived back at the airport, early hours of the morning. We were going through Customs as usual. Normally the Customs people don't even turn out when we get back from a European match. We get the VIP treatment.'

'And last night?'

'One of them pulled Pierre over, asked to look in his bag.'

'Just Pierre? Nobody else?'

'Just Pierre. They found the stuff in a plastic bag tucked down the side. It wasn't even hidden. Anyone could have opened the zip and tucked it in.'

'Another setup?'

'It has to be. Why pick on Bartola? They didn't even have to look for it. It wasn't pushed up his bum, or wherever drug-runners hide the stuff. Someone must have tipped them off.'

'Did you ask Customs who it was?'

'Yes, but they won't say.'

'He denies it, of course,' I said.

'Of course. This just confirms that someone is targeting the club. But what happened to your face?'

I told him.

'So whoever's behind this is prepared to go to extremes to stop us finding out.'

Until then I'd accepted my thumping as the price of being nosy, but Tomlinson was right. People who hang around outside your house to beat you up and who plant drugs in people's luggage are not just over-exuberant lads with a *Who are you lookin' at?* approach to human relationships. They're nasty and they're dangerous, and I was getting out of my depth. There is only so much I'm willing to do in the pursuit of justice, even for two hundred pounds a day plus legitimate expenses.

'Maybe it's time we called in the police,' I said.

'They've *been* called in,' said Tomlinson irritably, 'but as far as the police are concerned these are three separate incidents, all of which are being investigated. They say there's nothing that links them together. The police won't even get involved in Bartola's case. That is Customs and Excise. And unless he can prove he wasn't trying to smuggle a hundred grammes of a prohibited substance into the country, he's guilty.'

'If Pierre didn't put the stuff in his own bag, who could have planted it?'

'He was rooming with Gary Allen. He says he packed the bag himself in the hotel and carried it on to the coach. There was nobody on the coach or the plane but people from this club – players, officials, directors.'

'And none of them saw anything?'

'No.'

'Still,' I said, 'look on the bright side. We're not talking heroin with a street value of millions here. What's he going to get for possession of an ounce of coke? A hundred-pound fine?'

'There's something else you should know, Steve,' said Tomlinson. 'Something the press haven't picked up on yet, though it's only a matter of time. It was reported in the French papers. Pierre tested positive for drugs while he was playing in the French League. He was suspended for two months and had to pay a big fine – three months' wages.'

That *was* a big fine. On the kind of money players like Pierre Bartola earned, we were in National Debt territory.

'If this is proved, he'll be banned – probably for life. As it is, we'll have to leave him out of the side until this is settled. The football authorities have been getting tough on drugs. Setting a good example to the kids, that kind of thing, and as a club we can't afford to condone drug-taking.'

Most footballers are not much more than children themselves, but they're still expected to be role models for kids all over the world. It's a tough life being an icon.

Whoever was behind all this was clever. This wasn't just the work of the pair of heavies who had put their Doc Martens through my headlights. These were people who had done their research, picked their targets carefully, aimed their blows where the least effort would do the most damage.

And if they were trying to damage the people who ran the club by picking off the players, they were succeeding.

'Jack Cox's been on the phone from the Isle of Man,' said Tomlinson. 'He's starting to lose patience with all this. He wants it sorted out – fast.'

I could understand why Jack Cox was not a happy man. He'd put a lot of money into the club, and now a series of off-the-field incidents was threatening his investment. I could see that Tomlinson was worried, too. He was paid to run the club in Cox's absence. If Cox held him personally responsible for what was happening, Tomlinson's job was on the line. We might be entering the twenty-first century, but people like Cox can still wield an almost feudal power over their employees.

That made me angry. Tom Tomlinson seemed like a decent bloke, and he had handled City's affairs competently enough for years. But now the world of soccer was changing so fast that it had spun out of his control and he was losing his grip. As he sat behind his desk beneath all those photographs of long-forgotten footballers, he seemed almost pathetic, a figure left stranded in another time by the receding tide of history. I felt really sorry for him. Perhaps he reminded me too much of my dad.

Suddenly, I wanted to be back on the case.

'I'll sort it,' I said encouragingly, though I had no idea how.

'You'd better look sharp,' said Tomlinson. 'Jack's talking about bringing in a professional investigator.'

'*I'm* a professional,' I said, trying to sound as hurt as I could. 'I've got you the background you wanted on Karen Pearson.'

'He means an investigator with credentials,' said Tomlinson.

'I've got credentials. Didn't I tell you? I've been doing investigations and working in security and dealing with all sorts of vermin for years.'

All right, maybe TV researcher, security camera salesman and council pest exterminator were not exactly what he had in mind, but until one of our newer universities comes up with an honours degree in shamus studies we all have to get our education where we can. And I've read everything Raymond Chandler wrote, including his shopping lists.

Tomlinson looked at me with tired eyes. There was a copy of Yellow Pages on his desk, which contained several columns of detective agencies. But Tom had no way of knowing which of them were timewasters and which were any good. And I had a track record, of sorts. He knew me, and I was there, in the room, looking back at him. So he took the easy way out.

'All right,' he said. 'But you'd better get results, Steve, or I'm going to have to bring in somebody else. There's fifteen million pounds' worth of Jack's investment not earning its keep now. Bartola's out on Saturday, and Marty Weller's phoned Jimmy Farrell this morning to tell him Carlo Marconi has gone back to Italy because that model has thrown a wobbler over the indecent assault stories that are in all the Italian papers. And we'll lose Vince Naylor next week if he's sent down. Without those three for the return leg against Ajax, we go out of Europe. That will cost us at least as much again.'

So, if I understood him right, either I sorted this case out in the next fourteen days or City said goodbye to thirty million pounds. Now I know what football managers feel like when they're under pressure to get a result.

I didn't have time to stop and talk to Carol King as I passed the reception desk. Her face said plenty, though. Something along the lines of: 'Now you've been inside my knickers you think you can cast me off like a used condom.'

So I blew her a kiss and said: 'I'll call you.'

'That's what they all say,' she said.

I drove out to the airport. If you don't have an air ticket or a passport you are a prisoner in the coffee shop in these places. To get through any other door requires a piece of paper and a body search. Eventually, someone in a blue uniform escorted me into a glass cubicle that passed for an office and sat down behind a screen of officialdom.

'We have nothing at all to say to the press about Mr Bartola.'

His name was Stuart McDonald. It said so on his badge.

'I'm not the press. I work for City Football Club.'

'Mr Bartola has been released on bail and will receive a notice of prosecution in the usual way. If the club wish to engage a solicitor on his behalf . . .'

'Why were his bags searched? Who tipped you off?'

'He was searched as a result of information received.'

'From who?'

Yes, I know it should be 'whom', but I didn't feel like wasting a university education on this automaton.

'We never reveal our sources. We prefer to keep our informants alive. There are a lot of dangerous people in the drugs trade.'

If I'd been in the mood to pick it up I would have spotted the ironic sense of humour behind the officialspeak. And if I'd been writing a novel about Customs officers struggling to save the nation's youth from the tide of drugs engulfing the country I would probably be presenting Stuart McDonald as an honest and brave man who was refusing to be influenced by wealth and fame. But I wasn't, so I said: 'You made sure the media knew about it soon enough.'

'The *Post* story didn't come from us. Since it appeared, we've had every journalist in the country on the phone, and we've told them all the same: no comment.'

'Don't you think it strange that an international footballer should risk his career by smuggling a few pounds' worth of cocaine from Amsterdam? Isn't it obvious that he was set up?'

'If you provide us with evidence to that effect, we will, of course, investigate it. But drug-smuggling, no matter how socially acceptable the drug or how small the quantity, is a very serious threat to the social fabric of this country . . .'

I don't know how long the sermon lasted. I was out in Arrivals putting in a call to Tony Wilson at the *Post*.

'Same source,' he said. 'Anonymous tip again, but equally accurate.'

'These incidents are looking like something more than coincidence now, aren't they, Tony?'

'I was thinking the same thing, Steve.'

'What's the word on the street?'

'The street is uncharacteristically quiet. And Pierre Bartola doesn't speak to hacks like me. He's far too grand.'

'I'd better talk to him myself, then,' I said.

But first I had to take the MG round to Nick's to get the headlamps and the bodywork fixed. He operated out of a Victorian railway arch of soot-blackened brick that had been converted into a lockup. A couple of restored Morris Minors with optimistic price tags on their windscreens were parked on the forecourt, but he made most of his money from repairing 'period' vehicles like my own. I was one of his best customers, as well as being his best friend.

What I liked about Nick was that he was the free spirit I had always aspired to be but never quite had the nerve. He drifted from woman to woman without being tempted by the emotional security of marriage, and so he was under no pressure to get a 'proper' job. And because he was free he could also afford to be more honest or, to put it another way, to be less circumspect about what he said to people. I didn't want him running into Beth in the street and saying how sorry he was that I'd been beaten up round the back of the flat. So I lied when he saw my face and asked: 'What happened to you?'

'Had a bit of a shunt,' I said. 'Ran into the back of someone and banged my face on the steering wheel.'

He knew I was lying, of course. He also knew about the impending divorce, and probably thought Beth and I had had a fight, but he was too tactful to mention it so he said: 'It'll take me a few days to get the parts.'

'Fine,' I said. 'And don't bother gold-plating them this time. You seem to be under the mistaken impression that I'm a merchant bank.'

I arranged to meet Bartola in a coffee house near the university which tries to pretend it's in Stuttgart. The espresso they serve is like taking caffeine intravenously, though the delivery system is less painful. It's served with those Swiss cakes that contain a week's supply of calories and a lifetime's cholesterol by Scandinavian waitresses with an encouraging approach to life. The only bum note is the newspapers on sticks. On close inspection they turn out to be the *Express* and the *Mail*.

But Pierre had brought his own reading matter. It was a French film magazine – serious stuff, not *Film Fun*. I remembered reading his profile in the match programme, which asks players in-depth questions like which tape is in their car stereo and what (if anything) they read in bed. Oasis and *Loaded* are the usual answers, but Bartola had gone for the Modern Jazz Quartet and Camus' *The Outsider*.

'You are the detective?' he asked as I swam into his peripheral vision.

I nodded.

Bartola was what Vince Naylor would be if he had a brain and a bit of style. He had agreed to see me readily enough, but he had given Tom Tomlinson a hard time at the airport, and I was a bit apprehensive of his reputation as an *enfant terrible*.

It must have shown on my face, because he said: 'Don't worry. Last night I was angry. Today I am calm.'

He motioned me to sit opposite him, and in the same gesture caught a waitress's eye. I'm always the last person to get served at a bar, so I was impressed. If fame doesn't get you preferential treatment, it makes waiters aware of your presence, so it amounts to the same thing.

'Another espresso,' he said, and looked at me.

'The same for me, thanks.'

'OK, Maigret. What are you going to do?'

I wish people wouldn't keep asking me that question. It reminds me of my lack of progress. *I* should be asking the questions. That's the way it's always done in the movies.

So I asked him about the incident at the airport.

'I spend all night telling this to the Customs,' he said through a semaphore of Continental gestures. For someone who was calm, he gave a good imitation of the opposite.

'So now tell *me*.'

'Someone put it in my bag. You think I would try to smuggle that stuff?' he said, as though I had accused him of buying his underwear from an unfashionable store.

'But you do have a conviction for drug possession?'

He gave me the Gallic shrug I assume the French use on foreigners the way the English use frightfully refined accents in Sydney or New York. It sets them apart from the natives.

'It was nothing. Some stuff I was given at a party came up on a random test,' he said, knocking back his second espresso in a single gulp. If you ignored the Inspector Clouseau accent, his English was almost colloquial.

'So you admit to being a user?'

'Sure, I use coke sometimes for recreation. Good stuff only. At parties. What is wrong in that?'

We're talking prohibited substances here, but what would I know? I've seen *Trainspotting*, but sticking a slice of lemon down the neck of a bottle of Sol has been the limit of my personal experience of recreational drugs since I married Beth.

'This could be very serious for you,' I said.

'Sure, I could lose my boot contract and my advertising work. They are worth a lot of money.'

'And get banned from the game.'

He shrugged again. 'About that I do not care so much. All those arsehole journalists and fans wherever I go. And now this. In six months or a year I will be quitting anyway.'

'Quitting?'

That would come as a nasty shock to Jimmy Farrell and Jack Cox. Bartola was the club's biggest attraction, the sort of player who put thousands on the gate. And it wasn't just his skill people came to see. His unpredictable temperament and charisma had caught the imagination of the media and the fans. Even the distinctive little quiff he wore was becoming *de rigueur* on the kop.

He leaned back in his chair and became philosophical.

'How much of your life can you give to a game? A footballer should get out while people still want to watch him. I have been offered film parts. This time next year I will be a movie star. And if this business last night becomes too much hassle I will quit right now.'

It was the first time I had seen a really big ego in action. I thought of what Carol King had said about soccer players when they retired from the game. Well, Pierre Bartola had no intention of spending the twilight of his career in the lower divisions of the French League and going off to run a little *zinc* in Rennes or Auxerre.

'I've seen your TV ad,' I said. 'It's very good.'

He was in a knowingly post-modern commercial for a sporty French car, and was considerably more impressive than most telegenic pro footballers, who bring deep embarrassment to the sale of trainers and breakfast cereals. It was easy to envisage Bartola as a movie star. The Levi's and simple white T-shirt he was wearing showed off his body to good advantage, and the camera would love those bluish-grey eyes. He was currently squiring some pop chanteuse, according to the tabloids, so he already had more than one foot in showbiz.

'Maybe all this is not so bad for me,' he said. 'It is possible to earn much more as an actor if you have a little notoriety, yes?'

'That seems to be how it works,' I said.

The thought crossed my mind that Bartola had deliberately engineered this drugs charge to boost his reputation as the bad boy of soccer. It would do no harm to his chances of making the transition into a second career in films. But he wasn't that good an actor. His behaviour when the stuff was discovered in his bag was the real thing, according to Tomlinson.

I asked him the usual questions about who could have planted the stuff, but he hadn't a clue. Which made two of us. I sank my espresso in a single gulp and got up. I would have liked to have stayed and talked about movies, but I had more pressing things to do. If I didn't soon make some progress in this case, the last player on City's books would have turned out the lights and left.

The newspaper sellers outside the ground the following day were doing a roaring trade on the strength of a front-page headline:

ARE CITY JINXED?

Beside photographs of Vince Naylor, Carlo Marconi and Pierre Bartola was a panel recounting the charges against them, and a story by Tony Wilson which stopped just short of the conspiracy theory I was now convinced was the only explanation to all this.

I watched the match. Gary Allen scored another good goal, and Vince Naylor tackled and made overlapping runs down the wing as though he knew this could be his last match in a City shirt for some time. But you don't beat Manchester United with only one striker and a hole where your midfield general used to be, and City went down 3–1.

I went along to Jimmy Farrell's after-match conference in the press lounge. The manager kept the media hanging around for almost an hour before he appeared, as though he hoped they might go away. When he finally arrived he sat down wearily behind a carafe of water at a table on the raised dais at the front of the room. He didn't touch the water, though. Jimmy looked as though he was in need of something stronger to cope with the stresses of managership.

After a bit of fencing about how the game had gone, someone asked the inevitable question, the one every manager expects after a bad run.

'Five defeats on the trot now, Jim. Are you starting to feel the pressure?'

'This game's about winning. You get no prizes for coming second. At the end of the day, if we fail to deliver the results, my job is on the line. But I've not had the vote of confidence from the board yet, so I'll be here for at least another week.'

Five managerial clichés and some gallows humour in a single answer. I'd say Jimmy Farrell was under pressure, all right.

Chapter Ten

Jimmy Farrell wasn't the only one under pressure.

I left the press corps to file their copy and drifted out into the corridor under the main stand. The crowd had left and there was no one else much around: just a few stewards in Day-Glo jackets, someone sweeping plastic beer mugs and discarded betting slips from the floor around the bar, the crackle of a walkie-talkie echoing among cold concrete beams.

I went out into the stand and gazed across the deserted pitch. The floodlights were still on. The white lines stood out sharply against the unnatural emerald green of the grass. Now the spectators had gone, you could see that the bank of seats in the North Stand spelled out CITY in gold and black. Everything looked stark and simple and clear. Then an unseen hand flicked the switch that turned out the lights and suddenly the ground was in total darkness.

I knew how it felt.

It was as though I had been flung into space and was drifting through a vast, cold silence. Events at the football club seemed to be spinning out of control in the same way, and I was being paid to stop it. The responsibility for this vast stadium, for all this expensive equipment, for the hopes of the people who were now drifting home through shining streets and queuing in chip shops and getting the last orders in at the pubs, seemed to have come to rest on my shoulders. Suddenly, I was afraid of the responsibility, and I wanted to get out of it.

I needed moral support. If I'd been a middle manager in some big company instead of a half-arsed private investigator, I could have turned to my wife. Sympathy and encouragement were the kind of things Beth was good at, so long as what I was doing was in line with the marital mission statement. But this? She would just tell me to stop playing stupid games and jack it all in. And she might be right. But Beth was away on some weekend managerial course in the Lake District, which most people would regard as a nice skive but which she would be taking too seriously to enjoy, so I couldn't go home and tell her my troubles even if I wanted to.

I walked down the steps to the running track and went back through the players' tunnel into the foyer. Carol King was just leaving.

You know how it is when you've had an unexpected one-night stand with someone and the next time you meet you're not sure if it was a mistake or the gateway to something more permanent, and you say things like 'Hi' to each other and then leave long silences hanging in the air?

'Hi.'

'Hi.'

A sense of belonging surrounds people who work in public places when the public have finally left. Like an invisible gas, it was in the air now. Even the steward on the only exit that had not been locked had dropped his looking-for-trouble expression and was smiling and waiting to say good night knowing that the only people now left in the ground were insiders like us.

'Fancy a drink on the way home?' I said to Carol.

'All right.'

It wasn't really an invitation for a drink at all. It was an invitation for her to invite me back for tea and sympathy. But she said: 'Do you know that wine bar near the university?'

She had chosen neutral ground, but I wasn't too disappointed. At that moment I needed a mother more than I needed a tart.

That is one thing Beth has never understood – why men need mothering one moment and seducing the next. She thinks we should stop shillyshallying and make our minds up on the issue. But you can't get sex from your mother or understanding from a tart, so wives and girlfriends were invented to fill the vacuum. That Beth has not grasped this may be at the root of our problems.

The place was full of students drinking wine at two quid a glass to take their minds off how they were going to cope on their inadequate grants. You could tell they were students because a) they were in a wine bar and not a pub, and b) 'really' (spelled with several 'e's) rather than 'fucking' was their adjective of choice.

But the last thing I needed was the adolescent enthusiasm and naive optimism I remembered from my own student days, so I carried Carol's spritzer to a table in the corner.

'So,' she said, 'how's it going?'

'Badly,' I said. 'All I've established is that someone seems to be setting up City's best players one by one, but that could have been deduced by anyone who subscribes to a daily newspaper. It has to be someone who knows the players' backgrounds because every setup is very plausible. But I'm no nearer to finding out who it is or why. Who do we know who has a grudge against City players?'

'Me, for one,' said Carol. 'They're a bunch of sexist tossers.'

'Then where were you last Wednesday night, madam?'

'In bed with you. How quickly men forget.'

We smiled and our eyes met in the way they do when two people have broached the unmentionable subject. But she changed it quickly and slipped into something more comfortable.

'Who are we looking for? Someone who stands to gain if City go on losing. Have you ever seen a film called *Chinatown*?'

I perked up a bit. If this girl was willing to sleep with me *and* she knew about movies, life couldn't be as desperate as I thought.

'Roman Polanski,' I said, not only to confirm that I'd seen it but to establish my movie-buff credentials by knowing the director's name. 'You like movies?'

'Depends who's in them. I used to fancy Jack Nicholson. In *Chinatown* the bad guys made money by stopping the flow of water to the city. Does someone here think they can make money by stopping City's flow of success?'

'But who? And how? I don't get it.'

'There's so much money slushing around the club now you wouldn't believe it.'

'But there'd be even more if City won the championship or succeeded in Europe. Nobody would want to nobble the players if money is the motive. Unless another club is behind it.'

'They'd have to get at every other club in the Premiership, too. It doesn't make sense,' she said sensibly.

'What the hell made me think I could become a private eye?' I said. 'Agatha Christie would be assembling suspects in the library by now and running through a list of motives and opportunities.'

'Footballers can't read, so we don't have a library. You'll have to make do with the boot-room.'

'It's more than big enough for my list of suspects.'

'So you do have some?'

'Not really. Just a couple of people I could build a case against in desperation, like picking a question I could waffle through unconvincingly in an exam paper.'

'Waffle away.'

'There's your friend Marty Weller.'

'This juror says guilty. Insist on the death penalty.'

'But only because something about him doesn't feel right. When I spoke to him he didn't seem concerned that his client had a sex charge hanging over him. And he tried to buy me off in a crude sort of way. But Marco's his client, so what does he stand to gain? And there's absolutely nothing to link him to the Vince Naylor or Pierre Bartola incidents. I doubt if he spends his holidays in Blackpool, and he wasn't on the plane from Amsterdam.'

'Someone could have planted the dope for him.'

'And arranged to pick a fight with Vince Naylor?'

'Well, if you're going to be picky . . . Who's the other suspect?'

'Do you know Tony Wilson, the *Post* reporter?'

'Tony's a sweet little man. He's been around for years. He's in love with City. He wouldn't do anything to harm the club.'

'But he always gets the story first, and it always comes from an anonymous source. And the *Post* wanted to pension him off until he started to get this very convenient run of scoops. And he was on the Amsterdam plane.'

'And he's a client of Karen Pearson's and knows slot-machine operators in Blackpool, I suppose?'

'No, it doesn't feel right, does it?'

'What would feel right?' she asked softly, finishing her spritzer. Was this the sympathy I had been looking for, creeping in behind the conversational sparring that can sometimes be just a short step from foreplay? I replied by letting my gaze drift down to her breasts.

That was another set of signs misread.

'Not tonight. I'm washing my hair,' she said.

'You were keen enough the other night.'

'City had just scored and your face was all bloody. I was overexcited.'

Unless City started winning or I got beaten up again, scoring could become a big problem for me, too.

I was home by nine.

Beth phoned.

'I rang earlier. You were out.' She didn't ask where I'd been, which I suppose is a fairly good sign that a relationship is finally over. 'Have you filled in those job applications?'

She was in Mother mode, Scolding option. Why wasn't she in the bar, flirting with the chief accountant or whoever went on this sort of trip?

'I will. I haven't had time.'

'Make time, Steve. This is important. You need a proper job. Get those applications filled in and spend some time on them. We did the recruitment module this afternoon. The most difficult hurdle for any job applicant is getting off the slush pile and on to the shortlist. The way you present yourself at this stage is important. And the two key things employers are looking for are enthusiasm and commitment. I thought it was worth passing that on to you.'

'Thanks,' I said.

'When are you going to fill them in?'

'When I get a minute.'

'You're not still playing around with that football club business?'

'You've not reached the express-yourself-elegantly module, then?'

'Steve, I'm trying to help you, but when will you make the effort to be serious for once?'

And when will you make the effort to be flippant for once? I remember taking you to see *Chinatown*, Beth. You said you liked it. But you didn't like *Shallow Grave* or *Trainspotting*. You wouldn't even go to see *Reservoir Dogs*. You used to like sex in a Jacuzzi. Which one of us has changed?

But I didn't say it. Our ideas of what constituted the serious things in life had grown apart. That was our trouble.

'It's Sunday tomorrow,' I said. 'I'll have a run at it then.'

I took the application forms from behind the clock where I'd put them, and locked them in a drawer in my room. If she came back before I'd done them I would have time to prepare an excuse.

I went to bed and lay awake. I was trying to decide what I could do next to justify being paid two hundred pounds a day by the football club.

In the end I rummaged in the bedside cabinet, took out a book that might help solve both problems, and settled back to read, for the umpteenth time, *The Big Sleep*.

The trench in the road outside Karen Pearson's flat was deep. I couldn't get across it. The TV cables had been laid – hundreds of them, in all sorts of colours. Put your ear to them and, like a seashell, you could hear the voices of the commentators rising each time a goal was scored, and way beyond them hear the roar of the crowd like surf on a beach.

Marty Weller helped me over the trench and I climbed the stairs. The woman who had given me the key was standing on the landing, looking at me strangely. She made no move to bar my way or to let me into the flat. But when I pushed the door I found it was already open.

The floor of the sitting-room was covered in pieces of paper. They were receipts from expensive department stores, bank statements, cheques.

Karen's bedroom door was open. I looked in. She lay on the bed, smiling at me. She was wearing a City football shirt, black and gold stripes. It came below her waist like a short, sexy dress. I thought she was beckoning to me, but when I crossed the deep-pile carpet I realised I was wrong. Karen was dead.

As I reached out to touch her, she rolled from the bed and fell on her face on the floor. I bent over her. There was a name across the back of her shirt. Down at the club shop you can have any name you like for a pound a letter.

The phone started ringing in the other room. By the time I'd woken up and reached the phone I'd forgotten whose name was on the shirt.

Chapter Eleven

'Are you still in bed?' It was Carol.

'I was until you got me up.'

'This is something worth getting out of bed for. I'm at the stadium.'

'On a Sunday?'

'The tickets for the second leg against Ajax go on sale today. We're really busy.'

'That's fascinating,' I said, 'but not worth getting out of bed for.'

I'm not at my best in the mornings, and I was still smarting because she'd give me the brush-off the night before. I wouldn't have blamed her if she'd put the phone down, but she said: 'All the incoming calls come through my extension on a Sunday.'

'Have you been listening in to people's telephone conversations?'

'I thought you'd want me to.'

'You thought right. And what did you hear?'

'There was a call for Jimmy Farrell.'

'Do football managers work on Sunday mornings as well?'

'Not normally. But he was in his office this morning. And he seemed to be expecting the call.'

'From whom?'

'Such impeccable grammar so early in the morning! From that slug Carlo Marconi calls an agent.'

'Weller? What did he want?'

'Carlo Marconi is asking for a transfer. Farrell is meeting Weller this afternoon to talk it over.'

Now that was worth disturbing my sleep for. I could have kissed her. As a matter of fact, I could have kissed her anyway, but you know what I mean.

'Where's the meeting?'

'Service station near Leicester, three o'clock.'

'That's handy. Half-way between here and London.'

'But well out of the way if you don't want too many people to know what's going on.'

'Meaning?'

'Marco's only been with City since the start of the season. He's under contract. If he's going to leave, Jimmy Farrell will have to smooth the way. And agents have been known to offer managers bungs in motorway service stations. Don't you read the papers?'

I'd always known my friend Nick would come in handy if I kept him long enough. He'd done me a rush job on the MG's headlamps to make her roadworthy, so at least I had wheels at my disposal. He'd get round to the bodywork in his own sweet time. The kicking it had been given must have damaged the aerial so the radio was still on the blink. Luckily, Beth's Walkman was on the kitchen table. I picked it up as I went out. Unluckily, it contained a Simply Red tape, so I drove down the M1 in silence, thinking over what I knew about Jimmy Farrell.

His playing career had been in the lower divisions, but

when he turned to managership he showed a flair for winning promotion to the Premier League with teams that cost very little. They usually went straight back down, but with Jack Cox's millions behind him he had taken City into Europe. In football, though, success merely increases the burden of expectation. Now there was pressure on him to win the Championship or the FA Cup, and preferably both. Anything less would be regarded as failure, and managers who fail get the sack. Sooner rather than later. City's recent run of results meant that Jimmy Farrell was on borrowed time.

Marty Weller's Jag wasn't difficult to spot, even in a motorway car park. He wasn't in it, so I assumed they were meeting in the coffee shop.

They both knew me, so I fished in the glove compartment and pulled out my shades. Beth's baseball cap was on the back seat – the one she wore to her health club because she thought it made her look like the Princess of Wales, the fashion icon from beyond the grave. I put it on to cover what was left of my hair. Anyone looking for me would still be able to recognise me without any trouble. But Marty and Jimmy weren't looking for me.

People were pushing trays along the stainless-steel counter towards the till in the self-service coffee shop. I waited for someone else to join the queue and then slipped in behind them. The place was fairly empty, but Marty and Jimmy had chosen a table in the far corner, behind a pillar. They seemed anxious not to be seen.

So was I, so the pillar came in handy. It hid my approach, and when I sat down I was only a couple of feet from them. I could smell the smoke from Weller's cigar.

I leaned back and tuned in. The human ear can focus

121

as accurately as the eye. When it homes in on a source of sound, everything else becomes just white noise. I might as well have been sitting at their table.

'I see the vultures are gathering again, Jim,' said Weller.

The Sunday papers in the rack by the door were full of headlines like:

FIFTH DEFEAT PUTS PRESSURE ON FARRELL

'Yeah, the media campaign's started,' said Farrell. 'Once it gets into their ink supply it's like a virus. They won't be satisfied until I'm sacked. But I've been there before.'

'Stressful job, management. If the First World War hadn't finished, you'd all be queuing up to go in the trenches. Longer life expectancy.'

'You sound like my wife. She never comes to matches because she doesn't want to spend two hours in the cold watching me build up to a heart attack.'

'She might be right. Standing there in the dugout, every eye in the football ground on you, ready to blame you when something goes wrong. That or the booze will be the death of you, Jim.'

'Then either way I'll die happy, Marty.'

'The smart money's on you getting the push next week if you don't win the second leg against Ajax,' said Weller. 'You've lost five on the trot, you're in the relegation zone. Jack Cox isn't going to put up with that for ever.'

'Jack's a decent bloke. He'll give us a chance to recover. We've had some bad luck with key players recently.'

'But the pressure's on him as well, Jim. The other directors, the fans, the media. If you don't turn it round, you're on your way out.'

'Listen, with a full-strength side we can beat anybody.'

'You haven't even got a half-strength side at the moment.

122

And you're not getting any younger, Jim. At your age you might not get another Premiership club coming in for you. You could be spending the twilight of your career at Northampton or Walsall.'

'You asked me here to talk about Marco.'

'Yeah, well, the two subjects are connected in a way, Jim,' said Weller.

The smell of his cigar smoke would have spoiled the taste of my coffee if the coffee had any taste to spoil.

'I don't want to sell him,' said Farrell. 'He's a great little player. He's confident on the ball, he'll take on defenders and beat them, he's exciting to watch. You can't say that about many English players. They have it too soft in this country now. When I was a kid, I used to spend all my time kicking a ball around under the gas lamps. That's what makes these foreign players so skilful – kicking tennis balls round the slums of Naples.'

'Marco's father's a dentist and he comes from Florence,' said Weller.

'Whatever. He can win matches for us. Jack Cox won't let him go.'

'He can't win matches for you while he's in Italy, Jim. And he'll stay there until this business with the girl in the club is sorted out. It's upset his girlfriend. She's threatened to leave him. And Marco don't play well when his love life is in a mess.'

'Tom Tomlinson's put a private detective on the case. If Marco's being set up, it will be sorted.'

'Have you met the detective?' said Weller. 'I'd put more money on Doncaster Rovers winning the European Cup.'

Well, they say eavesdroppers never hear any good of themselves.

'Fair point,' said Farrell (of whom I'd thought better). 'So what's the deal?'

'I can sell him on to an Italian club for the ten million you paid for him – less commission.'

The windows vibrated as a juggernaut rolled past. The wagons out there were trading big all over Europe. Just like Marty Weller. Except that he could earn more than they did without leaving the car park. Agents like Weller made their money from percentages of their clients' transfer fees. The more often they were bought and sold, the more commission Weller made. Jimmy Farrell knew it, too.

'Sounds like a nice little earner for you, Marty.'

'Could be a nice little earner for both of us, Jimmy.'

'Are you offering me a bung, Marty?'

'Perish the thought! I'm offering you a broker's fee of one per cent of the sale value for assistance rendered towards the transaction. It's standard business practice.'

'That's not how the Football Association would see it, Marty.'

'The Football Association don't know, do they? Look on it as a pension plan. When you get the bullet from City, there may not be that many big pay days ahead for you.'

There was silence for a while, the clink of a spoon against a coffee cup. I couldn't see Jimmy Farrell, but I could imagine that florid face, the hundreds of burst blood vessels like the pixels on a television screen, the long, thinning hair pasted over his skull. He was thinking, and he probably thought better with a stiff drink in his hand than a cup of motorway coffee.

'One per cent?'

A hundred grand would buy a lot of stiff drinks when the doors to the TV hospitality rooms no longer opened for him as frequently as they did now. At last, something was beginning to make sense.

In the corner of the restaurant, a little red light blinked

on and off to show that the security camera was working. It felt like water dripping into the pool of silence that had gathered between Farrell and Weller again. The silence seemed to last an age – long enough for me to recall the days when I sold CCTV equipment to places like this, before the company discovered that hitting sales targets was not my strong suit. I'm still looking for my strong suit. Some day I may have to come to terms with the fact that God didn't deal me one.

'One per cent,' said Marty Weller. 'Take your time, Jim. Go away and thing about it.'

'All right. I'll be in touch, Marty,' said Farrell.

He didn't even glance at me as he left. Weller waited until the manager was well clear before getting up. I let him pass me and followed him into the car park.

The Jag had central locking. The thing about central locking is that it's central unlocking as well. All the doors unlock when the little gadget bleeps and the lights flash. I was sitting in the passenger seat before Marty Weller had eased his arse behind the wheel.

'Who the fuck . . . ?'

I took off the shades and cap. 'It's only me, Marty.'

'And what the fuck do you want?'

'I want to know what's going on.'

He took the cigar from his mouth and tossed it on to the tarmac.

'I'm going to drive to London, and if I wanted to travel sitting next to someone like you I'd use public transport. Now get out and piss off.'

'You're driving to London, and Jim Farrell's driving off in the opposite direction.'

'I'm a football agent; he's a football manager. We talk to each other. That's how we do business. Its like you talking to the checkout lady in Marks & Spencer.'

'I've never been offered a hundred grand cashback on a pair of boxer shorts in Marks & Spencer, Marty.'

The sarcastic smile froze on his face. His big fingers descended on the switch that winds up the electric windows and the switch that locks the doors. He swivelled round in his seat and looked at me steadily. Although it was winter and already getting dark, he was wearing a cream-coloured summer suit with puce slip-ons and a tie covered in blue and yellow flowers. Frightening. In a confined space, the size of the man was quite frightening, too. His thighs spread themselves all over the driver's seat, and his barrel chest put the seams of his jacket under some strain. The bulge under his left arm didn't help, either.

'So what do you want to know?'

The smile had gone now, and I started to wonder whether I had been as clever as I thought in jumping into a car with Marty Weller. People like Marty don't get where they are by bothering too much about the people they hurt along the way. I'd already been beaten up once, and for all I knew it might have been on Weller's instructions. And that bulge under his left arm worried me.

'I want to know why you're offering Jimmy Farrell large sums of money to sell Carlo Marconi. I was sitting behind the pillar when you did it.'

'That was careless of us. And who told you we were here? Is Jimmy having his phone tapped now?'

'It's my job to know these things. I'm a private eye. And a better one than you seem to give me credit for.'

It sounded tougher and more professional than I felt, but you don't need to wait outside someone's flat with a baseball bat to hurt them. What Marty had said about me in the restaurant had left bruises. I'm a sensitive guy.

'So you overheard a conversation. It's only your word against mine. Even private eyes need evidence. '

'I'm not a policeman, Marty. I'm not collecting evidence against you. Not yet, anyway. All I want to know is what's going on with Carlo Marconi.'

But he knew, and I knew, that I had no leverage over him unless I could prove he had offered Jimmy Farrell a bung. He wasn't going to admit it, and Jimmy Farrell wasn't, either. I thrust my hands into my jacket pockets. And felt Beth's Walkman.

'I could deny that this meeting ever took place,' said Weller.

'You could,' I said. I pulled the Walkman from my pocket. Fortunately, it was the type with a little condenser mike built in to it. It was typical of Beth to buy the top-of-the-range model, even though she would never use the mike. 'But not after I produce the tape.'

Weller looked at me for a moment, like a grandmaster reassessing the board after his opponent has made an unexpected though not necessarily very clever move.

'What did you say your name was?'

'Steve Strong.'

'You're smarter than I thought, Steve. You seemed a bit wet behind the ears when we met at the football ground. Now I think you could go a long way. What did I offer you then to keep out of all this?'

'I think two grand was the figure.'

'I'll give you four for that tape.'

I'll admit I thought about it. That was definitely the best offer I would ever get for a second-hand Simply Red tape.

'You seem to make a habit of offering people money, Marty.'

'It buys things. Anything at all. Believe me.'

'It doesn't buy this,' I said.

For a moment I thought he was going to grab the tape from me. He looked well annoyed. He was clearly used to being able to buy off people like me.

Instead, he moved his right hand across his chest. He slipped it inside his jacket, towards the bulge under his left arm. It was almost dark now. The sodium lamps in the car park had turned the Jag's long bonnet that yellow-grey colour that doesn't exist in daylight. Inside the car, all the colours had been knocked back to a bleached-out monochrome, black and white and fuzzy shades of grey.

The scarce light collected on anything pale and metallic, as water gathers in potholes. It settled on the silver-grey shape he withdrew from his jacket. Dull and metallic and cylindrical and quite heavy, it filled his palm. His hand slid between the seat and the door, where I could not see it properly. But I knew.

I felt the muscles in my arse begin to loosen. Sphincter muscles. What kind of word is that? Sphincter. It's the kind of word you know only because it's used to explain what it feels like to be shit-scared. And it's funny what rushes through your mind when you're shit-scared. Sphincter sounds like a statue near the pyramids. I've never seen the pyramids. Perhaps I never will now. Oh, shit!

I should have listened to Beth, applied for those jobs. I'm out of my depth as a private investigator. I've already been beaten up, and now this. You read about people with guns in the papers, people getting shot in pubs in Hackney or Moss Side. But you know they don't really exist, just as you know you will never die, even though everybody else will.

And now I know there *are* guns around, and that I could die. Very soon.

I pulled away from Weller, slewed round in my seat

with my back to the door. Not that a few extra inches of distance would make any difference if he decided to shoot me. He had been careful to lock the doors so I couldn't get away, even if running away from a man with a pistol in his fist was an option worth considering.

As I groped around in the dark, my mind searching for anything that might persuade Weller not to blow away this nosy little bastard in this quiet corner of a motorway car park, it occurred to me that the tiny red light blinking on the Jag's dashboard might be the last thing I would ever see. It signified that the car alarm was armed. And it reminded me of the little red light on the security camera in the coffee shop.

It was worth a try.

'If anything happens to me,' I said, 'the police will play back the CCTV tape in the coffee shop. I'm on it, you're on it, Farrell's on it.' Maybe. On the systems I used to sell, the coverage was so grainy you'd be pushed to spot a giraffe in a bikini, let alone a couple of middle-aged men hiding behind a pillar. Companies who would fork out thousands for the cameras were usually too mean to spend a couple of quid on a new tape. Most of them reused the same one over and over until it shredded. But did Marty Weller know that? And if he did, could he take the risk that this might be the only motorway service station in Britain that replaced its security tapes before they wore out?

Weller's hand came up from behind the seat.

'Why should anything happen to you, Steve?'

His hand caressed the shiny metal. Then he flipped open the lid of his silver cigar case, took one out and slid the dull metal cylinder back into his inside pocket.

The flame of Weller's lighter illuminated our faces as my eyes closed involuntarily with relief. Weller spotted my expression, and as he took in the first gulp of smoke he started to laugh. The smoke going in and the laughter coming out fell over each other and he began to choke. His jowly face darkened as the blood rushed to his head, and for a moment I thought it was Weller who was about to die. He slumped forward and I hit him on the back until his airway cleared.

'Here,' he said through his final spluttering, 'you ditn't think this was a shooter, did yer?' He took the silver case from his pocket again. 'You've been watching too much telly. You oughter get out more.'

'Just playing safe, Marty,' I said, as coolly as I could.

'Listen! Guns are for mugs. The people who use 'em end up either dead or inside, which in my book amounts to the same thing. The Kray twins came from my part of London and I saw what happened to them. You can make a lot more money with a lot less trouble on the legitimate side of the law, Steve.'

'Legitimate? Offering a bung to a football manager?'

'All right, that probably wouldn't go down well with the football authorities. And it would be embarrassing for me and Jim if it appeared in the papers. But it ain't illegal. And Carlo's my client. I've got to use my best endeavours to look after his welfare, ain't I?'

'He's been with City for only three months, so why does he want to leave?'

'He's been a bit homesick ever since he came. He's a warm-blooded Italian, and I don't think he realised how grim and cold it could be "oop north". This business with the girl who claims he groped her was the final straw.'

'You didn't put her up to it, by any chance?'

'Come on, Steve. I don't do things like that to my clients. But I'm an entrepreneur. When this thing came along I saw a chance to make a bit of money. Nothing wrong in that. You can't have a crime without a victim, and nobody will lose a penny from Carlo's transfer. City will get their money back for a player who's not happy here. Carlo will get another nice signing-on fee. Jimmy will get a few quid for his trouble. I'll make a bit myself. Even the girl will do all right out of it.'

'Meaning?'

'I've bought her off. As soon as the transfer goes through she'll drop all charges.'

'Isn't this called perverting the course of justice, Marty?'

'The very opposite. Carlo never laid a finger on her, but somebody's paying her to say he did.'

My surprise must have been obvious, even in the dark.

'And who might that be?'

'She didn't say – and I didn't ask.'

'So how much have you paid her to back off?'

'Five grand. And she's lucky to get that. She thought she could make money from the papers, but they've all pulled out. They know it will all come out in court if it gets that far, so she's got nothing to sell. The only people who've made any money out of her accusation are the model agency who owned the copyright of the topless shots. It's a mean old world, innit?'

'So whoever paid Karen Pearson to set up Carlo could be behind the setting up of Vince Naylor and Pierre Bartola.'

'If I was a private eye,' said Weller, 'that's the line of enquiry I'd be pursuing.'

'You're not thinking of transferring either of them?'

'They're not my clients. The Frenchman's got too much savvy to need people like me. And who'd pay good money for Vince Naylor? It would be cheaper to buy a chain saw.'

I sank back into the cream leather upholstery of Weller's Jag and watched the headlights streaming up the north-bound carriageway of the motorway like tracer bullets in those old black and white war films. Where the hell was everybody going? I didn't care, because at last I was getting somewhere with this case. I had survived the flak over Hamburg and was heading for home in my Lancaster with Richard Todd and Jack Hawkins, humming 'The Dambusters' March'.

Schizophrenic or what? Last night I was ready to pack the job in. Now I was rehearsing my next encounter with Tom Tomlinson. *There you are, Tom. The Karen Pearson case – sorted. One down, two to go.*

'I want Karen to drop the charges against Marco now – today,' I said. 'And I want Marco back in England, training with City.'

'This is going to hurt me, Steve,' said Weller. 'I'll be paying out five grand for no return. I don't suppose you'd reconsider selling me that tape?'

'That's right,' I said.

'I don't have much choice, do I?'

I could never get to like Marty Weller, but I almost felt sorry for him.

'I'll send you the tape when the charges have been dropped,' I said.

I hope he likes Simply Red more than I do.

Beth was back from her trip to the Lake District when I got home. It seemed to have done her good. She was more pleasant to me than she had been for ages. Not exactly pleased to see me, but more solicitous somehow, as though for some reason she felt sorry for me rather than annoyed with me. The prevailing wind had changed.

I hoped the good mood wasn't in anticipation of my having sent in those job applications. If she mentioned them, I would lie and say they were in the post.

But while my credit with Beth was good, I thought I'd

build up a few more bonus points on my loyalty card by telling her I'd cracked the Karen Pearson case. There was no harm in showing that I was capable of succeeding at *something*, even though it wasn't a proper job in Beth's book.

'Good,' she said. 'Good.' And nodded her head a lot in that abstracted way people have when they're not really listening and have half their mind on something else.

'And how was the weekend?' I asked.

'Good,' she said, with that upward inflection of the voice that signifies limited but not overwhelming approval. 'Good.' And she did a bit more nodding.

There was clearly a hidden agenda. Her trip had been either bloody awful or absolutely brilliant (which I found less likely, because Beth has a limited capacity for enjoyment). But she wasn't prepared to admit it, so she settled for this middle-of-the-road, head-nodding, all-things-considered 'good'.

I took this as a hint not to enquire further, which was just as well because I wasn't that interested in her management course, to be honest. In my experience, the highs and lows of team-building exercises and marketing strategies rarely give up their full fascination in the retelling.

'Is that it, then?' she said.

'Is what it?'

'Have you finished with this private investigator business now you've found out that the little tart you went to school with has been blackmailing the football player?'

'Pretty well,' I said. I didn't want the fact that the Naylor and Bartola cases still remained unsolved to detract from my success. I would go and see Karen Pearson the following day, make sure she'd withdrawn the charges against Carlo Marconi and find out what else she knew. There was bound to be a link.

'How much are the football club paying you?' Beth asked.

'Two hundred a day.'

'Two hundred a day?' She made it sound insignificant, even though a thousand a week was more than she was pulling down, for all her high-flying, middle-management credentials.

'Plus legitimate expenses,' I said.

She started unpacking the weekend bag she had taken to the Lakes with her and stuffing the contents into the washer. You wouldn't believe how many pairs of knickers some women find it necessary to wear over a weekend.

'It's not the best career plan ever devised, is it?'

'How do you mean?'

'Well, if I understand your terms and conditions correctly, the more successful you are the quicker you put yourself out of a job and the less money you earn.'

That had struck me as the principal drawback of my remuneration package, but I didn't care to admit it.

'Have you filled in those job applications yet?'

'They're in the post,' I said.

'Good. Now you've worked yourself out of this job, you're going to need another.'

I decided to go to my room, to make sure those applications were well hidden.

'And when you have a bath, clean the ring from round the sides when you get out,' she said.

If Weller had spoken to Karen, as he promised he would, I should get a decent reception when I went to her flat this time. But I wasn't exactly greeted as a long-lost friend, even though that figure of speech would, for once, have been accurate.

'What do you want, Steve?' said Karen when she opened the door.

'Let me in and I'll tell you.'

She didn't ask me to sit down, maybe because there were things on all the seats and most of the other flat surfaces – copies of *Cosmopolitan*, Danielle Steel and Jackie Collins paperbacks, Whitney Houston CDs, used ashtrays, mugs of cold coffee . . . The TV was talking to itself in the corner. She didn't bother to turn it off. Karen was still the girl I'd known on our council estate. Hers was a better class of mess, but she and Dumpy were still sisters under the skin.

'OK. You're in. Now what do you want?'

'I want you to tell me you're dropping the charges against Carlo Marconi.'

'All right. I'm dropping the charges against Carlo Marconi.'

'How did the police take it?'

'They weren't very pleased. *We've spent a lot of time on this enquiry, madam,*' she mimicked.

She made it sound as though having to endure the displeasure of the Yorkshire Constabulary was an extra service the five thousand quid Weller was paying her didn't cover, and I ought to be bloody grateful.

'So who put you up to it, Karen?'

'Fuck off, Steve.'

'Was it the same people who are now trying to set up Vince Naylor and Pierre Bartola?'

'How the fuck should I know? Listen, I was groped by that footballer. The only reason I'm not pressing charges is that I'm pissed off by all the publicity and by the police enquiry and by dickheads like you coming round pestering me every five minutes. And if I *do* take it to court, the football club will just hire a smart lawyer and he'll wriggle out of it. Satisfied?'

I wasn't, but there wasn't much I could do about it. I wondered if Weller had briefed her to say all that, or whether she was a good enough natural liar not to need coaching.

'Some of the other players are being set up now, just like Marco was. Is somebody trying to make hush-money out of them as well?'

'I've told you, I don't know,' she said. 'A lot of people are making more out of this than I am, even though I'm the one who's taken all the risks.'

'Like who?' I said.

'Did you see the photos of me in the *News of the World*, the *People*, the *Sunday Mirror*?'

'Some of them,' I said.

'I didn't make a fucking penny from any of them, Steve. My body was being gawped at over every breakfast table in Britain, and I got sod all out of it.'

'The elegant Estelle was hawking your pictures round the media,' I said.

'Yeah! She made a fortune and I got bugger all.'

'If she commissioned the photographer, I expect they're her copyright,' I said.

'They might be her copyright, but *they're my fucking tits*!'

The silence that followed was filled by the familiar jingle of a tea commercial, and there was Denise Talbot filling the screen.

It didn't amuse Karen.

'Look at that. Even that fat cow's making more money than I am.'

Chapter Twelve

If Beth thought I had worked myself out of a job, she was wrong. I was about to be given a different assignment.

I arranged to meet Tom Tomlinson in Jimmy Farrell's office to give him the good news about Marco. Because Jim was there, I gave him the edited version of my meeting with Weller. I didn't mention Farrell's discussion with Weller, and Jimmy certainly didn't volunteer the information.

From the wary look Farrell gave me, I deduced that he wasn't sure how much I knew about that meeting. I expected Tomlinson to congratulate me on getting Marco off the hook, but he didn't. He had been getting more grief from Jack Cox.

'You'd better tell Marty Weller to get Marco back over here sharpish, Jim,' he said. 'Jack wants him in the first team on Saturday. We still have two other players in trouble and Jack's losing patience.'

'They're big lads,' said Farrell. 'They're old enough to look after themselves.'

'Pretty obviously they can't. You're the bloody manager, Jim. You should be keeping them out of bother.'

'I'm a football manager, not a fucking baby-sitter. What do you expect me to do? Hold their hands whenever they go out?'

'Impose a curfew or something.'

'That's about the most fuckin' stupid thing I've ever heard from you, Tom,' said Farrell. 'And that's saying something.'

'Say that again!' said Tomlinson. He was no match physically for Farrell, but he stood and squared up to him across the desk.

The pressure was obviously getting to both of them. Farrell had a short fuse at the best of times. I had seen him lose his rag before, though it was usually on the touchline and generally with a referee. But the manager and the club secretary coming to blows wouldn't do much to improve morale.

'All right! *All right!*' I said, stepping between them. 'Just calm down and let's discuss this sensibly.' I was starting to sound like my wife.

They sat down, but the fact that I had shown them both a yellow card didn't placate Farrell.

'Bloody curfew! He's sending four of them to the opening of a bloody pub tonight.'

'That's a publicity thing,' said Tomlinson. 'Peter Collins and Eamon Doyle are opening a new bar.'

Footballers and free beer were a volatile mixture. A party was the last thing the club needed at the moment.

'Do they have to go?' I asked.

'They're both former City players. And we've put some sponsorship into the place. It won't go down well if the club isn't represented,' said Tomlinson.

'You'd think we were running a PR company, not a football club,' said Farrell.

'It's called doing our bit for the community, Jim.

They'll go to that bloody opening and they'll stay out of trouble.'

'You'd better read the Riot Act to them before they go, Jim,' I said.

'I want you to go with them, Steve,' said Tomlinson. 'Make sure they behave themselves. Jack Cox will go ballistic if anything else happens.'

'All right,' I said, but without much enthusiasm. Baby-sitting for four footballers on a free binge is the sort of job a spot of peacekeeping in Bosnia might be reasonable preparation for.

'They'll be no trouble,' said Farrell. 'We've got a strict alcohol ban for forty-eight hours before a match. They won't be drinking.'

'They better hadn't,' said Tomlinson. 'I want to know if any of them has as much as a swift half, Steve.'

He went off to phone Cox with the news about Marco.

'They'll behave if they know you're watching them, won't they?' I said to Farrell.

'You won't catch me there. It's the players who are banned alcohol. I didn't say I was. I don't suppose you fancy a snifter now?'

'It's a bit early for me, Jim.'

'Pity. I was going to ask how you knew Marty Weller was at that motorway service station.'

'I just ran into him by accident when I stopped for a coffee. Same as you did, I expect.'

His florid face went a deeper shade of crimson.

'And if you run into him again,' I said, 'make sure you don't accept any consultation fees.'

As I closed Farrell's office door I saw him lift a bottle of Grouse from his desk drawer and pour himself a stiff one.

I didn't fancy an alcohol-free evening in the company

of four players, but Beth says that every problem is an opportunity in disguise. She learned it on some management course or other, and for once she was right. It gave me an excuse to ask Carol to come with me.

I stopped at her desk on my way out of the stadium.

'Give me two good reasons why I should spend the evening with a bar full of sportsmen,' she said.

'The booze will be free.'

'OK. One to go.'

'I'll feel a right wallflower if you don't come with me.'

'As long as you don't turn into a right pansy, you can pick me up at eight.'

Scorer's Café-Bar was on the moors above the city. If you stepped outside you could see the lights spread out below, stretching away for ever. The city looked pretty by night. It was an electric Utopia. Each point of light had equal value. You couldn't distinguish the rotting council flats where people like Ann Humpage lived, or the steel security shutters over all the shop windows, or the dandelions growing from the top of abandoned factory chimneys from the reflector-glass skyscrapers of the banks and building societies, or the Doric-pillared executive homes in the western suburbs, or the golf clubs whose subscriptions were more than some people earned in a year. Night was the only time this sprawling web pulled itself together – except for five o'clock on a Saturday afternoon, when we all looked at the results to see how City had gone on.

But nobody spends much time outside a place like Scorer's when the drinks are free on opening night.

The press boys had already done their pictures of the owners – the two former City players, an ex-cricketer who had turned out in a couple of test matches for England and a moderately successful golfer on the European tour

– wearing smiles that barely concealed their anxiety about whether they were going to get back the money they had invested in the place.

One more, please. A photographer was snapping the four City players, who were wearing suits they would come to regret as much as Kevin Keegan regrets the perm and kipper tie when some spiteful picture editor resurrects one of those photographs from the 1970s. *Just one more.*

A sixteen-stone rugby prop and the net-minder from the ice hockey team, glasses in hand, were standing on a table singing rugby songs at the tops of their voices. Well, somebody had to make sure the free drinks the soccer players had turned down didn't go to waste.

The local TV channels had done their one-to-ones. None of the reporters asked whether the city needed another place to get pissed in, or whether it was out of town so that punters had further to drive home with a skin-ful. It wasn't that sort of night. The media just wanted a free shot at a room full of celebs. The owners just wanted the free publicity. It was all very incestuous and friendly.

'See what I mean,' said Carol over her third spritzer. 'When they get too old to kick a ball, they open a pub.'

She was right. Scorer's might be called a café-bar, but it was just another pub. Instead of horse brasses on the walls, there were photographs of City scoring goals and Rovers running in tries and hockey players beating shit out of each other on the ice. There was even a picture of the last Yorkshire cricket team to win the county championship. I didn't realise photography had been invented that long.

'You're just an old cynic,' I told her. She was a little pissed and was at the catty stage of enjoying herself. I was driving, so I had imposed the players' booze curfew on myself and was at the morose stage of being left out of a party.

'Less, of, the, old,' she said. She picked off each word carefully, as if she was shooting clay pigeons, and grabbed another spritzer from a passing tray. She was leaving me well behind. 'So why is Fat Marty paying your friend Karen to go away? And don't tell me it's his generosity and social conscience. He couldn't even spell them.'

'No. Just self-interest. It's cheaper to reach an out-of-court settlement.'

'I always knew that whoever said crime doesn't pay was a lying bastard.'

'Settling with Karen's cheap at the price,' I said. 'It's costing City a fortune for no return while Marco's sulking in Italy. Now he and his luscious lady can kiss and make up and he can come back and score loads of goals for us.'

'Bloody footballers. Just because they get their pictures in the papers and they've got money they think they can get away with anything.'

He hasn't done anything, I wanted to say, but I didn't. She was now reaching the belligerent stage she went through after a few glasses of wine. It was usually followed by a flirtatious stage, and even if I wasn't enjoying myself at the moment I was hopeful of a horizontal end to the evening back at her flat.

She'd been giving out the right signals ever since I picked her up. She wore a little red dress that dipped intriguingly at the front and slid half-way up her thighs when she manoeuvred herself into the low-slung passenger seat of the MG.

We'd followed Gary Allen out to Scorer's. He'd just taken delivery of a new sponsored car and volunteered to drive the other players so he could show it off. It was the sort of perk you get when you've just been selected for the

England squad – a tasteless Japanese job with Gary's name and some tacky advertising copy for a local garage down both sides.

'Nice motor,' said Carol. But a decent taste in cars has never been high on the list of qualities I look for in a woman.

'It's a bit flashy.'

'I can see it wouldn't be your choice,' she said. 'It's probably comfortable and reliable.'

'It's certainly fast.' Gary had lost us well before we hit the ring road.

'He's a footballer,' said Carol. 'He won't have got as far as speed limit signs in the *Janet and John* books. And bloody hell, why don't you do something about these seats. I've just snagged a hole in these tights.'

We stopped at an all-night chemist's and I bought her some more. I stuck a piece of tape over the protruding metal and pretended not to watch as she pulled her new tights on.

The evening turned out to be as cliquey as any other office outing. The City players – Gary Allen, Lee West and a couple of reserves I couldn't put names to – stood at the bar talking to each other. The barman kept bringing them bottles of lager, but they were sticking to the alco-free. You could neck that stuff all night with no effect, as I was finding out.

They all looked bored, apart from Gary Allen, whose voice grew louder as the evening went on. Or perhaps it was just an aural illusion, because he was the most famous person in the place. Your eye travelled to him automatically, as it travels along the line of Disciples in *The Last Supper* and ends up riveted to Jesus. When he laughed he pushed back his long, thick hair, which flopped stylishly on either side of his parting. He was fairly tall and fairly broad, and his face was as attractive as any young man's who is not specifically ugly. But the only thing that made him different from lads you see in steel-capped boots on building sites was his celebrity. There was a definite hierarchy among the sporting types in the room, with the cricketers at the bottom and the rugby players and the ice hockey players in the middle. But the footballers were at the top of the pyramid, and Gary Allen was its apex. The focal point of the room's perspective was wherever he was standing at the bar.

Other guests drifted towards the footballers and hovered on the fringe of whatever group they were in, waiting for an opening to slip in and absorb the glow for five minutes. The players chatted politely about golf handicaps. Gary cracked a few jokes. No trouble.

Every time one of the players went to the Gents I followed him and hung around self-consciously while he had a jimmy. Nothing happened. What would happen? Everybody in the place was an invited guest, and even though I had moved straight from the dole into the thousand-pounds-a-week bracket, most of them were earning more than me.

The bar's owners moved from group to group, glad-handing, hoping their fading reputations would be enough to drag the paying punters in when the free drink stopped flowing. I wouldn't have recognised any of them in the street, but I remembered Peter Collins and Eamon Doyle from the days when I watched City with Dad. It was Doyle who came to our table and put his hand on Carol's shoulder.

'You're looking foxy tonight, Carol.'

'Hiya, Eamon.'

'Long time no see.'

I didn't like the way his hand lingered on her bare flesh, and I didn't like the way she giggled about old times, as though they were part of a conspiracy I would never be in on. But before I could decide whether I was getting jealous, Lee West passed our table on his way for a slash and I got up and followed him.

Doyle was still there when I got back, but he ignored me. My face has never been in the papers, so I don't suppose I was of any commercial value to him.

Carol had reached the flirtatious stage now, but she seemed to be flirting with him, so I wasn't too disappointed when the players decided to leave. You couldn't fault them. They'd been a credit to the club. It was only about eleven, but these places are no fun if you're on the wagon. Only Gary Allen seemed to be having anything like a good time.

Doyle got up when he saw them leaving and did some obsequious handshaking at the door. 'Hope to see you in again, lads. Come back when you can drink something stronger.'

Doyle had been a big name himself a few years back. Irish international, played in the World Cup Finals. But in football fame doesn't stick much longer than the mud on your boots. Gary and Lee still had it, and if they drank here regularly, the fans would follow.

'And you, Carol,' said Doyle. 'Any time you're passing, come in and have a drink.' The invitation wasn't extended to me. It's not my sort of pub, anyway.

'Thanks,' she said.

'Take care!'

God, how I hate people who say 'take care'!

'He doesn't sound Irish,' I said as we left.

'Is he buggery,' said Carol. 'He's from Halifax. But the only qualifications you need to play for Ireland are that

145

you're not good enough to play for England and the grass on your front lawn is green.'

We stepped over the puddles of sick in the car park and got into the MG.

'Well,' I said, as we followed the players back towards the city, 'mission accomplished.'

'Yes,' said Carol, 'you're very good at riding shotgun. What other positions do you know?'

The Rover with the orange go-slower stripes down the side was lurking in a lay-by just outside the city boundary. Gary saw it and hit the brakes. He was well inside the limit before he got to the thirty-miles-an-hour signs, but the flashing blue lights came on anyway and the police car pulled him over. I came to a stop behind to find out what was going on.

Gary Allen was already blowing into the plastic bag when I reached him.

'He hasn't had a drink all night,' said Lee to the cop with the breathalyser.

'That's not what the crystals say, sir.'

'I've not,' said Gary. 'Just a few bottles of alco-free.'

The other players and the two traffic cops were standing round Gary. The sodium streetlights had bleached the colour out of their clothes, out of the cars, out of Gary Allen's face. It was a monochrome picture on which the yellow, Day-Glo anoraks of the policemen had been superimposed by a computer artist. The rest of the colour seemed to have drained into gold puddles on the wet tarmac.

'You can take a blood or a urine test down at headquarters, sir.'

'But I haven't been bloody drinking.'

'Calm down, Gary,' I said. 'They're only doing their

jobs.' Much more of this and I'd qualify for a referee's certificate.

'This is another bloody frame-up,' said Lee. 'Come on, Gary, let's get out of here.'

'I wouldn't advise you to try to drive that car in your condition, sir.' The traffic cop's sidekick reached into Gary's car and took the key from the ignition.

'Here, you. That's my fucking car.' Gary said he hadn't been drinking, and I knew he hadn't. But the slur in his voice said he had.

'Leave it, Gary,' I said.

The players were all big lads, and the police were out-numbered. This could turn nasty. And if Gary decided to do a runner, it could get very awkward for him.

'Why did you pull him over?' I said. 'He wasn't driving badly.'

'And who are you, sir?'

'I work for City Football Club. This is Gary Allen.'

'I know who he is. I'm a season-ticket holder. We received a report that the person driving this car was seen staggering out of a bar.'

'That's fuckin' rubbish,' said Lee. 'Gary were no more staggering than I was. He's been set up.'

'I wouldn't know about that, Mr West. But he's tested positive. He'll have to come down to Divisional HQ.'

'Get in the police car, Gary,' I said. 'I'll follow you down.'

I knew there was no point in hammering against this wall of police politeness. You only bruised your knuckles. 'Lee. Drive Gary's car back for him. And drop Carol off at her flat on the way.'

'But he wasn't drinking,' said Carol. 'You were watching him all evening.'

'Somebody must have been spiking his drinks.'

'Who?'

'The obvious answer would be the person who was pouring them. The barman.'

'Why?'

'Tomorrow, I'm going to ask him. Listen, Carol, will you do me a favour? Ring Eamon Doyle and find out who that barman was and where he hired him.'

'OK. Come round to the flat later?' She sounded like another woman feeling sorry for me, but I'm not proud.

I kissed her on the cheek and walked back to the MGB. They were putting Gary in the police car. He seemed to be crying. It wouldn't have been so bad if he wasn't such a golden boy. Somehow, the trendy suit and expensive haircut just made him look more pathetic. The golden puddles in the road were Gary Allen's cool, melting.

I sat with him in the nick while we waited for the police doctor to arrive.

It was a new building, all exposed brickwork and metal furniture. Easy to clean when the drunks threw up in it. A drunk had just thrown up in it.

Gary was crying again. 'I'll get fucking sent down for this.'

'Don't be daft. They don't put you in jail unless you're well over the limit.'

'They do if it's your second time.'

Oh, fuck!

'You've done this before?'

'Banned for a year. I only got me licence back three weeks ago.'

'Ring Tom Tomlinson. Tell him what's happened. Tell him to get down here,' I said.

I gave him Tom's number and he went to the payphone. No wonder he was crying. I'd be crying. This kid had everything to look forward to – money, cars, women, a place in the England squad. And what was he looking at now? Six months in jail if he was lucky, with remission for being top scorer in the prison football team. I'd be weeping buckets.

He came back from the payphone. 'He's on his way.'

'Don't worry,' I said. 'We'll sort it.'

I was lying. Would *you* believe a flash young kid who'd spent all night in a pub and claimed his drinks had been spiked when he was pulled over for drink-driving? Neither would I, especially if he's been done for it before. It's the sort of thing you read in the papers and wonder why anybody bothers to plead not guilty with an excuse as desperate as that.

'Let me smell your breath.'

He breathed on me. Nothing, except the faint odour of salt 'n' vinegar crisps. It must have been vodka they spiked his beer with.

'Didn't you taste anything in the lager? Didn't it taste stronger than usual?'

'Dunno. I never drink it. They all taste like piss.'

'Who served you?'

'Barman.'

'Did you see him opening the bottles?'

'Dunno. We were talking. He might have brought them through from the back room. Yeah! He did.'

'That's how they did it,' I said. 'Shot of vodka in each bottle.' The barman was the Judas figure in that nasty little tableau at Scorer's.

'I'll get off, won't I, Steve?' Tears of slightly drunken self-pity were rolling down his face again.

'Yeah!' I said. ''Course you will.'

They kept bringing in the real drunks, the pushers, the domestics bleeding all over the quarry tiles, the joy-riders, the street girls. We watched them come and go, sitting under posters warning people to lock their cars and beware of pickpockets. Me and England's next centre forward, worth about five million pounds at today's prices. And I was supposed to have been keeping him out of trouble.

I wished the doctor would come. I didn't want to be around when Tomlinson arrived. I didn't want to go back to Carol's flat, either. I felt I had let everybody down.

Still, he wasn't the first footballer to burst into tears. A bout of weeping was becoming an essential career move for any player who wanted to keep himself in the public eye.

Chapter Thirteen

'Jack Cox wants to see you.'

It was Tomlinson. He'd spent most of the night at police headquarters bailing out Gary Allen. He was not a happy man.

'Cox lives in the Isle of Man,' I said stupidly.

'You'll have heard of aeroplanes? Big metal boxes with wings. There's a flight at ten. Be on it. Your ticket's waiting at the airport. Jack will pick you up when you get there. And he's not best pleased.'

So this was where the shit hit the fan. It had already hit the fans, of course. Or at least those of them who read the *Post*. I picked up a copy from the kiosk where I caught the bus out to the airport.

> ENGLAND ACE FACES
> SECOND DRINK CHARGE

I didn't bother phoning Tony Wilson to find out where he had got the story from. He'd told me several times before.

* * *

You know how you build up a mental picture of somebody you've never met, and when you do meet them they turn out to be different and you can't believe you ever imagined them any other way? Well, Jack Cox was like that.

I'd expected to be met by a Roller with a chauffeur, but Cox himself turned up to meet me in a Ford Orion. And he hadn't sent for me to give me a bollocking. He wanted to know if Gary Allen was telling him the truth.

'He says someone spiked his drinks last night. You were with him. Is that right?'

'Yes.'

'I thought so. When you run a business you hear a lot of excuses. I can usually tell who's lying and who's telling t' truth.'

'You've talked to Gary?'

'Tom Tomlinson phoned to tell me what happened. We seem to be scoring a lot of own goals lately, Steve.'

It was the nearest he came to holding me responsible.

'So you phoned Gary?'

'I've got a soft spot for him. He's about the only first-team player who hasn't cost us silly money. Local lad, came up through the youth team. I know we have to buy these foreigners to stay competitive, but they're not football teams any more. They're gangs of mercenaries.'

'He's very upset,' I said. 'He's been set up, just like the others.'

'We'd better get him the best lawyers we can, then.'

Businessmen who retire to tax havens are supposed to wear polo shirts and those golfing sweaters with coloured diamonds all over them. Cox had on an old tweed jacket, grey flannels, one of those green checked shirts farmers wear to market and a drab brown tie. He could have been my father, if Dad ever had the ambition or ruthlessness to become a self-made millionaire.

Not that the rewards seemed too attractive as we drove to his home. The Isle of Man was shrouded in the sort of fine mist that comes out of one of those nozzles you spray pot plants with, and the bits of it I could see reminded me of the more godforsaken parts of the Pennine moors. Cox could only have come here to hide from the tax man. He was born in the city, like me, and you get used to it, even the ugly bits. Wild country like this stretches its past over a huge canvas, while big cities squeeze their entire history into the hundred years between their dark satanic mills and the building sites of their millennium projects. But it's the cities that contain the concentrated essence of life.

My first sight of the house told me he was a reluctant exile. It had a big picture window that looked over the Irish Sea towards England. Mrs Cox was framed in it as we arrived.

I would have to call her Mrs Cox, even if she offered me her first name. She was that sort of woman – small and neat, with her hair in a perm that was old-fashioned even for a woman of her age. Although she didn't shop at British Home Stores, she looked as though she went to the same designer, as though her husband's money was still as foreign to her as the island he had brought her to.

'Come through to t' kitchen,' she said.

Like her husband, she still had a strong Yorkshire accent.

Someone was vacuuming upstairs, but I guessed Mrs Cox felt guilty about having servants. She probably did the dusting before the cleaner arrived.

'Steve Strong, did you say? What part of town are you from?'

I told her.

'Gladstone Street? Strong? My sister used to live next

to your aunty in Benson Lane.' The cosy coincidence that she knew my family seemed to please Mrs Cox more than was reasonable, as though I had smuggled a phial of pure nostalgia through Customs, rolled up a twenty-pound note and let her snort.

'Your grandmother was a Webster and your grandad played the organ at Beck Bridge Methodists,' she said, as though I was a stamp she had identified and stuck on the correct page in her album.

'She never wanted to come away,' said Cox as his wife mashed the tea, 'but I've got my tax position to think about.'

'If you're thinking of making a lot of money, Steve,' said Mrs Cox, 'don't! You'll only get some accountant telling you where to live.'

'I'll bear it in mind,' I said.

'Give all your money to the government and they'll spend it on something worthy. I'd rather spend mine on summat trivial that makes folk's lives worth living,' said Jack Cox. 'My mother died from cancer. The health service could do no more for her, but *One Foot in the Grave* could still make her smile.'

His wife distributed the tea with the look of a cinema usherette who has seen this film several times before.

'When I was building up the business I used to have me dinner with the lads in the warehouse. All they talked about was football. It meant a lot to them that City should do well. They never did in them days, of course. We were always in the Second Division. I made my money from those blokes, and I want to give 'em summat back. If I have to live over here for a few years to do it, fair enough. It's not a bad spot when it stops raining.'

I don't like rich men on principle, though I haven't met that many. I like self-made rich men even less, though it would be more logical to dislike inherited wealth. And I like rich men who avoid paying taxes least of all. But in spite of myself I was beginning to like Jack Cox. He reminded me of Dad and stirred three sugars into his tea like my grandad.

And against all the odds, his outlook on life was the same as my own. It was a sort of philosophical hedonism that says that the things worth doing are those that will give the most pleasure to the greatest number. If he could only break the umbilical cord to his accountant, he might start enjoying life himself.

'You've got the squad to win something if we could keep them all out of trouble,' I said.

'We should have. Jimmy Farrell spends enough on their wages. Nobody's worth ten thousand pounds a week for kicking a ball about, but I've always paid the rate for the job. I'm getting tired of looking in that trophy cabinet and seeing nowt but the Yorkshire Senior Cup, though.'

'I wish they *would* hurry up and win something,' said Mrs Cox. 'Then you might be satisfied and we could spend a bit of time back home.'

'It's not just about winning cups, though,' said Cox. 'Some of my directors want to pull the stadium down and build a new one near the motorway. I grew up round that ground. I love that part of the city. If I had my way I'd bring back the terraces and give the game back to the working man.'

'You're too late,' I said. 'It's already been taken over by television companies and marketing executives who want to sell the kids a new replica shirt every three months.'

'Aye. There've been mutterings about Tom Tomlinson being behind the times. Tom's done a lot for City over the years. He's the last link with the way football clubs should be run. But I won't be able to defend him much longer if we don't get this business with the players sorted.'

'It's their mothers I feel sorry for,' said Mrs Cox. 'All that expense. And youngsters just pester until they get what they want.'

'I'm relying on you, Steve,' said Cox. 'I can't run the club from this distance, and if I thought Brian Deakin was capable of running it I wouldn't have bought him out. But I can do without much more of this aggravation. If it's not sorted soon, I might just take me bat home.'

You couldn't blame him. He was under pressure from his wife to return home from his tax exile. And there was somebody out there who clearly wasn't grateful for what his millions were doing for City.

'Have you any idea who's behind all this?' I asked. Though he lived in the Isle of Man, he was still the club chairman. If somebody had a grudge, or if there had been threats against the club, he would know.

'I've got my suspicions,' he said. 'But I've never accused anybody without proof. Besides, that's what we're paying you to find out. How much *are* we paying you, by the way?'

I told him

'Aye, well that's more than fair for a lad of your experience, though if you sort it quickly there might be a bonus in it for you. If you don't, we'll have to get somebody else in.'

It was the last thing he said to me, a tiny glimpse beneath the surface of an essentially decent man to the streak of ruthlessness without which nobody could build a business empire like Cox's Carriers.

He drove me back to the airport. Mrs Cox stood in the picture window, following us with her eyes as we headed towards the sea.

* * *

I needed to talk to the barman at Scorer's who had been spiking Gary Allen's drinks, but when I phoned they told me he wouldn't be working again until the following day, and they didn't have his address.

I can usually idle a day away with the best of them – put on a video, play a few CDs, go down the pub. I had three years' training for it when I was at university. But this thing was nagging at me now. I was restless for a result.

The one person I had been able to link positively to any of these incidents was Marty Weller. He'd denied being involved with the others, but he would, wouldn't he? He admitted his connection with Karen Pearson only because I had enough on him to make the soccer authorities show him the red card. I wouldn't trust Weller further than the end of one of his cigars. So I decided to fill in time with a trip to London.

My domestic arrangements have reached such a low ebb that it wasn't until I got on the train that I realised that Beth was also on it. She was going down for some flip-chart and brainstorming session with the rest of her company's middle managers, and she was more surprised to see me than I was to see her. When I joined her and her corporate briefcase I thought she might be impressed that my new job also involved executive awaydays, but thinking of me and a first-class compartment in the same context was too big a shock for her. She looked at me as though I was a pervert who had exposed myself to her in the park rather than someone who had chosen to sit next to her in a railway carriage.

'What the hell are you doing here, Steve?' were her actual words.

'I'm going to London to interview a suspect.'

'This is a first-class carriage.'

'And I've got a first-class ticket. Look.'

I was entitled to legitimate expenses, and City could afford it, so why not?

'You're not still on with that fantasy? It's ridiculous a man of your age playing at being a private eye. When will you grow up, Steve, and learn that life's about bread, not circuses? And take those sunglasses off.'

I was wearing them to cover my bruises, which felt better but looked worse.

I took them off.

'God!' she said. 'With them on you look like one of the Blues Brothers, and with them off you look like a giant panda. Either way, I don't want you sitting next to me.'

'Is that a request to move to second class where you obviously think I belong?'

'Steve, I have work to do. I have to prepare for my meeting.'

'OK,' I said. 'I'll just sit here quietly and read.'

Everyone else in the compartment was reading the *FT* or the business pages of the *Yorkshire Post*. But I had my own research to do. I got out the copy of *Four-Two-Four* I picked up on the station bookstall and settled back to enjoy the journey.

Weller's office was in a building in Haymarket. The usual thing: someone sitting at a desk just inside the glass entrance doors to guide you to the floor you want, another receptionist when you get there, somewhere to sit that feels like the waiting-room of a high-class private clinic. What I didn't expect was a security man. He wasn't the brown-uniformed variety they have in Marks & Spencer to stop you walking off with the knickers, but personal security. A big lad.

Interior designers must hate this. They take all that

trouble to specify the potted plants and the deep-pile carpet and the splashy repro watercolours and the chromeplated fittings, and then somebody in an XL fitting with a brutalist haircut is paid to stand around with his arms folded right in the middle of it all and ruin the effect. But if you allow people into buildings, that's what you get. Marty Weller's high-decibel suits wouldn't exactly complement the décor either.

I sat down in one of the black leather Bauhaus chairs with chrome arms and furtively looked at him furtively looking at me and wondered why Weller needed protection. I had taken off my shades, though it was difficult to tell because the bruises round my eyes made it look as though I was still wearing them.

After a while he walked over to the desk and spoke to the receptionist. It was obvious he was checking me out. The receptionist made a call. He took the phone from her and looked back at me as he spoke into it. I didn't blame him. I must have looked out of place there, too, unless the clients of Weller's sports management consultancy included unsuccessful middleweight boxers.

I had been feeling punch-drunk all week from the beating I'd got when I'd returned from Blackpool, and if I found out Weller was responsible for having me beaten up I was in the mood to give him a beating, protection or no protection. But someone else had got there before me.

Weller's head appeared round his office door, and his face was in a worse state than mine. His nose was split at either side, as though someone had taken a sharp instrument to his nostrils. The congealed blood had not yet darkened from red to black, which suggested his injuries were fresher than my own. And he wasn't pleased to see me.

'What the fuck do you want?'

I was getting used to that as an opening gambit from the people I went to see. Now I was a private eye maybe I had said goodbye to 'good morning' for ever.

'Invite me in and I'll tell you,' I said.

The security man hovered heavily, but Weller waved him aside.

'He's harmless,' he said. 'He shits himself if he sees a cigar case.'

I gave him my most insincere smile and stepped past him into his office.

It was exactly as I expected – desk the size of an aircraft carrier made out of some exotic timber with an unnaturally exaggerated grain, big leather chair that wrapped itself around him and tilted in all directions as he moved, drinks cabinet in the corner.

'Why the security? I didn't realise the West End was such a rough neighbourhood,' I said.

'It can be. I had a bit of trouble with some visitors recently. I don't want it to happen again.'

I looked at the pulp that had once been his nose. 'The words "horse" and "stable door" spring to mind.'

'Yeah, well I'm taking no chances until whatever is going on in your neck of the woods is sorted. And as you're the one City are paying to sort it, that could be some time.'

'The state of your face has something to do with what's going on at City?'

'A couple of lads with northern accents followed me home one night. They knew I'd paid Karen wassername to withdraw the charges against Marco, and they didn't like it. As you can see, they warned me off.'

'Who were they?'

'They didn't leave their business cards. And all northern accents sound alike to me.'

'But they knew you'd bought Karen off?' I said.

'Yeah.'

'How did they find out?'

'I don't know.'

He leaned forward and took a cigar from the silver box on his desk, buying himself time while he thought about what he was going to say next.

'Listen. I might as well level with you, Steve. I lied to you about Karen when we had that little talk on the motorway. It was me who paid her to set up Marco.'

I was getting somewhere at last, even if it had taken someone else to beat it out of him.

'OK,' I said, 'talk me through it again, and try to make contact with the truth once or twice this time. How did you get mixed up with Karen?'

'Where would *you* go if you wanted a woman in a strange town? I went to the local knocking-shop, though I think they called it an escort agency.'

'The White Rose Agency?'

'Something like that,' said Weller.

'And they said Karen would be willing to set Marco up?'

'Don't be daft. This was strictly between me and her. I just picked her out of a book of photographs. She was happy to do it when I told her how much she'd be paid. I made it easy for her. I knew Marco would be in the club that night.'

'And you arranged for a photographer to be there and bribed security at the club to call the police?'

'I've no idea where that cameraman came from, and I didn't want the police called in. All I wanted was a bit of low-key local publicity, to give Marco an excuse for wanting to leave City. But it got out of control.'

'You've lied to me before, Marty. Why should I believe you now? That photographer was a professional, with contacts in the media. And nightclubs don't call in the law if they can help it. That was deliberate.'

'I wasn't behind any of that, I promise you, Steve. What started out as an innocent little scam got taken over by somebody else very quickly.'

'But it also gave you an opportunity to blame somebody else for setting up Marco.'

'I've got my business to protect, Steve. But I swear I don't know who these people are or what they're up to. I only know they're rough boys and I don't want anything more to do with it. I just want out.'

'Well, like you said, Marty, it can be grim oop north.'

I was beginning to understand how football hooligans felt. Weller's professional Londoner act was bringing out the gritty professional Yorkshireman in me. There was no difference between the primitive tribal instincts stirring in me now and those of the lads who sat on the kop pointing at the opposition supporters and singing 'Come over 'ere if you think you're 'ard enough'. Except that neither Weller nor I were hard enough for the shadowy people who seemed to be behind all this, and we had the bruises to prove it.

'It looks as though somebody's been having a go at you,' he said, looking me in the eyes. 'Same people?'

'Maybe. That's what I intend to find out.'

He lit the cigar he had been rolling round in his fingers. Smoking it must have been difficult with his face the way it was.

'Seriously, Steve,' he said, coming on all sincere through the wreaths of Havana smoke, 'you're messing with seriously nasty geezers here. You wanna be careful.'

It could have been another veiled threat from somebody who still wasn't levelling with me, but it sounded more like genuine concern. Perhaps we weren't quite as far apart as

I'd thought. Now someone had smashed his face in, at last we had something in common.

As I left, his security man gave me one of those smiles only security men seem to be capable of. The facial muscles were all in the right place, but they had no visible means of support. No friendliness, no benevolence behind them. His smile was dead, like a body from which the soul has departed. But I mustn't get a complex about security men. He was probably good to his mum.

Chapter Fourteen

I went straight from the station to Karen's flat.

If the people who had attacked Weller and me got to her she could be in danger. But my concern wasn't entirely altruistic. Somebody wanted her to stick with her accusation against Carlo Marconi, and now she'd got her money from Weller there was no reason for her not to change her mind yet again about pressing charges. Especially if someone else was offering her cash. And if she did, I'd be right back where I started.

She didn't answer my knock.

I stood on the landing trying to decide what to do. I was under a court order to keep away from Karen's flat, and if I broke in I could be in big trouble. On the other hand, she could have been beaten up too. She might be lying unconscious or worse behind this door. The woman who lived in the next flat had a Neighbourhood Watch sticker in her window. I knocked at her door.

'Cable TV, love. Ms Pearson said you had a key.'

'She told me to be careful who I gave it to. But you've been before, haven't you?'

'That's right, love.' Someone really ought to do something about crime prevention.

I slid the key into Karen's lock and went in. Karen wasn't there.

I opened the drawer where she kept her bank statements and took out the paying-in book. The latest payment was a cheque for five thousand pounds drawn on the account of Weller Sporting Management.

There was no sign of a struggle or any indication of where Karen might be.

I was about to leave when I noticed the little red light blinking on the answerphone. I pressed PLAY and heard a man's voice. Local accent.

Hello, Karen. The acid on the car was just a gentle reminder. It has the same effect on people's skin. Think on.

The recorded click as the caller replaced the receiver reverberated round my head like water dripping into water in a great, dark cavern. I waited for half an hour but Karen didn't return. Then I went home and rang her number every hour until midnight, but there was nobody there.

I was on my way back to her flat first thing when the *Post* bill outside the newsagent's near my parents' house stopped me in my tracks.

CITY CRISIS:

DIRECTOR

HITS OUT

I picked up a copy from the counter and found myself standing next to Ann Humpage. She paid for her cigarettes and waited for me at the door.

'Give us twenny quid, Steve.'

'What?'

166

'Give us twenny quid.'

'What for?'

'I need to get something for the kid.'

'Is he all right?'

'What do you think? Are you going to give me twenny quid or not?'

It wasn't an approach I'd come across from any other charity, but I had to admit it was more effective than a flag day or a coffee morning. And Dumpy was only following a national tradition established by Dick Turpin and Robin Hood. I took out my wallet and gave her twenty pounds. God knows what she would spend it on, but she was in such a state that it hardly mattered. Besides, I could afford it, and I felt I owed her something.

And I needed to get away from her so that I could read the paper.

The story led the sports page under Tony Wilson's by-line.

City's absentee chairman Jack Cox was today blamed by a fellow director for the collapse of discipline among leading players which has sent the club plunging towards the Premiership relegation zone.

In what looks like a major boardroom split, his predecessor as chairman, Brian Deakin, lashed out: 'This club is now in free fall, both on and off the field, and the buck stops with Jack Cox.

'He is City's chairman and is responsible for the way the club is run. But no matter how much money you have, you cannot run a football club of this importance and complexity from the Isle of Man.

'We need a hands-on chairman, and if Jack Cox is not willing to come back and run the club properly, he should hand over to someone who will.'

There was a sidebar next to the story listing the charges facing Marconi, Naylor, Bartola and Allen. Jack Cox was not available for comment.

I forgot about Karen and went to the *Post*'s offices instead. They were in a narrow side-street near the cathedral. The machine-room had glass walls so you could see the papers coming off the big rotary press. I watched the afternoon edition being cut and folded, carried across the ceiling on a conveyor, tied into bundles and deposited in the loading bay, where the circulation vans were waiting to spread the story of the boardroom split all across the city.

The newspaper library was in a little room in the old part of the building. Mrs Mountfield remembered me.

'Can I see the cuttings on Brian Deakin?'

She pulled a stack of manila envelopes from the filing cabinet. 'I'll have to open a new envelope on him now he's started shooting his mouth off again.'

I sat at one of the desks, took out a notebook and went through the cuttings carefully, starting with the most recent. Mrs Mountfield hadn't filed that day's story yet, and the top one dated back a few months. It dealt with the financial problems of a packaging company Deakin owned. Unlike Cox, who had made his money from a single successful warehousing and transport company, Deakin dabbled widely and not always successfully.

There was a clutch of cuttings from a couple of years ago when Cox had bought most of Deakin's shares in City. Deakin seemed to have parted with them reluctantly, even though Cox was paying what was then a good price and Deakin needed the money to bail out another of his companies that was in trouble. As a sweetener, the club had awarded the contract for stewarding matches and providing bar staff to a security company Deakin took over at the same time. The registered office was down on the docks and its name, Quaynote, looked like a play on words by someone who ought not to be allowed to play with them unsupervised.

The bulk of the cuttings came from the six or seven years of Deakin's chairmanship. City were floundering in the lower divisions in those days, but their profile off the pitch had been high. There were a couple of planning applications to redevelop City's ground, one as a shopping mall, another as a multiplex cinema and leisure centre. The city council turned both of them down because of the effect the extra traffic would have on local residents.

Deakin had spent little of his own money on players, but he had worked hard at presenting himself as a pillar of the business community. There was an old photo of him with his dipso wife when she was still quite attractive. She was in a ball gown, he was in a dinner jacket and black tie, grinning for the camera from behind the big spectacles he wore. It was some Rotary Club do or businessmen's dinner, the sort of thing Jack Cox and his wife wouldn't have been seen dead at.

But the cutting I spent most time pondering came from the business pages. It was one of those advertising features the papers run which give you some free editorial space for a puff if you buy an ad. This one was about Deakin's security firm. It offered a wide range of services, including barmen and bouncers for pubs and clubs. And it had an office in Blackpool.

I put the cuttings back in their envelopes and returned them to Mrs Mountfield.

'Found what you want, love?'

'I think so.'

'I could have told you about Brian Deakin the last time you came if you'd asked. This paperclip's not as bent as he is. I've followed City for fifty years, and they were a disaster while he was chairman. Never spent any money on players. Deakin was never interested in putting anything into the club. He was only interested in what he could get out.'

I owed Tony Wilson a drink and this seemed like a good time to buy him one.

I stopped off at the sports desk and waited until he had finished writing his preview of that night's match. When we got to the Dove and Rainbow I said: 'What do you think of Brian Deakin, Tony?'

'He provides good copy.'

'Adolf Hitler provided good copy.'

'Reasonable point,' he said, licking the moustache of froth from his upper lip.

'Word has it he was always more interested in what he could get out of City than what he could put in.'

'It's a school of thought. The football ground is practically in the city centre. It's a valuable piece of real estate. Brian tried to redevelop it a couple of times while he was chairman. Said we needed to relocate nearer the motorway, where the access to the ground and car parking would be easier. A lot of other clubs have already done something similar. But rumour had it that Brian was going to use his own development company. That would have made him a lot of money out of the existing ground if he could have persuaded the council to give him planning permission.'

'Your librarian reckons he's bent.'

'You should always listen to people like Mrs Mountfield if you want the full story. Journos like me get inhibited by little things like libel laws. I have to pretend there's a dividing line between a crook and a businessman, even when it's difficult to locate. Deakin's been known to do a bit of asset-stripping in his time, though as far as I know that's legal. But I'm interested in football, not finance. If you want to know about his business dealings you should ask our business editor. Or Dave here. Same again?'

Dave was the barman. He pulled a couple of pints and set them on the towelling mat on the bar.

'You do a bit of moonlighting for Brian Deakin, don't you, Dave?' said Tony.

'I work for his security firm at weekends. Barman at the football or the rugby. Ice hockey or boxing sometimes. Never met Deakin, though. Bloke called Charlie Robey's in charge.'

'It sounds as though they've got all the sporting venues in the city sewn up,' I said.

'And the pubs and clubs,' said Dave. 'Anywhere that needs bar staff and doormen. Out of town as well. Deakin's got the contract for that new place just opened on the moors.'

'*Scorer's?*'

'Yeah. Well, there's not much competition, is there? Deakin's got every big lad in town on his payroll. Nobody else is going to try to muscle in on his territory.'

'There's something else you might want to know,' said Wilson. 'That lass who claims Marco touched her up is trying to flog her story again.'

'You what?'

I picked up my pint and downed half of it at a swallow. I needed it. Everything I had achieved so far, which wasn't much, had just evaporated.

'By heck,' said Wilson. 'And I thought I could sup a pint.'

'Are you buying?' I said.

'Her story's worth nowt to us. Anything she says about Marco is *sub judice* if the case is still going to court. That makes her just another small-time hooker with a few kiss-and-tell stories in her handbag. We wouldn't touch it with a bargepole. Most of the blokes she's been pleasuring are probably our best advertisers.'

I emptied my glass. 'I need another,' I said. 'Are you having one?'

'I shouldn't really,' said Wilson. 'I've got a match to cover tonight. But go on then.'

Beth was home when I got back to the flat. Before I could ask about her day she said: 'Some little tart's been round to see you.'

She didn't sound pleased. Maybe she'd come unstuck in the managerial bonding exercises.

'A tart?'

'Try to imagine a model in a Donna Summers catalogue with her clothes on.'

'If you'd encouraged my little fantasies earlier perhaps we could have saved our relationship,' I said.

She gave me a smile straight out of the frozen-food cabinet, but I've lived with Beth long enough to know that behind it was something not a million miles from sexual jealousy. It almost cheered me up.

'Did she have a name?'

'I wrote it down.'

She obviously felt her emotional territory was being threatened, though why that should worry her I had no idea, as we are about to be divorced. I'm trying to be a detective here, and I can't even fathom out the woman I've lived with for ten years.

But I didn't need the yellow Post-It note she had stuck on the fridge door to tell me she was talking about Karen Pearson.

'Did she say what she wanted?'

'Only that she wants you to go and see her. She sounded a bit disturbed.'

'She's involved with the case I'm on,' I said. Why am I explaining? It's over between us.

'I don't suppose you could go and see her now? I've got a business meeting here, and I don't want people thinking you're a victim who's strayed in from *Crimewatch*.'

Men are often accused, and with good reason, of wanting women for their bodies rather than their minds. Beth has turned the usual sexual imperatives on their heads. She doesn't want me, and it's my body she doesn't want me for.

She doesn't want it with an added passion at the moment because it has two black eyes, in the same way that a black suspender belt would make me want hers more. But she's pretty consistent in this area. Normally, she doesn't want it because it stays in bed late, doesn't wear the right clothes, likes to sit around watching old movies and is reluctant to imprison itself in a job it doesn't like.

And every reason Beth has found over the years for not liking me has given me a reason not to like her. In addition to her intolerance, there's her obsessive tidiness, and her sexual reluctance, and her general dislike of other people enjoying themselves and . . .

'And have you been drinking?' she said as I lurched within breathing distance of her. Admittedly, the session in the Dove and Rainbow had become a bit open-ended, but if either of us murders the other, the police won't be looking for a single motive. They'll need to assemble a thousand-piece jigsaw of them.

I had something to eat and drank a lot of coffee. When I had sobered up a bit I caught the bus out to Karen's place. The cable TV trench had reached the main road now, and the temporary traffic lights at either end of it were holding up the traffic. The bus crawled along behind a string of Cox's Carriers wagons whose overnight deliveries were being delayed. But Jack Cox would be making money whichever way you looked at it. The spread of cable TV meant that more people would soon be paying good money for the football matches they'd been getting free on the conventional channels until recently. Most of that money would filter through to the big soccer clubs like City, and then into the pockets of the people who ran them, like Cox. Or whoever took over from him if Brian Deakin forced him to resign.

Karen's car was parked in the road outside her flat. It was a fairly new Nissan Micra, but as I approached it I saw that there was something seriously wrong with the paint job on the front, nearside wing. The finish was blistered like a bad case of sunburn.

I rang Karen's bell. She was in, but she had put the chain on the door. She peered out at me through the crack, just as Dumpy had done when I went to her flat. When she saw who I was she took off the chain and let me in. It made a change to be able to get into Karen's flat the way normal people did.

She sat on the sofa and lit one of those long menthol cigarettes with the gold band round the tip. The sort they advertise in glossy women's magazines along with all the other accessories no girl can manage without.

'What's going on, Karen?' I asked.

She tossed back her hair, but it was not the calculated flourish of a fashion model being professionally provocative. It was the nervous gesture of a harassed woman. If she could see the worry lines on her forehead, worrying about them would produce even more. But whatever was troubling her hadn't stopped her putting on lipstick and varnishing her nails in matching pillar-box red. Old habits die hard.

'Long story, Steve,' she said.

'I've got plenty of time.'

'I dropped the charges against that football player because a bloke phoned a couple of days ago and offered me five thousand quid.'

'That was Marty Weller, Marco's agent.'

'You knew about him all the time?'

'He's the bloke who paid you to set Marco up in the first place, isn't he?'

She looked surprised.

'You may as well tell me everything, Karen. I know most of it anyway.'

'All right,' she said softly. 'I did set up Marco for the money.' It seemed to come as a relief to be telling the truth for once. It was a relief to me that I had finally got a confession out of her.

'So how come you're trying to sell the story to the papers?'

'You're well informed, aren't you?'

'It's my job to be,' I said.

She began absently to tidy up some of the detritus that was within reach. That was well out of character for Karen, a transparent displacement activity to buy herself a bit more time while she decided how much she could risk telling me.

'Somebody else phoned me out of the blue yesterday. Told me that if I withdrew the charges he'd be round to rearrange my face.'

My hand went involuntarily to my own bruises. So we were back in the frontage demolition business, and I had a feeling we were talking about the same firm of contractors. Now I understood why she was so scared. Karen's physical attributes were the only means she had of earning a decent living. She's seen what a few drops of acid could do to her car. No wonder she was scared. Any further damage to those fading looks really would put an end to her career. She'd be down at the pickle factory, peeling onions with all the other middle-aged women who were desperate for money, and Karen's tear ducts didn't need that kind of stimulation.

She was crying already. A tear rolled silently down her face, leaving a little runnel in the mask of make-up like a raindrop on a dusty windowpane.

I sat beside her on the sofa and put my arm round her. The blonde head fell against my shoulder. I could feel her body shaking, the soft movement of her breasts trembling against my arm, but I got no sexual charge from her at all. I just felt sorry for her. The adult shell seemed to have crumbled away, and underneath it was the little lass I had started school with at the age of five – a runny nose in scuffed sandals.

'Who was it, Karen?' I said.

'I don't know.'

'How did he know you were going to drop the charges? It's never been in the newspapers.'

'I don't know.'

'What did this bloke sound like?'

She hesitated for a moment, long enough for me to work out that she was again considering how much it would be safe to tell me.

'He had a local accent. He could have been anybody. I'm scared, Steve. I'd get out of here today if I had any money.'

If this was a subtle attempt to touch me for cash it wouldn't have the same success as Dumpy's more direct approach. I could afford to sub Dumpy for a carton of fags or whatever she intended to spend my twenty on, but I didn't have the sort of money Karen needed to run away

176

and hide. She would have to settle for words of comfort instead.

'Don't worry. I'll look after you,' I said.

She lifted her head and looked at my face. 'Like you looked after yourself?'

Karen Pearson was a lot of things, but she wasn't stupid.

'Somebody's already been snooping round the flat,' she said. 'Blagged their way in pretending to be from the cable TV people. Searched the place pretty thoroughly, but didn't take anything.'

I made the face everyone makes when they've been caught out but they don't give a toss.

'Yeah. Well. That was me, actually.'

'Fucking hell, Steve. Why?'

'I wanted you to tell me what you're telling me now. When you weren't in, I took the opportunity of confirming a few suspicions. I don't like going through other people's stuff, but what you did to Marco wasn't very nice either, was it?'

She sat up and stubbed out the cigarette. Now the worst was over she started to do what everyone does when they find themselves in a hole with dirty water in the bottom – try to scramble up the other side of the trench.

'It would never have come to court anyway. Marty Weller said from the start we were going to drop the charges after a few weeks. I would never have got involved otherwise.'

'A victimless crime,' I said. 'I know. But there have been three more victims at the club since you set up Marco. Does the bloke who's threatening you know anything about that?'

'I don't know.'

'That's what you said before. I want the truth this time, Karen.'

'Honest, Steve, all I did was set Marco up. Nothing else. That's the truth.'

She was another liar I had to decide whether I could now believe, and that was one life skill the education system couldn't teach you.

'Do you know why anyone would want to target City's star players?'

'Maybe they just want the team to lose. Maybe they're gamblers.'

'No gambler nobbles a horse and then announces it in all the papers. We're not dealing with gamblers, although the stakes are pretty high.'

She lit another cigarette with a little gold lighter. It was elegant and fragile and a bit too ornate, just like Karen.

She sucked the smoke deep into her lungs and released it in one of those long, powerful blasts steam engines used to give when the driver pulled on the whistle cord. Karen had more immediate things to worry about than cancerous tobacco tars.

'Have you told the police about this call?'

'And admit I'd been lying to them? Do you know what you get for lying to the police about something as serious as this?'

'You don't get your face altered,' I said. 'The police could give you some protection.'

'And they'd start asking all sorts of questions. You were right the first time you came here. I *have* asked some of the men I've been with for money.'

'Blackmail?' I said.

'They've got wives they don't want to find out about me – yes.'

I never thought I'd hear it in Karen Pearson's voice, but she sounded ashamed. What is it about being afraid that sharpens your sense of morality and makes you feel remorse? Perhaps it's because you feel closer to death, and even if you've lived as though the existence of God is about as likely as getting eight score-draws on your pools coupon, there's still that remote chance someone *will* be waiting on the other side with a pair of kitchen scales to weigh you in the balance. Maybe she was finally telling me the truth – but not the whole truth.

I remembered Tony Wilson's crack about her clients all being local businessmen. It was a long shot but worth a try.

'Do you know Brian Deakin?'

She looked blank. Evidently not a reader of newspapers, our Karen.

'But you *do* know who this is.' I went over to the answerphone, wound back the tape and pressed PLAY.

The voice that spoke of throwing acid over her car wasn't Brian Deakin's, but I could tell from Karen's face that she recognised it.

'Fuck off, Steve,' she said. She stubbed out her cigarette and came towards me. She wanted to take the tape from the machine, but you don't waste years of your life watching old movies on video without becoming an expert at removing tapes from their slots, and the cassette was in my pocket before she got near me.

'Listen,' I said, 'how can I help you if you won't help me?'

'They'll kill me,' she said quietly.

'Don't be daft, Karen,' I said. 'Things like that don't happen in this city.'

But fear is a high building, and it's not that easy to talk someone down. Karen Pearson was frightened for her life, and no matter how groundless I thought her fears were, they were real enough to her. She was not going to tell me whose voice was on this tape, and she was not going to go to the police.

That left me with no alternative. If I went to the police myself, they would waste hours dragging up Karen's stalking accusation again, and I didn't have that amount of time to spare. I had to sort this thing myself.

She turned away from me, lit another cigarette and went over to the window.

'Listen, Karen,' I said, 'I think I know who's behind this, and I think I know why. Keep your door locked and keep the chain on. Don't let anybody in unless you know them. Is there somebody you could go and stay with for a while?'

'My mam and dad won't have me. I've fallen out with them since all this hit the papers.'

I remembered my meeting with Dumpy in the newsagent's.

'Have you still got Ann Humpage's address? Nobody would look for you there.'

She'd have to be desperate to go and stay with Ann – but Karen was desperate. And seeing somebody worse off than herself might cheer her up. People are selfish bastards.

'I'll see,' she said. 'Where are you going?'

'I've got things to do. And I can't stay here all night, can I?'

Silly question. Plenty of men had done precisely that. But I didn't find Karen Pearson sexy in her present frame of mind.

'Give me a ring if you get any more threatening phone calls.'

'All right. And thanks, Steve.'

She gave me a chaste peck on the cheek, but I still felt a bit of a flush coming on.

'Can't let an old school friend down, can I?' I said.

Chapter Fifteen

I didn't like deserting her to go to a football match, but this was work, not pleasure.

It was also a game City badly needed to win – Southampton at home.

The run of defeats was having its effect on the crowd figures. The season-ticket holders had paid upfront, so they came anyway, but lots of supporters who bought their tickets at the gate seemed to have found better things to do on a wet Wednesday evening in November than watch their team lose again. Fewer than twenty-five thousand fans were in the ground when the match kicked off, and you could still make out the letters CITY among the bodies in the south stand.

I sat next to Tony Wilson in the press box, which was high up in the main stand and had the best view in the stadium. We were almost at the level of the floodlight pylons, and looking straight down on the half-way line. The plastic seats had little tip-up tables in front of them, just big enough to take a notebook and a telephone, but with no room for your elbows. The cramped conditions and the superb view reflected the schizophrenic attitude most football clubs had to journalists: they were a necessary evil for businesses that depend more than most on the oxygen of publicity.

The company in the press box wasn't much better than that in the directors' box, but you found out what people were saying about each other by listening to journalists. Not what was going on, necessarily, but what people were saying. None of it may be true, but some of it would appear in tomorrow's papers and acquire a validity that was more powerful than the truth.

We sat behind the coven of journos from the tabloids. They did everything together, like the witches in *Macbeth*. The trivia of the football world was a cutthroat business. They found it safer to share their information than to risk being scooped by one of the others.

'Gary Allen's not in the squad.'

'I heard they're drying him out. If he's not careful he'll become another George Best.'

'Another precocious talent who burned himself out young. How old is he? Twenty? And he's already in the England squad and been done twice for drink-driving.'

'What's the strength of the drying-out story?'

'Got it from a board member. They've got to do something to give the magistrates an excuse not to send him down. It's two strikes and out for drink-driving.'

'Jimmy Farrell's running out of players. Marco's still in Italy trying to calm Supertits down. Bartola's been sent to his bedroom in case he tempts the kids to spend their money on coke instead of ecstasy. If anybody gets injured tonight, one of us will have to go on as sub.'

'And this match could be Vince Naylor's swan-song. His case comes up next week.'

'Vince isn't bothered. A conviction for GBH would be one career move nearer to getting his own chat show on Channel 4.'

The gossip mattered to them more than the football. Soccer was a soap opera that wrote its own plot every week.

But they were right about the effect all this was having on City's play. Once the game started it was obvious that they missed Marco's pace upfront and the width Gary Allen gave them on the wing. Without Pierre Bartola they had nobody to distribute the ball from midfield, and Vince Naylor was too busy defending to make his overlapping forward runs. The makeshift side played reasonably well considering. They forced a few corners and Lee West hit the crossbar, but I was rehearsing Jimmy Farrell's post-match press conference speech in my head well before the final whistle.

It was always going to be a tough one for us. We had to shuffle players around, bring in a few youngsters who are not quite ready for it. The lads defended well. Young Westie was unlucky hitting the woodwork. I thought we done enough to win it, but at the end of the day what matters is the result.

I couldn't have put it better myself. What mattered was not the poetry of the play on the pitch or the permed prose with which the reporters described it. What mattered was that simple, tabulated statistic that would appear at the bottom of the sports pages tomorrow, as dry as the Stock Exchange closing prices, and just as important. What mattered was that split second towards the end of the second half which made the agency reporter pick up his phone and say: 'Match number four. I've got a scorer for you. Eighty-four minutes, Le Tissier for Southampton.'

You may as well watch football on Ceefax.

That made it five defeats on the trot for City.

There was no reaction from the crowd at first. Their little bursts of desperate encouragement gradually had been superseded as the match wore on by stretches of silent gloom that were as palpable as the auroras of grey mist that gathered round the floodlights.

The players had already left the pitch when we heard it begin, towards the front of the east bank. Low, staccato, but echoing between the emptying stands like a galloping horse. It was the reporter on my other side who picked it up, the tall, blond freelance working for the *Independent*.

'Cocks out? Have we missed a streaker or is this the kop's alternative to "Get your tits out for the lads"?'

The chant was accompanied by that straight-armed pointing gesture that can make a soccer ground uncomfortably like a Nuremberg rally.

'Cox out. Cox Out. COX OUT!'

The stewards were supposed to remain in place until all the spectators had left, but for some reason there were none at that end of the ground. Some of the fans began climbing over the advertising boards and making their way round the pitch towards the directors' box, where Jack Cox and Brian Deakin sat a few feet from each other, watching what was going on and ostentatiously ignoring each other.

The ringleaders came first, but they were followed by a couple of hundred youths who didn't want to miss the only excitement they were likely to get that evening. It could have been an experiment in group behaviour designed to show how easy it was for someone like Adolf Hitler to collect followers and get them to do what he wanted. By the time the demonstrators reached the players' tunnel they were aiming their Nazi salutes at the directors' box in unison.

The police had been taken by surprise. It was five minutes before they had assembled in sufficient numbers to disperse the demonstrators. Plenty of time for the photographers and the TV cameras to get their pictures and the journos to realise they had something more significant to write about than a dull evening game that had ended 1–0.

The press box is next to the directors' box, and we had a grandstand view. So good, in fact, that I thought I recognised one or two of the faces at the front of the crowd. But it was like seeing someone in the street you normally come across in a different context. You know you know them, but you can't think where from.

'It doesn't take them long to bite the hand that feeds them, does it?' said Tony Wilson. 'Jack Cox won't like this.'

'Do you think he'll resign?'

Wilson shrugged. 'No idea. I've told you – Jack Cox doesn't share his thoughts with the press.'

'How soon will your photographer have prints of this, Tony?'

'It's all digital these days. He wires his stuff back to the office straight from the ground. I'll get him to do you some hard copies in the morning if you like.'

I didn't bother going to Farrell's press conference. I needed to talk to Tom Tomlinson.

I found him in the corridor beneath the stand, surrounded by reporters. They'd decided they would rather talk to Tom, too, and for the same reasons.

'Where's Jack Cox, Tom?'

'Didn't you hear the helicopter? He's already left. You know his time on the mainland is limited.'

'What was his reaction to the crowd protest tonight?'

'He didn't tell me. If he's got anything to say he'll issue a statement.'

Brian Deakin came out of the directors' lounge with his

wife. This was not the way directors normally left the ground. The press pack saw him, which seemed to be what he intended. 'Did you see the demo tonight, Mr Deakin?'

'I'm not blind.'

'The fans seem to share your opinion of what's happening at the club.'

'As a director it's my job to reflect the views of the supporters. Of course, it's difficult to know what their views are if you don't live in this country.'

'If Jack Cox steps down, would you consider taking over the chairmanship again?'

'Jack owns the majority shareholding now, not me. But if he decides to put his shares on the market at a sensible price, I might consider making an offer.'

Brenda Deakin looked as though she'd been road-testing the hospitality again. But she smiled as she caught sight of me through the cluster of heads. She was probably wondering where she'd seen me before, just as I was still wondering where I'd seen the big lads who had been leading the demonstration.

When the reporters dispersed to file their copy, I followed Tom out to the car park.

'There are no microphones around,' I said, 'so how *did* Jack take it tonight?'

'I thought he was going to cry,' said Tomlinson. 'I think this was the last straw for him. He's ready to get out and cut his losses. And I'm off home to get my golf clubs out of the loft. I'll probably have plenty of time on my hands to use them soon.'

In most of the novels I've read, the private investigator is an ex-cop with friends on the inside who owe him favours. That must be handy when you need to know the registered owner of a vehicle or check someone's criminal record.

My arrest for stalking Karen Pearson wasn't the sort of networking that breeds that kind of familiarity with cops. But don't think I'm entirely without contacts in high places. I know Ken Welsh of the city council planning department.

All right, *know* is perhaps pitching it a bit high. But during my brief career in the public health department I once rang him to find out which builder had been tipping his waste cement into the sewers, and he once rang me to find out if the site the parks department had chosen for a kiddies' playground was polluted by heavy metals.

'I once dumped a pile of of AC/DC LPs there,' I replied wittily.

It was when I had to explain the joke that I decided a career in local government was not for me. People like Ken only saw jokes by appointment.

But even boring old farts can come in useful if you keep them long enough. It was a relationship of sorts, and enough to get me round the wall of confidentiality and bureaucracy town planners operate behind. The city council was such a big organisation that with any luck he wouldn't have heard that I no longer work for them.

He hadn't heard, but he kept me hanging on for ages when I rang. Eventually he said: 'The file on the City ground seems to be out, Steve. Somebody must be working on it. I'll track it down and ring you back in ten minutes. What extension are you on?'

'I might be out of the office, Ken,' I said. 'All right if I pop round in an hour?'

When I got to City Hall I took the long way round to the planning department, in case anybody from public health stopped me in the corridor to ask what I'd been doing since I left.

The file Ken Welsh handed me was marked STRICTLY CONFIDENTIAL. I know this isn't saying much, but it turned out to be the most interesting thing I had ever come across in City Hall.

It contained a planning application by a firm called Rosebud Developments from what looked suspiciously like an accommodation address in London. They wanted to demolish the football ground and the disused council abattoir that stood between it and the river and build a shopping mall, a multiplex cinema and some waterfront lofts on the site.

I wasn't sure any of this was an improvement, even on the abattoir. How many more shopping malls do we need? And Arnold Schwarzenegger and Bruce Willis wouldn't get any better no matter how many multiplexes you could watch them in.

But what did I know about property development? Just enough to realise that this was a massive scheme, and that whoever controlled this site would stand to make millions of pounds if it went ahead.

'I take it this will be thrown out, Ken,' I said.

'The recommendation is for approval.'

'But we've always turned down redevelopment plans for the football ground.'

'That was before the abattoir closed. The council's strapped for cash. We'll never sell that site as long as it's next to a soccer ground. But this deal gives us a good price for it. We're snatching their hands off.'

'And when does this become public knowledge?'

'It goes to the planning committee for approval in a couple of weeks. I didn't realise public health had any interest since the abattoir closed.'

'Rats,' I said. 'That whole area seems to be full of them.'

I walked into the city centre, avoiding eye contact with a couple of beggars in shop doorways and then buying a copy of the *Big Issue* to salve my conscience. I side-stepped the market researchers in the pedestrian precinct and went to an Italian coffee shop to suck on a cappuccino while I decided what to do next.

I knew what a real PI would do next: check the ownership of Rosebud Developments with Companies House. But I had no idea how to do that, and I was too idle to find out. Besides, there was an easier way. I would go to the house of the man I guessed was behind Rosebud Developments and ask him.

For someone who has stumbled into one of the sleazier professions, I spend a lot of time in the more desirable postal districts. The place was only a few streets away from Karen Pearson's flat, except that the streets around here were called anything but streets. Avenues and drives are the nomenclature of choice. This one was a drive, lined with big detached houses in white stucco with unfeasibly large amounts of roof attached at odd angles. They look as though they would cost a fortune to maintain, but if you can afford to live round here you either have a fortune or an appointment with the bankruptcy court. The space in between that is occupied by builders and roofers doesn't concern you.

The gravel in the drive was so deep my feet left dimples in it. When I rang the bell, a woman answered.

'He's not in, I'm afraid.'

Well, it was the middle of the afternoon. What did I expect? To be honest, I expected him not to be in, because I thought I might find out more from his wife.

I let her have a good look at my face. She'd remembered it the night before. If she wasn't too sozzled, she might remember it again now.

'I know you, don't I?'

'I'm a colleague of your husband's,' I said.

It wasn't a direct lie. It was – how did Shakespeare put it? – the lie circumstantial. I was a temporary employee of City Football Club, and Brian Deakin was one of its directors. We're colleagues, circumstantially speaking. And what's good enough for Shakespeare is good enough for me.

'Would you like to come in and wait?'

Brenda Deakin was alone in the house, apart from lots of what can only be called *objets* – smoothly imprecise models of animals or naked women cast in brass or bronze or polished out of shiny black stone. The sort of thing Henry Moore might have made if he made prizes for amusement arcades. You fell over them and their ludicrously large price tags in the home-furnishing sections of expensive department stores. A large ceramic spotted dog stood guard at either side of a white and gold tiled fireplace. Ornate little lamps with tasselled shades hung from the walls. But the focal point of the room for Brenda Deakin was the gilt drinks trolley under the window, on which cut-glass decanters reflected the light from the chandelier.

'Can I get you a drink?'

'Thanks.'

'Gin all right?'

'Plenty of tonic, please.'

She was already ahead of me, of course. There was a glass on the arm of the sofa, next to the copy of *Vogue* she had been reading. She found its twin on the trolley and wiped it fastidiously with a cloth. Brenda Deakin took her drinking seriously.

She was wearing an expensive tailored suit in some bright, flowered material, a riot of reds and yellows. The red perfectly matched her lipstick. She passed me to go into the kitchen and a split second later her perfume hit me, like thunder rolling in after a lightning flash.

Seeing her made me change my mind about fashion designers. I had always filed them away under Con Artist on the grounds that you could dress Claudia Schiffer in my granny's bathroom curtains and she would look great. In the chain-store polyester most women of her age in this city would be wearing, Brenda Deakin would look fat and frumpish; in this outfit, she looked almost fanciable.

She came back with a fresh lemon and some ice. The gins she poured were big ones, though the tonic seemed to be in short supply. She sliced the lemon with the expertise of one whose only job over the past twenty years has been entertaining her husband's business associates.

'Cheers!'

I raised my expensive tumbler.

'Is Brian due back soon?'

'I doubt it. He spends a lot of time at the football club these days. But if he wasn't there, he'd be spending a lot of time somewhere else. Anywhere but with me, in fact.'

Oh dear. I suspected Brenda Deakin was the kind of woman who became maudlin when she drank alone and had invited me in to give me the sob story that had driven her to drink. But if I had to sit through that to get to the information I wanted, I'd grin and bear it. She crossed her legs, which were still quite good for a woman of her age. I crossed mine, and sank further back into the puffy cream leather sofa.

'Don't worry, I'm not going to make a pass at you.'

She'd interpreted my body language correctly. I'd obviously got hers all wrong.

'You've been watching too many movies about bored housewives. I invited you in because I've got no one to talk to, and I enjoy a conversation with someone who'll bloody listen now and again.'

'I came to talk to Brian about Rosebud Developments.'

I watched her reaction carefully. I didn't want to frighten her off by becoming too nosy too soon. She glanced at me quickly, just long enough to let me know I'd set an alarm bell ringing. Then she sidestepped me as neatly as I'd avoided those market researchers.

'Now I remember where I know you from. We met in the bar at the football ground. I expect you thought I was a lush?'

'Not at all,' I said.

'Liar. That's the impression most people down there have of me. But as a matter of fact, I'm not. Drunks are those fellers you see lying about with bottles of British sherry in the station concourse. They're trying to forget. I'm not trying to forget. I just like a drink because it helps the conversation flow, makes life less bloody boring.'

I think it's called being in denial. It was obvious she spent most days nursing a glass among all these smooth, rounded things, using a bottle of Gordon's to plane the sharp edges off her life.

'You've got a comfortable place in which to be bored,' I said. I looked past her out of the bay window at the horse chestnut tree at the end of the long lawn.

'Oh, I wouldn't swap it,' she said. 'Not on your life. I like all this. I'm not one of those rich bitches who thinks she'd be happier if she were poor. Would I buggery.'

I thought of the women in my life: Beth, Karen Pearson, Carol King, even Ann Humpage. They were all very different personalities, and all discontented in different ways. But they were also sisters under the skin. They were all searching for the kind of security Brenda Deakin had found. So why the hell was I feeling sorry for this woman sitting opposite me with a glass in her hand? She was probably as content as any of them.

'Rosebud Developments is one of Brian's companies?' I asked.

She swirled the ice cubes round in her glass and peered at me through them. 'Fascinating, aren't they? I've spent hours watching the shapes made by melting ice cubes. Never the same twice. Brian says they've influenced my taste in sculpture. Would you like another drink?'

'You didn't answer my question.'

'You didn't answer mine.'

I held out my glass. I was working on the assumption that if drink loosens my tongue, it probably had the same effect on her. At least she hadn't thrown me out yet.

'I've forgotten your name,' she said as she unscrewed the metal top from the square, green bottle.

'A lot of people do. It's Steve Strong.'

'But I remember why you're at the football club. Tom Tomlinson wants you to find out why all these football players keep getting themselves in trouble. And you think it might have something to do with Rosebud Developments?'

'Maybe.'

She sank back slowly into the sofa and put down her drink very carefully on the little occasional table, as if buying herself time in which to make an important decision. When she spoke again, it was as if she was talking to herself rather than to me.

'Brian's not really much good at making money. But he enjoys trying. It makes him feel as though he's one of the big hitters. That's why he was chairman of the football club all those years. He doesn't actually like football.

Never watches it on TV. But he likes seeing his name in the papers.'

I looked round. 'He seems to have done all right.'

'This place is mortgaged to the hilt. Brian collects companies like kids collect those pictures of footballers they stick in books. If we're lucky, the successful companies make enough money to pay off the debts of the others. He's like a kid under a conker tree. If he keeps throwing sticks up at it, he thinks a big one will eventually fall off.'

I looked down the garden. This late in the year, the conkers had long since fallen from the Deakins' horse chestnut.

'He'll be able to buy an awful lot of football stickers if the stadium development comes off.'

'You *have* been doing your homework,' she said. 'That's not supposed to be common knowledge.'

'Word gets about,' I said modestly.

'Brian thinks a football stadium in the city centre is a waste of a valuable site. He wanted to develop it while he was chairman, but the council wouldn't let him. So he got out. Then as soon as Jack Cox took over, the TV companies started throwing money at football. Brian put a lot of time in at that club. He thinks he's entitled to a return on his investment.'

I wondered why he had chosen the name Rosebud. Did he see himself as Citizen Kane? Brian Deakin didn't strike me as an Orson Welles fan. His metaphor was more likely to be drawn from nature, as Dr Chasuble would say. But it was well chosen. If this bit of asset-stripping came off, the white rose would certainly bloom again in this part of Yorkshire.

'We're talking serious money here, Mrs Deakin,' I said. 'In my experience there are three ways to make serious money. Either you graft away at something worthy and

194

keep your head down, like Jack Cox . . . or you're very clever . . .'

'. . . which Brian isn't,' she said.

'Or you're a crook . . .'

I let the unanswered question hang in the air, and Brenda Deakin lifted it down.

'. . . which Brian isn't. Brian's done some daft things in his time, sailed a bit close to the wind on a few projects. But he's never actually broken the law. So far.'

'Meaning?'

'Brian owns a security firm – Quaynote Securities. There's money to be made in security, if you're not too fussy how you do it. The word covers a multitude of sins.'

I could have given her a list: protection rackets . . . bouncers on commission from drug-dealers . . . escort agencies who provide blackmail demands as part of their after-sales service . . .

'Brian doesn't run it himself. He injected some capital into it when he sold the shares in the football club, and now business is booming. We've even opened an out-of-town office.'

'Yes, in Blackpool,' I said. 'Handy for the illuminations.'

She gave me a look that showed I had impressed her again and took another long pull at her G&T. That was fine by me. She was reaching that state of alcoholic relaxation in which the tongue begins to loosen, and a little more *vino* might produce a little more *veritas*.

'Brian doesn't get involved with the day-to-day operation of the company,' she said.

'As long as the money keeps rolling in, he doesn't care too much about how it's made?'

She thought about this for a while, took another drink and said: 'The manager is an ambitious man. He's persuaded Brian they can make really big money together.

Brian provides the respectable front and the business contacts, and he does whatever else is necessary.'

'The dirty work?'

'Brian told me about Rosebud Developments last night, after he'd offered to buy out Jack Cox. He has to get the money to buy Jack's shares in the club from somewhere, and the banks will give it to him on the strength of the property deal. The rest I've picked up. Just because I've got a glass in my hand when you see me in the directors' bar at the club doesn't mean I don't listen to what's going on.'

'And why are you telling me?'

'I'm telling you so that you can stop it before Brian gets in too deep.'

She finished her drink and poured herself another. She didn't offer me one this time. She was like an athlete out training with a less energetic partner. She had realised I would never keep pace and had given up waiting for me.

I could read the signs. Having reached the maudlin phase some people get to early on when they go on a bender, she now wanted to get to the other side of it as quickly as possible. Women and drink, eh? If I went on *Mastermind* it would be my specialist subject.

'I've been married to Brian for twenty-six years,' she said. 'We don't have much in common any more. I'm not that interested in sex. He's been making his own arrangements about that for years. When he bought into the security business he also bought the knocking-shop next door, although they call it a massage parlour. And Brian goes to Pakistan a lot. Hot weather's good for the libido, and you can buy anything there for the price of a packet of fags. But he's still my husband. I don't want him ending up in jail. If he didn't come home at night you probably *would* find me sleeping with a bottle of VP on the station concourse.'

'What's his name? The man who runs Quaynote Securities for him?'

'Charlie Robey.'

The name seemed familiar, though I couldn't remember why. But at least I'd remembered where I'd seen the ringleaders of the protest at the match last night.

'Now you've got what you came for, stay for another drink.'

'All right,' I said.

Drinking in the daytime was getting to be a habit, but I felt I owed her that. She might view the world through the bottom of a glass, but Brenda Deakin is one of the most clear-sighted people I've ever met.

Tony Wilson had the photographs waiting for me, as promised.

I took the black and white prints out of the envelope and looked at the faces of the ringleaders of last night's demonstration against Jack Cox. Yes, my hunch was right: I knew where I'd seen them before.

'Can I use your phone?' I asked Tony.

I put in a call to the club's solicitors to find out the names of the two witnesses who had seen Vince Naylor inflict grievous bodily harm on Kevin Carter in a Blackpool pub. Then I called a company in Blackpool to see whether the same people worked for them. They did, though they weren't in. They usually worked at night.

I put the receiver down with a certain satisfaction which Tony Wilson sensed.

'You're starting to get somewhere with this business, aren't you, Steve?'

'Yeah, but there's a difference between knowing something and being able to prove it,' I said.

'I know the feeling. If I can't prove something, I can't

print it. But don't forget you owe me one. By the way, have you heard that City's next match has been put back until Monday?'

'Why?'

'Satellite TV have decided to broadcast it live. The vultures have started gathering. If City lose again, they'll get Jimmy Farrell's head. Or Jack Cox's. Possibly both. Either way, it'll make great television.'

'Thanks for these, Tony,' I said. 'I'll try to get you an even better story before Monday. Something you can print.'

It was downhill all the way from the blinding mirror-glass of the *Post* building to the prefabricated warehouse by the docks which housed Quaynote Securities. Though it was walking distance, the contrast couldn't have been greater – unless you count that between the airy suburb where Brian Deakin lived and the place where he made the money to pay the mortgage. The place smelled of oil and fish and salt and sin. No wonder Deakin employed a manager to keep it at arm's length.

It was one of those run-down inner-city areas where you don't feel safe even in broad daylight. The wind funnelled up the long, straight roads that gave out at the waterside. There were not many other funnels around. The dockside buildings seemed to echo with abandonment – even those that were still in use. There were scrap yards and cheap car repair yards it was hard to tell apart, and half-demolished pubs whose bedroom fireplaces hung in the air, still surrounded by hideous wallpaper. Even the graffiti artists and flyposters had given up bothering with it. It was so far downmarket it could only be a matter of time before the warehouses were redeveloped into executive waterside apartments. Deakin had better get his riverside condos built in a hurry.

But Brenda Deakin had been wrong about one thing. Quaynote Securities was not next door to the Aphrodite Massage Parlour. It shared the same building and the same entrance. The girls who worked at Aphrodite's must have felt ever so protected having so many big lads within screaming distance. The financial pages would call it a symbiotic business arrangement.

Just inside the door was a glass display case of the kind you used to see outside cinemas filled with stills of the forthcoming attractions. This one contained photographs of women in interesting poses, like the takeaway menu in a restaurant. Most of them would have looked very ordinary with their clothes on, and the photographer had used plenty of Vaseline on his lens. But you could still see the desperation in some of their eyes, and the bruises where the needles went into the veins. If Karen Pearson represented the glossy mail-order end of the market, this was where they piled 'em high and sold 'em cheap. I could understand why Karen was tempted by easy money if this was what the future held for a faded glamour-girl.

The photographs hung above one of those lift-up counters they have in old-fashioned builders' merchants where you order your screws. I'll leave you to make up your own joke at this point while I describe the rest of the place.

Behind the counter was a flush-panelled door which had been painted grey some years ago. A peeling vinyl sticker announced APHRODITE'S LOUNGE, and there was a peephole which allowed those inside to look over whoever wanted to come in.

There was a glassed-in office with a desk and the sort of still life Braque would have painted if he'd been around today: a plastic jug kettle, an opened bag of granulated sugar, a jar of Co-op instant, a tin of powdered milk, a girlie calendar on the wall, a folded copy of the *Sun*. There was also a girl in a short skirt drinking coffee from a mug, and a big lad with a neo-brutalist haircut reading the *Daily Sport*.

It was the girl who came out, switching on her smile as she did so, as if it was a light as she entered a darkened room.

'Can I 'elp you?'

She was a cropped bottle-blonde with half an inch of dark roots showing and enough facial jewellery to make you speculate which other parts of her anatomy she'd had pierced. She looked about sixteen. Didn't she realise she'd probably end up like the women in the photographs if she stayed here long? Or perhaps she was just grateful for whatever job she could get. I knew the feeling.

The smile had only two settings: on and off. The eyes told me more. They looked surprised to see me, and a little suspicious. My understated look of black T-shirt, leather jacket and jeans was evidently not *de rigueur* in these parts, but the dirty mac that would have made me invisible was at the cleaners.

Over her shoulder I could see the well-hard one in the office watching me, letting me know he had seen me. Do these people all go on the same training course, or is it just instinctive?

'I'm looking for Quaynote Securities.'

She nodded towards another door, which had a Quaynote Securities letterhead taped to it. 'But Charlie's not in. Do you want to talk to Darren?'

If Darren was the *Daily Sport* reader, I didn't.

'I'm here on behalf of a new club that's opening soon. We're looking for doormen.'

'You need to talk to Charlie,' she said. 'I just look after Aphrodite's customers.'

'We're in the same sort of business,' I said. 'We're only

200

taking on good-looking doormen. It helps pull the ladies in, if you know what I mean.'

'You won't want Darren, then,' she said.

'Have you got a register, with photographs?'

'It's security, not a model agency.'

'I know we're being fussy, but clubs are in a competitive market. Your staff must have ID photos.'

She was thinking about it. The cover story I'd made up on the way here sounded great in my head but felt a bit flimsy now I was trying to hide behind it. I didn't want her rattling Darren's bars. I preferred him in his glass cage.

'I'll have a look,' she said.

She went into the Quaynote Securities office and, to avoid Darren's eye, I made a close study of the photographs in the glass case.

'That's all I can find,' she said.

She handed me a cardboard-backed manila envelope containing a few strips of photographs taken in a passport booth. What I assumed had been the most flattering image had been cut away from each strip, presumably for use on identity cards. Those that remained had the slightly startled stares of the photo-booth, but they were good enough for my purposes.

The dodgy blonde had gone back to her coffee, so I spread them out on the counter, slid the photograph Tony Wilson had given me from its envelope and compared the faces.

I had matched three of the ID pictures with those taken at the protest at the football ground when I discovered why certain types of shoes are known as brothel creepers.

'Can I help you, pal?'

He must have come in from Aphrodite's Lounge. He frightened me, though he wasn't as big and menacing as Darren. He had red hair, and I realised he was the man I had seen in the directors' bar with Deakin the first time I'd visited the football ground. But it was his speech patterns rather than his appearance which interested me most. There was something familiar about his voice. A single word echoed around my head for a moment.

Pal . . . pal . . . *pal.*

You know how a pop song can preserve the precise moment and specific place in which you heard it as perfectly as the impression of a fossil in limestone? I was suddenly back on the service road at the rear of Beth's flat, being thrown against the wall by two men, hearing the tinkle of glass as my headlights were kicked in, and the drip of my own blood as it splashed on the bonnet of the MGB.

This must be Charlie Robey, the man who managed Quaynote Securities for Brian Deakin. So that was how they found me so quickly after my trip to Blackpool. Kevin Carter had phoned the people at Quaynote Securities' Blackpool office who were collecting his protection money to tell them about my call. They phoned Charlie, who phoned Deakin at the football club, who got my address from the club records, and Charlie had come round with one of his employees to put the frighteners on me. Which suggested Deakin wasn't quite as innocent as his wife believed.

'It's OK,' I said. 'Your young lady has been very helpful.'

But the frighteners had been more effective than I'd realised. My hands were trembling. If he recognised me now, I was in trouble.

I tried to slip the *Post* photograph back into its envelope, but I knew he must have seen it.

'What are you up to, pal? Mandy! Get out here.'

She came out. She had that look which dogs have when they're beaten by their masters.

202

'We don't give these photos out to anybody, Mand. Think on!'

I could hear another echo, now. He had a local accent, not unlike thousands of others in the city. But I recognised the tone. The quiet, threatening anger I had heard slightly distorted by the howl-round of a cheap telephone answering machine, saying: *The acid on the car was just a gentle reminder. It has the same effect on people's skin. Think on!*

'He's after doormen.'

'I don't care what he's after.'

He was looking at me closely now.

'I know you, don't I? You'd better come in the office.'

'I was just leaving.'

'Darren! I want you.'

Darren put his paper down. He looked even bigger standing up.

The street door behind me opened. If this was another member of Quaynote Securities' staff, there was no escape. I was surrounded.

A middle-aged man with a slightly furtive look came in and trod on my heel. 'Sorry!'

If he was looking for a good time, he'd come to the wrong place.

'Sorry!' I echoed as I pushed past him. Polite to the last. I'll probably apologise to the vicar at my funeral for the inconvenience I've caused.

I slammed the door behind me and took off up the deserted street towards the safety of the main road. A sheet of newspaper blew towards me like tumbleweed, and I made a ludicrous attempt to read the headline as it scurried past in case some other disaster had befallen the football club which I didn't yet know about.

When I looked back I saw Darren coming after me. The

adrenaline injection it gave me had the same effect as pressing the overdrive button on the gear lever of the MGB, which was back in Nick's garage having the dents hammered out. Still, it was encouraging to know I still had that much power under my own bonnet, and when I looked back again Darren had given up the chase. Big men are fast over short distances, but they soon run out of steam. I didn't know I was this fit. But I did know that if this was going to become a regular part of the job, I needed my wheels back.

Nick's head was under the bonnet of a Morris 1000 when I got to the railway arches. Fiddling with car engines was what he enjoyed. Selling them to make a living was a necessary evil. Nick preferred things when they were dysfunctional. Once he had them running smoothly he just wanted to get rid. I wondered how his relationship with the redhead was prospering.

My MG was parked across the double yellows out in the street.

'It's all done,' said Nick when he saw me. 'What's up with you? You look as though someone's been chasing you.'

I told him the story, and his face grew serious, which is a very bad sign with Nick. He's not a serious bloke.

'Shit, Steve. You want to be careful there, mate.'

'You know these reptiles?'

'I know *of* them. I'm in the motor trade, remember. Most of it runs above ground, but certain stops offer direct connections to the underworld.'

'And?'

'And there are some pretty frightening stories about Quaynote Securities. They're into sex and drugs, though no convictions for rock 'n' roll so far as I know.'

'Can we conduct this conversation in English?'

'If you like. They run a knocking-shop behind their office, as you probably know, but they've also got the drug distribution network in the pubs and clubs sewn up. And apparently they weren't too fussy how they did it. The water started tasting funny one day, and when the police looked in the reservoir, the boss of a rival outfit was floating on the top. One or two people who've tried to muscle in on the drugs trade have taken an early bath as well.'

'Can't the police pin anything on them?'

'Rumour has it they haven't been trying too hard. They've got enough to worry about with the ordinary, decent crime in this city. I expect they take the view that if the rats are eating each other it keeps the vermin down. But if you take my advice you won't get mixed up with them.'

'It's a bit late for that. I already am.'

'They were responsible for the broken headlights and the black eyes, eh? Well, I knew you were lying to me about that. Nobody smashes headlights in a shunt and leaves the bumper and numberplate unscathed. And even a deformed midget like you couldn't black his eyes on the steering wheel.'

Do I lie that badly? I must practise harder.

'Just gimme the keys, Nick,' I said. A traffic warden was looking over the MG and reaching for his book of tickets.

'There you go, mate,' he said, throwing them at me. 'Drive carefully.'

I drove to City's ground to see Tom Tomlinson. He was paying me two hundred pounds a day plus legitimate expenses, so he had to be the first person I told about my suspicions. And the more people I told about Robey, the less likely I was to find myself in traction in the infirmary. Or apologising to the vicar in the crem.

Carol was behind the reception desk.

'Will you do me a favour?' I said.

'I was willing to do you a favour the other night, but you preferred to spend it at the police station.'

'Yeah. Sorry about that. Will you ring your friend Eamon Doyle at Scorer's and find out where he hires his bar staff?'

She made the call without having to look up the number, which was quite impressive. I could tell she had been put through to Doyle because she started to giggle a little, the way she had the other night. But she eventually got round to asking for the information I wanted, wrote Doyle's reply down on a yellow Post-It note and stuck it to my leather jacket. Luckily, it was already quite distressed. Then she had the sort of oblique conversation that was designed to stop me guessing what Doyle was saying to her and put the phone down. It was an effective demonstration of the methods women have of obtaining information that are not available to a man. If I ever get good enough at this game to take on staff I'll remember that.

'Now put the answerphone on and come with me,' I said.

'You're so masterful, Popeye,' she said, though I've heard better imitations of Olive Oyl.

I spread the photographs on Tomlinson's desk and pointed out one or two faces.

'Recognise anyone?' I asked.

Tomlinson shook his head.

'This one seems familiar,' said Carol.

'He should be. He was the barman serving Gary Allen at Scorer's the other night.'

'So he is!'

'And who do Peter Collins and Eamon Doyle get their bar staff from?'

'Quaynote Securities.'

'Brian Deakin's firm?' said Tomlinson.

'Precisely. The firm that provides the stewards here on match days. Stewards who were conspicuously absent when this protest took place last night.'

'The Chief Constable's already asking for an explanation.'

'I can give him one. The people who were shouting loudest for Jack Cox to go are employed by Quaynote Securities. The stewards who should have stopped them getting on the pitch are employed by Quaynote Securities.'

'And the guy who spiked Gary's beer is employed by Quaynote Securities,' said Carol.

'There's more,' I said. 'Recognise him, Tom?'

'He was at that club where Marco was arrested.'

'He was the steward who called the police, despite the fact that navy-blue uniforms with the Queen's initials on them have never featured in the dress code of any other club I've been into. And do you know who supplies the bouncers at the Double Two?'

'Quaynote Securities?' said Carol.

'They also operate in Blackpool. Plenty of pubs and clubs needing bouncers there. And there's scope for a bit of overtime in the day, offering protection to amusement arcades who don't want their expensive machines smashing up. I can't prove it, but I'll bet Quaynote Securities put Kevin Carter up to having a go at Vince Naylor.'

'That still leaves Bartola,' said Tomlinson. 'Who set him up? Brian Deakin wasn't on that plane from Amsterdam. He never travels to away games.'

'That's puzzling me,' I said. 'Who was on that plane?'

'Only club people. It was a special charter. There was the first-team squad, of course: the manager, the head coach, the physio, the club doctor.'

207

Phil Andrews

'Nobody else?'

'We always take a couple of stewards to handle the bags and the kit.'

'Provided by Quaynote Securities!' said Carol.

So now we had a full house, aces and kings. But Tomlinson didn't seem entirely convinced.

'I've never liked Brian Deakin,' he said. 'When he was chairman he was never interested in football. He was always in it for what he could get out of the club. But that's not unusual in soccer – especially these days. I didn't have him down as crooked enough or clever enough to do this, though – not to plant dope on an innocent man or get a young player drunk and put him behind the wheel of a car.'

'I don't think he is,' I said. 'Deakin's just a front man for somebody else who's a lot more unscrupulous than he is. The world's full of people who pretend they don't know about the ruthlessness of the people who are working for them. They're normally called politicians or shareholders. You'd better phone Jack Cox and tell him not to do anything hasty with his shareholding in the club.'

'All right, Steve,' said Tomlinson. 'You've made out a plausible case. But you've still got to prove it.'

'I'll prove it. Whoever set your players up probably did this to me,' I said. The bruises round my eyes had now turned an unflattering snot-yellow. 'I'm going to see Brian Deakin. He won't admit anything, but if he knows I'm on to him it should stop him trying to get to any of the other players. Then I'll go and see Karen Pearson and tell her I know who's making threatening phone calls to her. And then I'll go to the police.'

'I wish you'd go to the police first,' said Carol as we left Tomlinson's office. I was quite touched. But I said:

'And get put into the queue behind all the rapes and

208

murders and housebreakings and armed robberies? Do you know how many crimes take place in this city every day of the week?'

'No.'

'It was a rhetorical question,' I said. 'I don't know, either, but I'm a private eye. Tom Tomlinson is paying me good money to sort this case. The only reason for going private is that you get preferential treatment. Ask the National Health Service.'

For the first time since Tomlinson had asked me to make enquiries about Karen Pearson, I felt like a professional. It wasn't just pin money. It was a job, and I was starting to feel the pride and insufferable self-satisfaction of someone who likes his job and believes he is good at it. I was beginning to feel like Beth.

So it was ironic that it should be another woman who was putting her hand on my arm and saying, 'Be careful, Steve.'

'You sound like the script of a bad movie,' I said quietly.

The low evening sun was streaming in through the plate-glass doors in the foyer. The words CITY FOOTBALL CLUB etched in the glass broke the light into bundles of iron rods. My shadow stretched itself out on the tiled floor and leaned up against the wall like a folded paper cutout. It was a shame that the gold stripes in the wallpaper ruined the *film noir* effect. Pity City don't play in black and white.

But it reminded me that they were showing *The Blue Dahlia* on Channel 4 tonight. Script by Raymond Chandler. Starring Alan Ladd.

FAVOURITE FILM STARS: Alan Ladd, Glenn Ford, Dustin Hoffman, Tom Cruise, Leonardo DiCaprio.

GIVE REASONS: They're all smaller than I am, but they still get the girls.

I thought we might watch it at her place with a bottle

of Australian Cabernet Sauvignon. I could further her knowledge of film classics, and I'd be safe from the attentions of Quaynote Securities, who knew where I lived.

As if on cue, Carol touched the bruises on my face and I felt a pink flush surround the snot-yellow.

'I just don't want you to get hurt again,' she said.

'I thought you liked damaged men.'

'Only if they're still in working order. If they're too damaged to do the job, I bin them.'

I knew this scene off by heart from a thousand movies. The sexual sub-text has become one of the clichés of film-making. You can bet your bottom dollar that when the conversation starts to go like this, the star will be in bed with the girl before the end of the reel.

'I thought we might make an evening of it,' I said confidently. 'Watch a video, bottle of wine?'

'I'd love to, Steve,' she said. 'Only I can't tonight. I'm going out.'

Beth was out when I got back and the flat was cold. Or perhaps I was shivering because I was scared.

I had parked the MG a couple of blocks away and approached the flat along the main street in case the boys from Quaynote Securities had thought of staking out the back alley again. When I got in I locked the doors and slid the bolts across.

There was nothing in the freezer but a pizza that was past its sell-by date, but I stuck it under the grill anyway. There was a bottle of cheap wine in the fridge. Naturally, as I was under the jurisdiction of Sod's Law, it was red wine. Beth must have put it there because she knew we would never drink it. One of our friends with some month left at the end of his money had brought it to a party.

I stuck it under the grill with the pizza. It couldn't do it any harm.

I sat the phone down on the arm of the sofa, just in case I needed to call the police in a hurry, and started to watch *The Blue Dahlia*.

Why is watching a classic movie sprawled on the sofa with a woman and a bottle of something rugged and colonial like Rocky Ridge or Stony Creek cool and sophisticated, but watching it on your own with a bottle of Spanish plonk makes you feel like a sad, nostalgic anorak?

I burned my fingers on the hot metal cap of the wine and settled back to count the scenes in which Ladd has to stand on a box to kiss Veronica Lake.

When I woke up, the bottle was empty, the hard bits from the edge of the pizza were strewn across the carpet and someone was trying to break down the front door.

I looked at my watch. It was one o'clock in the morning. I picked up the phone and thought about dialling 999. I'd never dialled 999 before, and it seemed a bit extreme and girlie, and probably had the same sort of dire consequences in the event of misuse as pulling the communication cord on a train.

I decided to look out of the window to see who was there.

There was a shadowy figure moving around the little square of grass that passes for a garden. As I twitched the curtain back, the figure looked up. I let the curtain fall again to avoid being seen, but I was too late.

'Stephen. What the fuck do you think you're playing at locking me out of my own fucking flat?'

Beth never swears unless she's really angry.

'Sorry. Must have bolted the door by mistake and dropped off.'

As I went to let her in I stood on something hard and crumbly. Twice.

And how often have I told you about getting pizza crumbs in the carpet?

Chapter Sixteen

Beth had gone to work when I got up in the morning, and there was a note on the kitchen table telling me to hoover the carpet. *Properly!*

I was on my second cup of coffee, getting my strength up to get the vacuum cleaner out, when the phone rang.

It was Brian Deakin.

'I think we should talk, Steve,' he said.

'So do I, Brian,' I said.

'Can you come to my office? Quaynote Securities. By the docks.'

I laughed. I hoped it sounded hollow.

'I'll meet you at the football ground,' I said. 'Half an hour. Don't bring any of your business associates.'

Carol was at her desk when I got there.

'How was your evening?'

'Great movie,' I said. 'Lousy company. And yours?'

'Fine.'

All right, don't tell me what you were doing. See if I care.

'Have you seen Brian Deakin?' I asked.

'He's out on the pitch. He asked me to tell you.'

'On the pitch? Why?'

'Clairvoyant wasn't part of my job description,' she said.

I went through the swing doors to the dressing-rooms and walked down the muddy strip of astroturf in the players' tunnel. I fantasised about doing this as a kid, emerging into the glare of the floodlights with eighty thousand eyes on me. It wasn't quite as good as I'd imagined, mainly because the stands were empty and the only person around was a middle-aged man in a camel-hair overcoat with a mobile phone welded to his ear.

It still felt great, though. This is pretentious, and I will blush about it in the privacy of my room, but it was almost a religious experience. I could understand how football grounds had replaced churches as places of worship all over the world, and why grown men chose to celebrate their rites of passage here – getting married in the centre circle, having their ashes scattered in the penalty area. And as I stepped on to the turf I felt I had a mission to pre-serve its sanctity. (Well, I did say this was pretentious.)

Deakin was alone. He collapsed the aerial on his mobile and offered his hand as though I were just another businessman with whom he was about to strike a deal. I kept my hands in my pockets.

'Training for the match, Brian?' I said. 'Have we lost some more players I haven't heard about yet?'

'I thought we could chat more freely out here. I wouldn't want our conversation overheard. Or recorded. I under-stand you're clever like that.'

I held my jacket open. 'I haven't even got my Walkman with me.'

'My wife tells me you paid her a visit yesterday.'

'I expect your pals at Quaynote Securities did, too. And I know they've been visiting Karen Pearson, and they've been to London to visit Marty Weller. They're not very nice people, Brian.'

'If there's been any rough stuff it's had nothing to do with me. I'm a businessman, not a thug. But you've upset some dangerous people, Steve. They wanted to go round to your place and give you a warning last night. I persuaded them not to. You ought to be grateful.'

I was, but I didn't tell him that.

'Four players have been set up by your associates, and we both know why. So let's not play the innocent, Brian.'

We walked towards the goalmouth in front of the kop. Workmen were doing something to one of the floodlight pylons between the stands. There was so much money in the game now that the ground was usually a building site unless a match was being played.

'I'm going to be straight with you, Steve. But if you try to use anything I say now against me I'll deny I said it. I've put a lot of time, money and effort into this club over the years and got nothing for it. Now there's a chance for me to do the club and the fans a favour and to get something back on my investment, but Jack Cox is standing in the way.'

'You put the careers of four professional footballers in jeopardy so that you can get Jack Cox out?'

'As soon as Jack goes, the charges will be dropped.'

'But you can't drop the publicity they've had.'

'Publicity comes with the territory. If they were grease monkeys at the corner repair shop, what they did wouldn't have rated a paragraph on page twenty-two. But grease monkeys don't get upwards of ten grand a week. It's obscene really, isn't it? All that money just for kicking a bag of wind about. They get well compensated for hitting the headlines occasionally.'

This was the first time I'd looked at Brian Deakin closely. He was in his mid-fifties and wore glasses with a designer name on the frame which made them expensive without being stylish. His thinning hair was dragged in a vanity-slick across his bald patch and his burgundy slip-ons had a gold bar across the front. He spent money on clothes that gave out all the wrong signals. They told you that Deakin was a man who needed props for his self-image. Whereas the seriously rich like Jack Cox can afford to look downhome and comfortable.

'Look, Steve, everybody knows this ground is too small for a club with our ambitions, and it's in the wrong place. We need to move with the times. Lots of other clubs have moved to new stadiums – Derby County, Bolton Wanderers, Middlesbrough, even Huddersfield.'

'But Jack Cox has got a sentimental attachment to this old place and doesn't need the money?'

'He's standing in the way of progress, of the good of the city.'

'And of you getting your hands on all the TV money that's coming into the club.'

'I told you, I've earned some of that. But you're right. This place is awash with cash, and there's plenty to go round. There could be something in it for you if you're sensible.'

I know what you're thinking. This scene is like the climax of a hundred movies. Private eye comes face to face with Mr Big for the first time. There'll be lots of tough talking and a few wisecracks. Except that Deakin wasn't Mr Big. He was Mr Average. He didn't even make jokes, unless you count his taste in shoes. Brian Deakin was a mid-range wheeler-dealer who had sold the goose he had been fattening to Jack Cox just before it began to lay golden eggs. Now he was using someone with even more dodgy morals to try to get it back, and I was in his way.

But don't worry. At least I've read the script. My role now

is to keep to the high moral ground and hold out against whatever temptations the bad guy throws in my way. The fact that I still have the scars his employees inflicted on me makes it easier.

'Somebody tries to bribe me every time I set foot in this place,' I said.

'We're not talking Co-op stamps here, Steve. If this deal goes through we're looking at ten million quid.'

'You've got to buy Cox's shares first.'

'They're a depreciating investment as long at the team are losing and my credit's good. I can buy Jack out, put this deal together and still be left with the gross national product of several banana republics.'

'I'm a monarchist and I don't like bananas,' I said, though I'm not and I do, but it was the sort of thing Humphrey Bogart would have said in these circumstances.

'Then how do you like a hundred grand?' That was the sort of thing Mr Big would have said. Maybe I had misjudged Brian Deakin. And a hundred grand would be more than fair compensation for a couple of black eyes.

'I'm serious, Steve. Drop this case and there's a hundred thousand quid in it for you.'

I looked at Deakin. He wasn't somebody I would want to spend much time with, but a number of people would regard him as successful. Certainly my dad would love to be able to afford his Rolex watch. Let's be honest, *I'd* love to be able to afford it. But people like Deakin and the others in fancy overcoats who joined the boards of football clubs had different goals, greater expectations than most people. Deakin was a middle-aged, middle-ranking businessman who had spent his life waiting for the right deal that would put him into Jack Cox's league. Now he was looking at his last chance slipping away. This was

Deakin's midlife crisis. I haven't reached mine yet, but I know they make people do wild things.

It was my turn to feel what Jimmy Farrell must have felt when Marty Weller dangled the same amount of money in front of him at the motorway service area.

I won't pretend I didn't think about it.

I thought about it.

I stared at the pitch. There were stud marks drilled as neat as washers in the mud, and jagged bayonet holes where the groundsman had been spiking the turf. The pitch marking turned individual blades of grass into abstract patterns of green and white. Damien Hirst could slice the pitch up, put it in glass cases and sell it as modern art.

And with a hundred grand, I'd be able to buy it.

But all those old movies had filled me as full of simplistic morality as any other religion would have. I knew what Philip Marlowe would have done.

'Trying to pervert the course of justice is a very serious offence, Brian. It doesn't go down at all well with the judiciary. It's a sending-off offence, like tackling from behind when a forward's through on goal. It's red card and off you go time.'

For the first time he looked worried.

'You can't prove any of this, you know.'

'I can prove Marty Weller was beaten up and that threats have been made against Karen Pearson.'

'I had nothing to do with any of that. But the people who did are dangerous. Don't mess with them, Steve.'

'People keep telling me that, Brian. Who's running Quaynote Securities and Rosebud Developments? You – or Charlie Robey?'

'You've heard my offer, Steve. If Charlie asks you to back off, it won't be money he's offering you. I'll be at the ground again this evening if you change your mind.'

Brian Deakin was caught between a rock and a hard case and he was scared. And when people are scared they are unpredictable.

'I'm more likely to be back with the police,' I said. 'When Karen Pearson tells them Charlie Robey has been threatening her, the game will be up. He's covered his tracks pretty well so far, but leaving a threatening message on an answering machine was either arrogant or daft.'

Producing your trump card is always a satisfying experience, and I enjoyed it for as long as it took to walk back to the players' tunnel. When I looked back, Deakin had his mobile phone to his ear and I realised at once that I should have kept my mouth shut. If Robey decided to go back to her flat to retrieve the tape, I could have put Karen in danger.

I asked Carol King if I could use her phone.

'Help yourself.'

The number was engaged. I hit the redial button over and over until the quaver of the engaged signal changed to the semi-quaver of the ringing tone. But that was as good as it got. When the ringing stopped, it was replaced by the sound of an answerphone kicking in. I didn't respond to Karen Pearson's request to leave a message. Something had made her leave in a hurry, and I needed to know why. I had to get to her flat quickly.

'Time for a coffee?' said Carol when I put the receiver down. 'You can tell me where the fire is and I'll tell you about my evening.'

'Sorry. Can't stop,' I said.

As I ran to my car I knew that wasn't likely to improve our relationship. But I needed to get to Karen now before somebody else did.

The thought of ringing the police crossed my mind,

but I decided it wasn't a good idea. As far as they were concerned, I was a loony with a fixation about Karen. They'd probably try to intercept me on the way there, and wasted time could be very dangerous for Karen.

For once, the MG started first time and I made a mental note to pay Nick's bill. But it didn't get me very far.

Heading out of the city I got stuck behind a bus that stopped every thirty seconds. I crawled behind it punching my fist into the steering wheel and a few more holes in the ozone layer. Eventually, the bus veered off towards the university, but then everything else stopped. The road ahead as far as I could see was a flare path of brake lights. The traffic helicopter throbbing overhead wasn't encouraging.

I was freezing, and I realised that the heater in the car had packed in, but at least Nick had made the radio work. I tuned to Ridings Radio to find out what the hold-up was.

The programme was into one of those brainless phone-in competitions local radio run with questions like: What's the capital of France? Is it Paris, London or New York?

Come on, get off the line!

The third caller got it right and was insanely grateful to win a T-shirt and a Ridings Radio car sticker. When the traffic news finally came on, the eye-in-the-sky was forecasting long delays on all westbound arterials because a lorry had shed its load of electrical goods at the Fiveways roundabout. Why didn't the police just leave it to the looters? They'd have it cleared in no time.

I mounted the pavement, executed an illegal U-turn and cut through a bus-gate. The city-centre traffic system is so bizarre that the only way to get to the ring road was to go the wrong way down a one-way street and over a pedestrian precinct.

Any other day I would be hearing sirens and picking up

flashes of blue in my mirror, but just when I could have done with arriving outside Karen's flat with a police squad car in close attendance there was nothing.

I crawled round the ring road. Every light was at red, and it took me half an hour to cover the three miles to Karen's flat. I didn't have to bother the neighbours for a key. The door was open, but Karen wasn't there.

She certainly had left in a hurry.

A gold-tipped cigarette had burned itself out in the ashtray. The last inch of coffee was still warm in a mug on the table. A copy of *Hello!* lay on the carpet, open at the page she had been reading.

I looked on all the flat surfaces to see if she had left a note. There was nothing. I played back the answering machine, but there was nothing on that, either, except the hissing silence that must have been me calling from the football ground.

The situation demanded something dramatic, like a message scrawled on the bedroom mirror in lipstick. I went to the bedroom door. Something made me hesitate before I opened it. I had a weird feeling about what I might find inside. You can sense what is going to happen in particular circumstances by extrapolating from your previous experiences, but I had never been in a situation like this. I had never opened the bedroom door of an empty flat and found a woman sprawled out on the bed with her throat cut, but it can be difficult to separate popular culture from real life, and I *do* watch too many movies.

I opened the door quietly and stuck my head round. There was a shape on the bed, and a face staring at me.

The shape was Karen's coat, tossed casually across the duvet. The face was my own, staring back at me from her dressing-table mirror. But there was no message in lipstick. And no body.

I told myself not to be so melodramatic. I was dealing with some nasty people here, who were not above maiming women and beating up men, and who made their livings by selling sex and drugs and perverting the course of justice. According to Nick, when they killed people their *modus operandi* involved water.

I slid back the door of the en suite bathroom. I knew the bath would be full of bloody water broken by a bloated face with staring eyes.

It was empty.

There were no clues here. Nothing but the smells you expect in women's bedrooms: perfume, talcum powder, the glue they pour in the bath. I found myself sniffing the air like one of those posers who claim they can taste grass cuttings and fig biscuits in Bulgarian Chardonnay.

But even my own untutored nose was picking up subtle and unexpected undertones. They became stronger the closer I got to the coat that lay on the bed. I picked it up and thrust it under my nostrils. I was getting Dettol. I was getting diarrhoea. I was getting . . . Dumpy!

Of course. Karen had taken my advice and was hiding out at Dumpy's, where Robey would never think to look. Ann Humpage's vile maisonette was the last place anyone would think of looking for a girl like Karen.

The accident at Fiveways was clogging the roads for miles around, and it took me an hour to get to Dumpy's place on the other side of the city. But as soon as I got there I knew my hunch had been right. Karen's Micra with its blistered paintwork was parked on the verge outside.

There was no bell, so I rapped on the three-ply that had been used to board up the door the last time Dumpy was burgled. There was no reply, though I could hear movement inside.

I tried the door and it opened. Any portable electrical goods in the flat probably belonged to a rental company or had already been recycled from some more affluent neighbourhood, but leaving your door unlocked in this part of town is still not recommended practice. I remembered the security chain and the pale face appearing in the gap the last time I was here. Ann Humpage had become careless.

I went inside. There seemed to be no one around, although the smell of shit was even stronger than I remembered. There was a packet of cigarettes of the brand Karen smoked next to the electric kettle, and a plastic pouch of what I took to be Ann's tobacco. But no sign of either woman.

The noises were coming from upstairs. There was a low, aimless moaning which had to be Ann's son. There was also a rustling sound I could not identify and the occasional footstep vibrating the ceiling over my head.

'Anybody home?'

No reply.

I went to the foot of the stairs and shouted again.

'Anybody in?'

The rustling stopped for a few moments and then began again, but nobody answered me.

There were three rooms off the landing. One was a bathroom with a plastic bath that had a brown stain where the tap dripped, a washbasin in need of a wash and a lavatory bowl with a loose plastic seat. There was a bedroom with a melamine wardrobe and a single bed with the covers thrown back, which I took to be where Ann slept. The door to the third room was closed and the moaning and rustling came from behind it.

I tapped on the gloss-painted hardboard, but no one opened the door. I pressed down the metal handle and pushed. The door resisted me. There was something wedged beneath it. When I pushed harder it slid open slowly, pushing away the old khaki blanket that had been rolled against the bottom of the door like a draught excluder.

There were two people in the room. The boy on the bed was about fourteen and completely naked. He saw me come in, but there was no change in his blank expression or in the regular pattern of seal-like noises he was making. He lay in the foetal position with his arms wrapped round his knees, though the room was warm because the gas fire on the wall was turned full on. The mattress on which he lay was stained, but there were no sheets on the bed. They were covered in shit and piled in the middle of the floor like a pyre, along with the toilet paper and washing-up bowl someone had used to clean the boy up.

But the stench was masked by other smells – the Dettol I had recognised in Karen's flat and something else, sweet and sickly. It was the joint Ann Humpage was smoking as she tore strips from a newspaper and wedged them into the cracks in the window frames. She had obviously put my twenty quid to good use.

'Hello, Ann,' I said. 'I've come to find Karen.'

She gave me the benign smile of someone who is well relaxed on dope and turned back to her task at the window. I wondered why she had chosen today to shut out the draughts. It was warm for November and, outside, the sun shone. It struck me that housekeeping was out of character for Ann, but it wasn't until much later that I was to discover the real significance of what she was doing.

'Where is she, Ann?'

Her naked son turned over and grunted at the wall.

He was as big as Ann. How did she manage to lift him and clean him up every morning? And how much longer would she be condemned to looking after him because of that one mistake fourteen years ago? Apart from the vacant face, he seemed strong and healthy enough to outlive her.

'Where is she?'

'Who?'

'You know who. Where's Karen?'

'Gone.'

She tore and folded another strip of paper slowly and deliberately and pushed it into the last crack in the window.

'Gone where?'

She was wearing the tracksuit and scuffed trainers she always wore. She went to the bed and put her arm round the boy. He stopped grunting. I forgave her for spending the money I had given her on dope. She needed it more than the kid needed a bag of Mars bars.

'Gone where, Ann?'

She looked almost content sitting beside him. He began to moan again, and she kissed him on the forehead with as much tenderness as any mother for her child. Perhaps Beth would be mellower if we had children. Not like this, of course, but the carefully planned, comfortably middle-class nuclear family. Not that it would ever happen. She was too attached to her career, and I was too fond of my freedom for us ever to experience a moment like that. But I suspected such moments were rare interludes in the wall-to-wall misery of Ann Humpage's existence.

'They came for her,' she said.

'Who came for her?'

One of my failings is that, when I should be focused

on something important, something trivial but equally interesting comes and elbows it out of my thoughts. I should have been concentrating on who had come for Karen, but Ann's doped-up reactions to my questions set me thinking about a term I had used a hundred times without really appreciating its meaning. Now I saw that 'spaced out' described perfectly the time-lag between the receipt, cognition and response to information of someone on a spliff-high. My questions seemed to set off a complex chain reaction in Ann's brain, like knocking over the first domino in one of those intricate patterns that make any sense only when all the others in the sequence have fallen over.

It seemed ages before the final domino fell and she said: 'Two fellers.'

She sucked at the last inch of her joint, flipped the tab on the lino and crushed it beneath her trainer.

'Which two fellers, Ann?'

She didn't reply. She had both arms round the boy now, and she lifted up her feet and curled round him in the same foetal position. They were like a pair of spoons lying side by side in a drawer. He was making animal noises again. She was silent, and crying.

I put my hand on her shoulder, but she shook it off.

'Piss off, Steve.'

I tried a different approach. I took a twenty-pound note from my pocket and held it towards her.

'Which fellers, Ann?'

I hated doing it. It was exactly what Marty Weller and Brian Deakin had tried to do to me – offering a bribe to get what I wanted. But everybody I had met on this case had found some way of justifying the creepy things they did. My excuse for bribery was that Karen Pearson's safety, and possibly her life, depended on it.

I had intended giving Ann some money anyway. I thought about it as I drove here from Karen's flat. On what City were paying me I could afford to do something for her and for the kid. It would take more than twenty quid to make any lasting difference to Dumpy's life, of course, but if I'm honest that wasn't the object of the exercise. Twenty quid was enough to buy off a bit of the guilt I felt about the way she lived.

But Ann's mood had changed.

She ignored the note I held out and got off the bed and went downstairs.

I followed her.

She went into the kitchen and picked up the plastic wallet that lay beside Karen's cigarettes.

'I don't need your fucking money, Steve.'

She took out the makings and began rolling herself another joint. The wallet was full. It was a big stash for someone on Ann's finances – certainly more than the money I had given her would buy.

'Where did you get that?'

She gave me the drowsy smile of someone who has switched off, of someone who has let go of the greasy pole and decided to enjoy the descent and the hell with what will happen when she hits the bottom.

'She said they were going to kill her.'

'Christ, Ann! Who was going to kill her?'

She had no matches to light her roll-up so she picked up one of those battery-operated gadgets my mother keeps beside the stove and lit the gas ring. This was the poverty trap springing into action. She couldn't afford the basics, and her improvisation cost her ten times as much. And because her credit was no good she would be paying for her gas the most expensive way, by feeding pound coins into a meter.

'Ann! Listen to me! Karen said that here, this afternoon?'

'Yeah,' she said, exhaling sweet smoke over me.

'Who said they were going to kill her? Where is she now?'

She nodded towards the phone. Yellow Pages lay open on the floor beside it.

Ann was perfectly calm again now. She leaned against the melamine kitchen units with the fake-wood veneer and watched me pick up the directory. It was open at the section headed SECURITY SERVICES, and someone had underlined *Quaynote Securities* in felt-tip pen. So Karen had known all along who was threatening her and had been too scared to tell me. But she had made the mistake of telling Dumpy, and that could prove fatal.

'You rang them up and told them where she was?'

The sour smile that spread across her face gave me my answer. She had betrayed Karen to Robey, and she had equalised a little of life's unfairness.

Shit! Effectively, I had sent Karen to Dumpy's flat. I was responsible for whatever trouble she was in at this moment. But how could I have known Ann hated Karen this much? The disappointment when Karen left her to go modelling in London must have turned to resentment when she had the child and had been festering for the last ten years. And there were plenty of places for things to fester in this filthy hole.

I doubt if Karen had helped. I could imagine her sweeping in here in her smart clothes with her nose turned up, desperate for somewhere Robey could not reach her yet unable to conceal her distaste for what the woman who had once been her best friend had allowed herself to become. That would have made Ann's resentment worse. But if I hadn't brought them together there would have been no opportunity for Dumpy to betray her best friend. Not for thirty pieces of silver, but for a plastic bag full of weed.

She showed no sign of remorse. If you ignored the reefer in her fingers, the years seemed to have slipped away from her. She was a schoolgirl again, caught by the teacher doing something she shouldn't and responding with the smug, dumb insolence of a child. She had as little power as a child, but she had learned the rudiments of guerrilla warfare – wait for the right opportunity and strike without pity and you could still beat the bastards in the end.

'Did they come for her, Ann?'

She released the information slowly, making me wait.

'Two blokes. Big blokes.'

'Where did they take her?'

She shrugged. 'They just said: "come on, Karen, we're taking you home."'

I was almost out of the door when Ann said: 'Steve?'

'What?'

'Got any pound coins? This gas will run out soon.'

I scooped all the change I had from my pocket, threw it on the worktop and left.

Road rage? It's for wimps.

I knew I had to get back to Karen's flat, quickly. So I drove down the white line in the middle of the road, forced the oncoming traffic up on to the pavement, overtook queues at junctions, flashed my headlamps and leaned on my horn and shot every red light I came to. All I got in return was enquiring looks from behind the tinted windscreens of other people's comfort zones. But no rage. Road rage is reserved for the inconsiderate and inadequate – drivers who stall at junctions and delay other people's progress by one nanosecond, or who hoot at them because they're slow getting away when the lights turn green and put a dent in the bumper of their self-esteem. But if you chuck the Highway Code out of the window and throw road safety to the winds, people just look puzzled and get out of your way.

I punched in the local radio news just in case Karen's body had already been thrown from a car down an embankment, but it was just the usual crap – cats up trees, some band I'd never heard of splitting up, Richard Branson's latest publicity stunt. I felt like biting the first dog I saw just to give them a decent story.

I reached Karen's flat in twenty-five minutes. But it wasn't fast enough. I couldn't have done it any quicker if it had been three in the morning, when the overcrowded roads in this city are as empty as they ever get.

A car with two figures in it was pulling away as I turned into the street. It was too far away for me to get the number or even the make. I parked in the spot it had vacated and went into Karen's block.

The door of the flat was still on the latch, as I had left it. There were signs that someone had left in a hurry. But it wasn't Karen.

Her body was on the bedroom floor, face-down near the dressing-table. I turned her over. The side of her face was a dark-purple pulp, as though someone had squashed a bunch of black grapes on her cheek.

I shook her, hoping her eyes would open. But something about the weight of her, the way her limbs had lost their articulation and no longer moved separately when I shook her, told me she was dead.

In a bizarre way, this was like looking at Dumpy again. This was not the body of a woman whose fading beauty had been violated; it was the body of the kid I had gone to school with. All those little snapshots of her that had stayed in my mind, moments of animation that had no significance in themselves but which had deposited themselves in my memory bank in the random way memories do, were now frozen in my arms. It was as though the video image of a child had been stop-framed and now the machine was broken and would never start again.

I stretched out my fingers and touched the bloody sponge that was her right cheek. She must have fallen and hit her head on the sharp angle of the dressing-table. Pushed by Robey or one of his pals? And when they realised she was dead they had left.

When I drew my hand away it was covered in blood. I looked at it, not knowing what to do. Some ludicrous sense of propriety stopped me wiping it clean on one of the soft, white towels in the en suite bathroom. Instead, I hauled the bottom of my T-shirt out of my jeans and wiped the blood off on that.

I laid her gently down on the pink pile of the carpet. I knew I had to phone the police.

I went into the sitting-room. The postman must have been while I was at Dumpy's, and a letter lay on the doormat. I have never been able to resist putting my boot into a virgin snowdrift. I picked the letter up and transferred a perfect set of fingerprints to the envelope. In Karen's blood.

Maybe calling the police wasn't such a good idea.

To them, I was the man Karen Pearson had accused of stalking her. I also had a vested interest in getting her to withdraw her allegations against Carlo Marconi. And now I was in her flat, with her dead body and her blood all over my clothes. If I were a policeman in these circumstances I know what I'd be saying: *I think you'd better come quietly, sir.*

Maybe I could prove it wasn't me eventually, but you

only have to read the papers to know that innocent people have spent years in jail on the strength of much flimsier evidence than this.

I stuffed the letter in my jacket pocket and flipped the catch on the Yale lock. I was about to close the door behind me when something made me go back to the bedroom, strip a sheet from the bed and lay it like a shroud over Karen's body. I was probably destroying vital forensic evidence, but what the hell? She deserved that much, for old times' sake.

The woman in the next-door flat was peering round her door as I left. I made a face at her that I hoped would give her no clue as to what lay behind Karen's door but which might be interpreted in retrospect as a reverent expression. Then I ran down the stairs.

If I was going to nail Robey for this and clear my own name, it would have to be through Brian Deakin. Now that Karen was dead, the gaps I had been peering under were all nailed down again. Deakin was the only person who could stick a crowbar under them and start prising up the boards that would eventually uncover who had murdered Karen Pearson and get me off the hook.

It was getting dark. Deakin had said he would be at the football ground all evening. I drove there slowly and carefully. The last thing I wanted was to be pulled over by a zealous traffic cop.

In the city centre I hit the evening rush. As I sat in the motionless traffic I took Karen's letter from my pocket and opened it. It was from the White Rose Model Agency. It contained a cheque for a few hundred pounds and an itemised account for 'escort' duties over the past few weeks. But it was the name on the letterhead that held my attention. I knew the woman who ran the agency was called Estelle. What I didn't know was that she was called Estelle Robey.

It was a useless piece of information now, but as I stared at the mortgage offers in the windows of the building societies and the kids eating fries from cardboard containers in Burger King I felt the satisfaction of someone who has finally found the missing number in an abstract theorem. I understood it all now – how Charlie Robey had known in advance that Karen would accuse Carlo Marconi of sexual assault at the Double Two club, and how he had been able to arrange for a photographer to be there and to tip off his doorman to call the police. The missing link was in my hands. The circle had closed.

Chapter Seventeen

It was already dark when I arrived at the stadium, and there were only two vehicles in the car park. One of them was Deakin's BMW; the other was an obsolete Escort which probably belonged to one of the groundsmen. There was a lot of money sloshing around in the game, but the bulkheads between the upper decks and the lower were tighter than an oil tanker's. Not much of it trickled down to the groundstaff.

There was a light on in the foyer, and another high up in the stand where the chairman's office was. The banks of turnstile gates along the base of the stand were all securely barred and padlocked. Even the main entrance was locked, but as I rattled the door one of the groundstaff appeared in the foyer on his way home.

'Lock it behind you, mate. We don't want anybody running off with the European Cup, do we?'

I glanced at the almost-empty trophy cabinet, bent my face into a smile to show I appreciated the joke, and watched him get into the Escort and drive away. Then I secured the Yale lock in the open position. I wanted to be very sure that the door *wasn't* locked. The long corridor beneath the stand, with its concrete walls and regularly spaced, firmly locked exits and metal staircases, was like the landing of a prison. If Robey or his hired muscle followed me here, I wanted to leave myself an escape route.

My footsteps sounded hollow in the long corridor beneath the stand as I passed the silent betting shops and deserted bars and hot-dog kiosks. The social geography changed when I reached the directors' entrance. The floor and stairs were carpeted in a tasteful, specially woven, thick-piled job in gold with the club badge picked out in black. Like the military, the decorative imagination of sports clubs never extends beyond their own insignia.

I went up silently to the next floor and through the directors' bar to the chairman's office. Judging by the startled look on Deakin's face, he hadn't heard me coming.

'What's the matter, Brian?' I said. 'Were you expecting someone else?'

'I wasn't expecting anybody at this time in the evening.'

'You phoned Robey as soon as I left this afternoon, didn't you?'

'Who I phone is my own business.'

He was sitting behind Jack Cox's big walnut desk going through a pile of newspaper clippings filed in plastic loose-leaf envelopes. I could see from where I stood that they were recent. They were the cuttings from the *Post* and the national dailies about the off-field activities of Marco and Naylor and Bartola and Gary Allen.

I had already guessed who had been tipping Tony Wilson off. Deakin would have Wilson's home telephone number from his self-publicising days as club chairman. Wilson knew his voice, of course, so it was probably Charlie Robey who had been making the calls which resulted in all these stories.

'Checking how much of that stuff can be pinned on you?'

'I'm just bringing myself up to date,' he said.

'There's something else you need to get up to date with. Karen Pearson is dead.'

The shock on Deakin's face was genuine. If he could fake it that well he'd have a little gold statue called Oscar among the other smooth sculptures his wife had assembled in their living-room. Not that I'd ever thought Deakin capable of murder. He may have colluded with Robey in setting up the players, but in football parlance he was an opportunist, not a hatchet man.

'Dead?'

I told him what had happened. When I showed him the blood on my T-shirt, most of his drained from his face and I thought he was going to faint.

Deakin got up from behind the desk.

'Do you want a drink?' he said. 'Because I do.'

I realised that I did. I had driven from Karen's flat on auto-pilot. Now I had landed in Deakin's office I was shaking. I'm not used to seeing bodies, particularly when they are lying in a pool of blood. And as I was the last person to see this one, dead or alive, I was in a jam.

A sliding door at the back of the office led through to the bar. I hadn't noticed it before. At first glance it looked like one of the panels which formed the office walls.

Deakin went through it and came back with a bottle of Bell's and two glasses. If his wife found out about this useful arrangement, she might want to spend more time at the stadium with him.

Deakin poured out a couple of stiff ones – closer to a fist than two fingers.

'Now, do you want to tell me about your call to Robey?' I

said. 'You might find a practice run useful. You're going to have to tell the police pretty soon.'

He knocked back a digit of Scotch.

'I didn't know they were going to kill the girl, Steve. Believe me.'

'You must have known what Robey was capable of. He's into prostitution, drugs, protection rackets. You don't keep other people's scooters off your lawn in that business without using violence.'

'Look, I bought Quaynote Securities as an investment with the money Jack Cox paid me for my City shares. Maybe I was naive, but I didn't know it was a front for any of that stuff.'

'Come on. Most of the blokes he employs have got longer records than Wagner.'

'All right, I knew a few of the staff had convictions for violence, but that comes with the territory in the security business. And I knew there was a knocking-shop on the premises, but these places are just sexual safety valves. Without them, there'd be more rapes and interference with little boys.'

Everybody else in this case could justify their morally dubious activities to themselves. Why should Deakin be any different?

'I don't know why the council bothers employing social workers when we've got public-spirited citizens like you around,' I said.

'I'm not a pimp, Steve. The girls rent space from us to run their businesses, and they feel safe because there are always a couple of big lads on hand to sort out punters who step out of line.'

'And I suppose using child labour to make footballs in Pakistan was another charitable gesture.'

'As a matter of fact, you're right. Work for those kids was

the alternative to begging on the streets of Islamabad. If I hadn't employed them, somebody else would have. You're making the mistake of trying to impose Western values on a Third World society, Steve.'

You couldn't shame a man like Deakin. The way to hurt him, it turned out, was to suggest that Charlie Robey was responsible for his business success.

'You don't seem to have too many values, Brian. You were happy to turn a blind eye to what was going on at Quaynote Securities as long as Robey was making money for you.'

'Listen, Quaynote Securities was eating sand on the seabed when I bought in. I made that company successful and I made it profitable. Everything came on the back of the stadium contract I got for them. Robey seemed like a good manager. I knew he leaned on people, sent the heavy mob round if somebody needed a final bit of persuading to move his business to us. But I don't know anything about drugs or protection rackets.'

'And I bet you haven't done much to find out. Was that the deal? You provided the money and the respectable front so that Quaynote Securities could corner the security market in this city. And you relied on Robey's muscle to protect your empire and turned a blind eye to his freelance activities round the edges?'

He poured himself another drink and waved the bottle in my direction. But the first couple of mouthfuls had calmed the shakes, and I wanted to keep a clear head.

'Once this property deal has gone through it will all be different. I'm a respectable businessman, Steve. But I've never had the breaks. Once you're in the big-time property business, money prints itself. I just need this break to get in. You can't blame me for that.'

Deakin took his drink to the window and looked out

239

across the desolate abattoir towards the river. Until today, he must have been seeing riverside apartments and spacious lofts. Now they were just rusting cattle pens and dilapidated slaughterhouses again. He leaned forward, as though something had caught his eye in the car park, and then turned to face me again.

'Have you told the police what's happened to Karen?'

'Not yet. Karen's dead, and another half-hour won't make any difference to her. But the way things stand, I'm on the hook for this, and you're going to get me off it.'

I could see that he was trying to decide what to do. He lowered himself into the big swivel chair behind the walnut desk again. This corporate opulence was the habitat Brian Deakin must always have imagined himself in, but he didn't look right in it. The chair was too big for him, and he seemed to have shrunk since I walked into the office and implicated him in a murder.

'What do you want me to do?' he said.

'Ring the police. Tell them what you and Robey have been up to. And tell them about the call you made to Robey this afternoon to warn him that I was going to get Karen Pearson to blow the whistle on you both. Tell them about the methods Robey uses on people who get in his way. And I'll send them to talk to Ann Humpage. She can give them a description of the men who took Karen away. I'll still have to spend a couple of days in the cells explaining this away,' I said, holding out my bloodstained hands. 'But if you and Ann back me up they'll get to the truth in the end.'

I handed him the phone. 'The number's 999. A dead woman and a couple of killers roaming the city should count as an emergency.'

I was standing with my back to the door. Before Deakin could dial, the handle hit me in the middle of the back and knocked me over. City buy quality carpets, I'll give them that. I hadn't heard anyone coming, either.

'Put it down, Brian.'

It was the first time I had the chance to study Robey closely. Looking up at him from a prone position on Jack Cox's carpet, he seemed bigger than I remembered. He wore a suit that was somewhere between the Bond Street tailoring Deakin favoured and the razor sharpness in vogue with the players. He looked like the kind of used-car dealer who would sell you a car in the morning and then come round and steal it back at night. He wore a glass smile, the sort you can see right through to the tough sneer behind it. Robey was the type whose personality needs twin lines of defence in case one of them breaks down. Like Weller, he also needed jewellery to increase his sense of self-worth, although he might have been wearing the rings on his right hand because a knuckle-duster was too conspicuous.

A pair of feet passed my head, and someone reached down and pulled the telephone plug from its socket. The feet belonged to Darren, last seen reading the tabloids in the glass booth at Quaynote Securities. He wrapped the cord neatly round the phone and placed it on the windowsill. Then he took up his position with his arms folded and his back to the door, to stop either of us getting past him. It was a task he seemed comfortable with. He probably began his career as a bouncer.

'Get up,' said Robey.

I got up and looked at Deakin. I should have guessed that he had seen Robey's car turning into the car park. Deakin seemed relieved that Robey had arrived and taken on the responsibility for what to do about me and the inconvenient matter of Karen Pearson's murder. Robey was clearly the stronger character in their partnership.

'What's he been telling you, Brian?' asked Robey.

'That the girl is dead. Why the hell did you get mixed up with her, Charlie? If you'd left her alone nobody could have traced anything back to us.'

'I can tell you why, Brian,' I said. 'Charlie doesn't let his employees step out of line.'

It was clear that Deakin didn't know what I was talking about.

'You thought all this was your own idea, didn't you, Brian? When you heard that Karen had set Marco up, you realised that by getting Charlie here to set up some of the other key players, you could force Jack Cox out and take over the chairmanship again. But Charlie was one step ahead of you. He'd already started perverting the course of justice, hadn't you, Charlie?'

I didn't feel as tough as I sounded. Robey was a danger-ous man at the best of times. With an undiscovered corpse on his mind, it was impossible to predict how he might react. But for the moment he let his fixed grin widen into what passed for a bitter laugh.

'Justice? Do you know how much the blokes who work for me get for being up all night, having people puke down their dinner jackets and pushing beer glasses in their faces? Two pounds twenty a fucking hour, that's how much. And the fucking footballers at this club get paid a fortune for putting in ninety minutes on a Saturday afternoon. Where's the justice in that?'

'Somebody else with a social conscience,' I said. 'I bet the only reason they won't have you in the Salvation Army is that their dress sense is better than yours.'

'Don't try to be funny,' said Robey. 'Darren doesn't like comedians. But don't let me stop you telling Brian why I couldn't let Karen back out of the deal with Marty Weller. When I know how much you know, I can decide what to do with you.'

He would have guessed anyway, so I looked at Deakin and said: 'Karen Pearson was a model and an upmarket tart employed by the White Rose Agency. Have you met the agency's proprietor, the starry Estelle?'

'Estelle Robey?' said Deakin.

'How many Estelles can there be?' I asked.

'You've been, told not to be funny,' said Darren. He jabbed his finger into my shoulder and it felt like a broom handle.

'You knew this scam was already in the family, didn't you, Robey? Estelle had supplied Karen to Weller. If she dropped the charges against Marco, the police might have wanted to know why. And Estelle might have found herself in the dock for anything from running a brothel to perverting the course of justice. Karen had to be persuaded to come back on board.'

'Karen Pearson was a little tart who'd do anything for money,' said Robey. 'Nobody will lose much sleep over her. There are plenty more where she came from.'

'Listen,' said Deakin. 'I don't want anything to do with this. I told you a hundred times that your strong-arm tactics would get us into trouble.'

'Shut up, Brian,' said Robey. 'You've needed a steel rod up your arse for years. If you'd been tougher when you owned this football club you'd be a rich man now, instead of Jack Cox's office boy. You could have bought a distillery for that dipso wife of yours. You owe what money you've got to me. I built up Quaynote Securities for you. Do you think you can do that without a few people getting hurt? It's a war out there in the security business, but you sit here in your comfortable office and pretend you haven't noticed.'

'But you needed Brian as much as he needed you, Charlie,' I said. 'Until he bought into Quaynote Securities and gave you a sniff of the biggest property deal in town, you'd had to scrape a living where you could – selling drugs in the clubs, pimping for the girls at the sauna, running the odd protection racket . . . It was better than working for a living, but it was never going to make you a rich man, was it? That's why you couldn't afford to let anybody get in the way of Brian taking over the football club again – not even one of your wife's high-class tarts.'

'You *have* been doing your research, haven't you?' said Robey.

'But do you think Brian would have kept you on the payroll once he got his hands on Jack Cox's shares?' I said. 'You would have become superfluous to his requirements once the property deal went through. He would have dumped you, Charlie. Brian would have been a respectable businessman then, a real mover and shaker. He wouldn't want to be associated with a torpedo like you.'

Torpedo? I know, I've been watching too much Jimmy Cagney. But if I could drive a wedge between them I might be able to divide and rule. Except this wasn't a dispute between equals. Robey was the President of the United States with an aircraft carrier on station in the gulf between this office and the bar, and Deakin was the commodore of the Isle of Wight yacht club.

'Is that right, Brian?' said Robey. The toughness flashed through the smile like the beam of a lighthouse.

'Listen, a woman's been killed, Charlie. We're in big trouble. We need to work this out together or we all go down for a very long time.'

'What's this "we", Paleface?' said Robey.

In different circumstances I might have smiled and revised my opinion of Charlie Robey. A man who watches *The Lone Ranger* and has the bottle to use the Tonto joke under stress is worth two stars in my classification system, although being a pimp, drug-dealer, extortionist, blackmailer and generally corrupt and violent bastard does admittedly count against him a bit.

'Seems like you and the Singing Detective here are the ones in trouble. If that's Karen Pearson's blood all over his hands and vest, his fingerprints will be all over her flat. And I wouldn't be surprised if the nosy cow who lives next door saw him leaving.'

'There's nothing to connect me to that girl's murder,' said Deakin. He was starting to panic now. And even Darren was turning out to be less tough than he looked.

'It wasn't murder,' he said. 'It was an accident. She fell.'

But Robey was still in control. 'Shut up, Darren! The only person who's got anything to worry about is Steve here.'

He turned to Deakin. 'Listen, Brian. If we stick to the same story, we're in the clear.'

'We haven't got a story.'

'Yes, we have. You'd lost patience because Jack Cox was doing fuck all about the accusations against top players. You said so to all the papers. So you sent Steve here to persuade Karen to withdraw the charges against Marco. Unfortunately, he got a bit heavy-handed, and now she's dead.'

'Do you think the police will believe that?' I said.

'With all the evidence stacked against you, why should they believe anything else?' said Robey.

'Somebody probably saw you arriving at her flat with Karen in the back of the car.'

'So what? Like you said, she works for my wife. Estelle likes to look after her girls. The streets of this city can be dangerous after dark. We were just seeing she got home safely. When we left her flat, she was alive and well.'

It seemed a flawless argument. There was still Dumpy, of course. They had told her they were going to kill Karen. But for all I knew they had been back to Dumpy's maisonette already to keep her quiet. My prints were all over her place, too. It wasn't looking good for me.

But it would get worse.

'Listen, Charlie, if I start lying to the police, that makes me an accessory,' said Deakin. 'You're not getting me involved in this. I don't want anything to do with murder. I'm going to the police now, before we get in any deeper.'

'No, you're not, Brian,' said Robey. 'You're going to tell the story I've just given you.'

He glanced at Darren, who placed his hand on Deakin's chest and pushed him back into the swivel chair. Robey's scheme had clearly bucked Darren up. It would get him off a manslaughter charge at the very least. His face was already showing that happiness and nastiness are not necessarily conflicting emotions.

'You can't cover something like this up for ever,' I said. 'You can't kill somebody and leave no trace. There'll be some of her blood on your clothes, some dirt from your fingernails in her wounds. They'll find it. Forensic science is brilliant these days.'

Who was I kidding? I watch *Rough Justice*. I know how many people are eating prison food for crimes they didn't commit.

I seemed to have convinced Brian Deakin, though.

'Steve's right. And I'm not going down with you, Charlie. I'll put my hand up to getting you to set the players up, but murder is another thing altogether.'

Robey perched his backside on the corner of the desk, and the smile took centre stage on his face. And that's not just a lazy theatrical metaphor. I could see, now, what Shakespeare meant when he said that a man could smile and smile and be a villain.

'Brian, you don't fucking well deserve it, but I'm going to get you off the hook *and* keep the property deal on the stocks,' said Robey.

That kind of self-satisfaction is annoying enough at the best of times, but more so when it comes from someone who has every justification for being a smug git. Robey had the power to do what he was threatening, and I knew he was ruthless enough.

And Deakin's expression showed that the prospect of a lifeline still interested him. Robey raised his hands and eyebrows and gave that ironic little shrug of the shoulders that means *I'm going to do something nasty but nobody will be able to blame me for it.*

'We're going to hand Karen Pearson's murderer over to the police ourselves. And he won't contradict your story or ask them to carry out DNA tests on us all. Because he'll be dead.'

Deakin looked more frightened than ever. 'What do you mean?'

'We're paid to provide security in this stadium. Steve's broken in here after dark. If we were to chase him and he fell from the TV gantry at the top of the stand and ended up in bits in the car park, we'd only be doing our job, wouldn't we?'

It was my turn to feel the fear churning up my stomach. 'Listen . . .' I said. I made a move towards the door, but I didn't get far. Darren had years of experience dealing with drunks who wanted to get into the Roxy without a pass-out. I presented no problem at all.

Deakin poured himself another drink. 'I'm not being party to anybody getting killed . . .'

But Robey wasn't listening. He clearly liked the sound of his own plan, and you couldn't blame him. The only fault I could find in it was that it was my body that would be spread over several parking bays. And these Levi's were almost new.

'It'll be more bad publicity for the club, of course. But when the police find Karen Pearson's blood mixed with his own on Steve's T-shirt, and then they find Karen dead in her flat, we'll have put a killer out of circulation and saved the legal system the cost of a trial. It won't do Quaynote Securities' reputation any harm at all.'

Deakin swallowed another finger of Bell's. I could tell he was thinking about Robey's suggestion. The man was smarter than I had given him credit for. From everybody's point of view but my own it was neat. Get me out of the way and Karen's death would be accounted for, Jack Cox would sell his shares in City to Deakin and the property deal would go ahead.

But to his credit Deakin couldn't stomach the thought of cold-blooded murder, even after half a pint of Scotch.

'Come on, Charlie. You can't be serious.'

'Never more so, Brian,' said Robey. 'I'm not asking you to shove him over yourself. All you need to do is keep your mouth shut. That shouldn't be difficult when the choice is between going to jail for ten years or making ten million quid on a land deal.'

He didn't wait for Deakin to reply. He turned to Darren.

'Pour him another drink and lock him in the liquor store until it's all over. And make sure he doesn't take his mobile in there with him. We don't want to put temptation his way, do we?'

Darren took Deakin's phone from his inside pocket. His future was no longer Orange, but mine was looking distinctly black.

'Check Mr Strong's pockets for a mobile as well.'

'I haven't got one,' I said.

'No, you don't look successful enough,' said Robey, 'but

we'll just check anyway. And don't touch his shirt, Darren.
We don't want to destroy any evidence, do we?'

Darren stood in front of me, blocking out the light. I
wondered what was going through his mind. If he'd already
killed Karen Pearson today, a second killing wouldn't make
much difference to him, particularly if it conveniently
removed the only person who could convict him. There
was now no evidence of the panic that had briefly flawed
the polyurethane paint-job of this hard case a few moments
before. It wasn't murder that had been troubling him but
the prospect of getting caught. I raised my arms while he
ran his hands over my jacket. They were strong hands. If
he squeezed any harder I would have burst open like a
pea pod.

'He's clean,' said Darren.

It was life imitating art again – the sign of another misspent youth watching television. You can pick up language like that only from movies. Unfortunately, they are
usually violent movies, and just now I would have preferred Darren to have misspent his youth in a snooker
hall or behind the school bike sheds with the wrong sort
of girl.

He led Deakin out through the bar to the liquor store,
clutching his tumbler of Scotch. Maybe the liquor was
softening the edges of his conscience anyway, but I sensed
he was relieved at the way things were turning out. Robey
was doing his dirty work for him again, and by locking him
up was absolving him of blame and guilt and giving him an
alibi for my own impending death, which was worthy of the
Lavender Hill Mob.

Robey stood guard on the office door. I wondered if he
could see that I was shaking with fear. The Scotch bottle
was open on the desk, but I knew that what I needed was
a clear head, not a drink.

Robey watched me patiently and silently, indifferently even, like a member of a firing squad for whom a dawn execution was something to pass the time until breakfast. He had let the smile slip. It must have been hard work holding it there, because the malevolent look was his natural expression, the bedrock to his Mount Rushmore.

I sat on the desk, facing him, remembering the time I had first seen him in the directors' bar, chatting conspiratorially to Brian Deakin. Almost everyone else had ignored them, because all eyes were on Jack Cox. But Charlie Robey was the sort of man you ignored at your peril.

Any moment at all, Darren would be back, and they would frogmarch me up to the television gantry at the top of the stand. Struggling would do me no good because the pair of them were far too strong for me, and shouting would be useless because there was no one else in this vast stadium. If I were to get away from them, it had to be now. Robey was too big for me to get past. But at least there was only one of him. I gave Darren thirty seconds to reach the liquor store. Then I made my move.

The bottle of Bell's crashed to the floor as I swung my legs across Cox's desk. It was a shocking waste of good whisky, but in desperate times sacrifices have to be made.

I yanked open the sliding door and ran through the bar. The element of surprise had given me a few yards' start on Robey, and Darren was still pulling down the steel shutter on the stockroom. I took the stairs three at a time and sprinted along the corridor beneath the stand to the main entrance through which I had entered the stadium. The catch was still up on the Yale lock. I pulled on the door, expecting it to open, but it didn't. I hadn't noticed that there was a Chubb further down the doorframe. Robey must have had a key and locked it.

There was a phone on Carol's desk. I would call the police. But even as I picked it up Robey burst into the foyer. My first instinct was to throw the phone at him, but it was one of those flimsy lightweight things and you'd need to chuck a red kiosk at Robey to make any impression. Then I had a better idea.

I jerked the phone from its socket and ran to the trophy cabinet. There were wires coming through the glass at the top. With any luck, it would be alarmed.

The phone was heavy enough to smash the glass at the second attempt. It crashed in icy slivers to the floor, but after that there was a deathly silence. No jangling bells, no flashing lights. Shit! I should have known. Would you bother switching on the alarm when all that was in the cabinet was the Yorkshire Senior Cup?

I looked round in panic. There's nowhere more crowded and comforting than a football ground at three o'clock on a Saturday afternoon, but there's nowhere emptier or more frightening when you are sharing it with two men who are out to kill you.

Robey stood at the end of the corridor, patiently watching me again. The grin was back on his face, and Darren was now coming towards us as fast as sixteen stone of muscle can move. The only way out was down the players' tunnel and on to the pitch.

It gave a whole new meaning to the term 'pitch black'. With no crowd and no floodlights, it was a dark, silent void.

I ran to the centre circle. It was the most visible spot in the city on a Saturday afternoon. Now it was the only place to hide. As I looked around me, the vast roofs of the stands blocked out all the light except for the ambient glow of the city beyond the stadium's rim. It was like watching a hundred-and-eighty-degree sunset that would last all night.

They didn't follow me at once, and that made me uneasy. I wanted to know where they were. I stood listening to the silence and to the dull hum of traffic in the distance. But silence is like a vacuum. Things keep trying to get in: the creak of a girder contracting in the cold, the rattle of an insecure window in the breeze, the scratching of pigeons' feet under the metal roofs of the stands . . . Then the tunnel doors were flung open, and a shaft of light shot *noir*ishly out along the half-way line like a searchlight beam. They were in no hurry; they knew I couldn't get away.

But I felt safer out in the open and in the dark. I couldn't see them, but they couldn't see me, either. If I climbed into the stands and hid under one of the banks of seats and didn't freeze to death through the remaining twelve cold hours of a November night, I might be able to stay hidden until morning, when the groundstaff would turn up for work again.

I was clambering over the advertisement boards that ran the length of the touchline on the other side of the ground when the flaw in this logic became blindingly apparent. One by one, somebody was switching on the floodlights. And with the unlikely irony you would never believe if you read it in a novel, I found myself silhouetted astride a billboard advertising life insurance.

I dropped down behind the board, but I knew Robey had seen me. He was standing at the mouth of the players' tunnel waiting for Darren, who I assumed had been sent to switch on the lights. I had no idea what to do now, but running away was what came instinctively. So I did.

I've always wanted to run down the middle of the City pitch with an open goal in front of me, but this wasn't exactly what I had in mind. I was running towards the kop end, where as a kid I used to stand on the concrete terraces with my dad before they put the seats in and the admission prices up.

They say your past life flashes through your head when you are about to die. Well, I was getting the edited version. I remembered the little piles of grassy shit left by the police horses in the streets as we walked to the ground. I remembered bouncing up and down to the pop songs that came over the Tannoy before the game started. I remembered queuing for Bovril and meat pies at half-time and watching tiny flames flickering all round the darkened stands as people lit cigarettes in the crowd. (And to think I gave up smoking because I didn't want it to shorten my life expectancy.)

I glanced over my shoulder and heard Kenneth Wolstenholme utter yet again the most famous words of the twentieth century. *There are people on the pitch; they think it's all over*: Please, God, don't let Robey and Darren complete the sentence for him.

They were following me, but without much urgency. They knew there was no way I could get out. My stomach felt as though I had just eaten a five-course meal in an Indian restaurant after a night at the pub, and my legs seemed unable to carry the extra weight. My thighs were like jelly.

A song came into my head, because cheap music has always been there before you no matter what the circumstances. 'Nowhere to Run'. I had heard Martha Reeves singing it over the Tannoy in the good old days when City were getting beaten at home by Tranmere Rovers and Crewe Alexandra.

I was still singing it manically to myself as I scrambled over the advertising boards behind the goal, a classic piece of displacement activity from a man whose true predicament was too awful to contemplate. I realised I was heading instinctively towards the one floodlight pylon that wasn't lit up, the one I'd seen men working on earlier in the day.

Whoever said you should always trust your instincts was talking through the wrong orifice. It was the one place in the ground I shouldn't have gone to. In any of the other corners, the glare of the lights might have dazzled Robey and Darren and given me the few minutes' invisibility I needed to think my way out of this. Instead, I was in full view and cornered.

I stood beneath the pylon's galvanised girders watching the two of them come towards me. At my back, the turnstile gates were all closed and secured with chains and padlocks. To both left and right my escape was barred by high steel fences put up to deter hooligans from hand-to-hand fighting with the opposition supporters.

As I stood there, Martha and the Vandellas faded out to make way for Yazz, whose only hit had also been blasted over the Tannoy in the years when City were languishing in the lower divisions. 'The Only Way is Up'.

I took Yazz's advice and started climbing.

The new floodlights were the latest expensive ground improvement Jack Cox's millions were paying for. The girders felt icy beneath my palms, and I noticed that the intricate pattern the galvanisation process left on the steel looked like fresh frost on a car roof.

I knew the trivia that kept entering my brain was part of some deep-seated psychological defence mechanism, implanted to take my mind off my own impending death. But I couldn't block it out for ever. All I would achieve by climbing this pylon was a few extra minutes before Darren followed me. And being flung from the top of a floodlight pylon by big Darren would have the same effect as falling from the TV gantry. My talents would be spread over a wide area.

As I climbed I felt something digging into my thigh. I put my hand in the pocket of my jeans and touched the tape I'd taken from Karen's answerphone. I'd forgotten I had it, although it wouldn't do me much good now. When the police scraped me up from the terraces they'd find it and play it back and recognise Charlie Robey's voice and search his car and put strands of Karen's hair into plastic bags like they do in the movies and piece together her last hours, and I would be transformed from murderer to saint. Some consolation. I've never wanted to be a hero, but I've wanted to be a posthumous hero even less.

About twelve feet from the ground a notice said DANGER OF DEATH BY ELECTROCUTION with a picture of a skull and crossbones to emphasise the point. Beyond that was the ladder the electricians used to reach the maintenance platform and the bank of lamp units at the top of the structure. I grabbed hold of the bottom rung of the ladder and paused.

Robey and Darren were approaching as calmly as a couple of workmen arriving to finish a job. I knew that people who went out and killed other people in cold blood existed. I've read about them in the newspapers. But they belonged to a parallel universe, not the comfortable place I'd always known.

I could now see over the stadium wall to the rooftops of the city in which I was born and grew up. Things like this didn't happen here, not in the world of department stores and offices and quiet residential suburbs in which I lived. But I had strayed outside that world and was discovering it was just part of a big, anarchic anthill full of people looking for that bit of extra leverage that would carry them to the top. And if it meant treading on the bodies of others, that was the way it was.

Half-way up a floodlight pylon on a freezing November

night probably isn't the best time to contemplate the nature of evil, but I realised I was dealing with evil here.

Deakin and Weller and Jimmy Farrell were all bent in their own ways, but they still belonged to the same world as Beth and me. They weren't above a bit of ankle-tapping when the referee wasn't looking, but they knew the rules and there were limits to how far they were willing to bend them. Robey was different. Robey had the courage to ignore the rules if they got in his way. Robey was playing a different ball game. If his only means of getting where he wanted was by picking up the ball and running with it, Robey would invent rugby.

He and Darren had reached the foot of the pylon and were looking up at me. Next to them was the yellow generator the workmen had been using and a few bits of broken concrete. Robey was wearing his insincere smile again.

'You ought to be careful going up there, Steve,' he shouted. 'You might fall.'

From where I was standing I was looking down on the face of evil, but if I'd learned anything from this case it was that we all have our own justification for breaking the rules. I doubt if Charlie Robey knows anything about philosophy, but if he did he would probably describe himself as a utilitarian, a subscriber to the belief that the end always justifies the means. From Robey's point of view, killing me was just the lesser of two evils, a single, audacious act that would put an end to something worse, like dropping the atom bomb on Hiroshima.

I was all that stood between Robey and a share in ten million pounds that would mean he would never again have to demand protection money or deal in drugs and women. My death would provide him with enough to keep his wife Estelle in designer outfits for ever and to convert him at a stroke from a gangster and a pimp into a legitimate businessman. But this gravy train would pass his station only once, and if he missed it he would remain a petty crook for the rest of his life. If I were standing where he was, killing me might seem like a perfectly reasonable proposition.

So there was no point in trying to plead or reason with him. I knew what would happen next. I've seen *North by Northwest* fourteen times. Darren would climb the pylon after me. We'd grapple at the highest point. One of us would slip and tumble to his death, and the law of averages dictated that this time it wouldn't be the bad guy.

I took a few more steps up the ladder and watched the city extending beneath me, stretching away as far as I could see. It was bleak and cold out there, and the clear sky was full of stars. There was nothing to stop this puny pool of light being sucked into the vast, frozen emptiness of the universe. Even the psychological comfort blankets were being withdrawn. Communism has crumbled. The churches are empty. Mere anarchy is loosed on the world. I think somebody may have used that line already, but you get the idea. This city was no different from any other big city in the world. Cold-blooded killings happen every day in Johannesburg and Rio and Miami, so why not here?

I reached the maintenance platform, but they were making no attempt to follow me. Instead, Darren was doing something with the generator, while in that parallel world beyond the stadium walls, life went on as normal. I could see the headlights of the traffic sliding by on the main road.

And if I could see them, they could see me.

It was worth a try.

I climbed on to the frame that supports the floodlamps and inched my way along it, my petrified face staring back at me out of each of the chrome reflectors. The last bloke

I saw do this had a Millwall scarf round his neck and eight pints of lager in him. But if I could get to the end and lean out and wave, I would be silhouetted against the most powerful lights in the city. Someone might see me and think I was another hooligan and call the police. Or more likely the fire brigade to get me down. I didn't care. Any emergency service would do. Even an AA man on a motorbike would be very acceptable.

The generator started up with a throaty roar that almost startled me into losing my balance. What the hell were they up to? I peered down between my feet and wished I hadn't. It gave me vertigo, and my hands were so numb I could barely feel the safety rail.

Oh, shit! Why hadn't I realised that they would think of this? It was so simple, such an elegant solution to their problem. They didn't need to climb up after me and risk the struggle at the top of Mount Rushmore. All they had to do was get the generator started, hook a piece of live cable round the pylon and I would light up like a neon sign.

Darren was already hauling some cable towards the base of the pylon.

The klaxon they use in all those U-boat movies began sounding in my head. *Dive! Dive! Dive!*

I scrambled back along the gantry and reached the top of the ladder. Darren was now getting ready to lash the bare wires to the steelwork.

I didn't know whether to walk or slide down the ladder. All I knew was that if Darren connected the cable to the generator, I would vaporise in a split second. I wondered if the rubber soles on my shoes would protect me if I tried not to touch the ladder with my hands. Or would I just fall off and break my neck? Don't think, Steve, I told myself. Just get the fuck down from here as quickly as you can.

When I reached the bottom of the ladder I would jump. I might break my leg on the concrete, but what the hell?

Darren was on the point of connecting the cable to the generator. I got ready to jump. The ten thousand volts that would surge through my body would probably throw me off anyway.

But before I had summoned up the courage to leap, there was a blue flash and I knew that was it. It was Goodnight Vienna, as they say in soccer circles. I never did understand what it meant, and now it was too late to find out.

It was followed by another blue flash. And another. And another. And by the sound of a siren in the car park.

I saw Darren look at Robey, wondering what to do.

And I heard Robey say: 'Just do it. *Now!*'

But the moment's hesitation was long enough. I let go of the pylon and leaped. As I did so I heard the crackle of a powerful electric current surging through the metal. There were more blue flashes as the high voltage arced across the gaps between the steel girders.

And then the wind was knocked out of me.

But Robey had broken my fall. I was winded, but I could stand up. Beyond the stadium wall were more flashing lights, fusing together into a solid wall of blue light. There was a symphony of sirens, and then a deafening bang as the fusebox in the generator blew and the surge of power died away.

Robey was clutching his shoulder. He seemed to have fallen badly. Darren was running down the cinder track at the edge of the pitch. But the only way out was the way we had come in, down the players' tunnel. And four policemen were now emerging from it into the floodlights' glare.

He didn't bother trying to evade them. He knew there were reinforcements in the car park. They arrested him

as calmly as if he were a fan who had run on to the pitch
during a match to remonstrate with the referee, and they
led him down the tunnel.

I started to walk towards the two remaining policemen,
but I seemed to be floating over the cinders. The rush that
a reprieve from certain death brings is incredible: better
than any drug, better than alcohol, better than sex. At
that moment I understood why people played Russian
roulette, knowing how good it must feel to hear the soft
metallic click of the firing mechanism that tells you your
brains haven't been blown out. I even envied prisoners
on Death Row, who live with the exquisite possibility that
someone will walk in to their cell one day with a paper
signed by the governor and release this tremendous high.
I had been suddenly handed another thirty or forty years
of life. It was the best present I would ever get, and the
only people I could thank for it were these two coppers.
I could have thrown my arms round them, but an English-
man's restraint is not a matter of life and death. It's more
important than that. So I settled for shaking them by the
hand. The nearest of them responded. But when he held
his own hand out there was a handcuff round his left wrist,
and he snapped the other end round my right one.

Even that didn't bring me down. Nor did the realisation
that Sod's Law was in operation again, and the copper to
whom I was handcuffed was one of those who had arrested
me as a stalker in Karen Pearson's flat.

He said: 'You keep turning up like last night's curry in
somebody else's flowerbed.'

I said: 'Am I fucking glad to see *you*. They were going to
electrocute me.'

His colleague said: 'Another one been let out under Care
in the Community?'

'We had this one in a week or so ago. Stalking some lass

whose picture had been in the papers. He seemed fairly sane then.'

His mate said: 'They usually do.'

'Did you spot me up there on the floodlight gantry?'

'We were already on our way. When a burglar alarm goes off in the police station we generally respond if we're not too busy.'

'I thought it wasn't wired up,' I said. 'It didn't go off when I smashed the glass.'

They looked at each other as though I were a bit simple.

'We've found that gives the game away a bit. People put two and two together and run away before we arrive. Even people like you.'

He wasn't calling me 'sir' this time, which should have warned me of what to expect. But it didn't. When you know you've done nothing wrong, you forget that policemen trained to be suspicious can jump to the wrong conclusion when they find you on somebody else's property with a couple of known criminals and broken glass all over the hall and blood down your shirt.

'Listen,' I said. 'You've got the wrong end of the stick.'

There was a sergeant in the foyer and four or five squad cars outside the door. They were putting Darren in one of them.

'Take 'em both down in the same car,' said the sergeant.

'Hang on a minute . . .' I said.

'Are there any more out there?'

'There's another down on the kop, sarge. He looks to have broken his arm. This one reckons they were climbing up the floodlight pylons. I've radioed for an ambulance.'

The sergeant looked at me. 'Bit old for that sort of game, aren't you, son?'

'You should see some of the ageing hooligans we get at matches, sarge.'

They started to take me out to one of the cars.

'You can't just take me away. They've locked Brian Deakin in a storeroom behind the bar!'

'You what?'

They made me show them where he was. The sergeant came with us, and I told my story as we climbed the stairs to the directors' bar. When I got to the bit about Karen Pearson lying dead in her flat we stopped in mid-flight. The pocket radio came out and there was a lot of static and some serious conversation with senior officers. One of the constables was sent to release Deakin, and I was taken back to the foyer. They handcuffed my left wrist to a second policeman. The mood had changed dramatically. I had ceased to be a nuisance, an amusing incident in a night's work, and become a suspected murderer. They were particularly interested in the blood on my shirt.

'Right, you. Let's get you down to the station.'

'I can still walk,' I said, as they dragged me towards the door. Our wrists were rubbing together, which is more intimate than I care to be with a man in a uniform.

'Listen, Robey and Darren killed Karen.'

You can only stay grateful for so long. Now the high was wearing off and I was starting to get angry.

They were used to it. They probably learned the technique for dealing with it in basic training. Well, it was a pretty basic technique, as it happens: they just ignored me.

The Yorkshire Senior Cup stood among the shattered glass in the trophy cabinet.

'One of these days City will win summat worth pinching,' said one of my escorts as they threw me into the back seat of a police car.

'The police haven't been getting great results lately, have they?' I said. 'What's the latest score? Birmingham Six, Guildford Three?'

Chapter Eighteen

It seemed quite witty at the time, though it cost me an extra couple of hours in the cells. Still, what's two more hours when you've already been there two days? And it was beginning to feel quite homely. I was having the papers delivered and everything.

It took the police that long to eliminate me from their inquiries. They hardly mentioned the incident at the football ground. All they were interested in was the murder of Karen Pearson, and because I was seen leaving her flat ten minutes after she died with her blood all over my shirt the idea that I had killed her took some shifting.

They trained the big guns on me to begin with, a detective chief inspector and a sergeant who did the nice guy/nasty guy routine you thought TV scriptwriters had made up. Tom Tomlinson sent me a lawyer, and he was good, but it didn't exactly level the playing field. The interview procedure had a satisfying symmetry from the police's point of view: I was expected to tell them everything; they told me nothing at all.

I didn't know what Robey or Darren or Deakin were saying. I didn't know if the police had spoken to Ann Humpage or Marty Weller. It was like needing three points to avoid relegation on the last day of the season and not knowing how the other teams were getting on.

So I lay on the cot in my cell between interviews, staring at the ceiling and calculating my place in the suspects' league table from the stray bits of information that drifted into my possession.

1. The woman in the flat next to Karen's had heard a struggle and had seen me leaving some time later. She recognised me as the man who'd tricked her into giving me the key to Karen's flat before. *(Source: the police.)*

2. Jack Cox was paying for my lawyer so they knew I was on the club payroll and not just a homicidal maniac with an obsessional interest in blondes and football. But that wasn't enough to lift me off the bottom of the league.

3. The *Post* carried a story saying that City would be at full strength for the second leg against Ajax. The charges against Naylor, Bartola and Gary Allen had all been dropped, though they didn't seem to know why. 'Mystery surrounds' was the term Tony Wilson used. But I knew it meant that Deakin had come clean. I made a mental note to phone Tony Wilson with the full story when I got out. I owed him that.

4. Beth started to be nasty to me again.

She was surprisingly wifely and solicitous when she came to see me the morning after I was arrested, and for once her immaculate grooming and the expensively subtle scent she wore didn't seem like self-indulgence but a breath of fresh air, a lifeline to civilisation.

When she saw the inside of my cell she burst into tears, as though she couldn't believe how far the standards of décor and soft furnishings fell below those of the hotel she'd stayed at in the Lake District. She had brought clean socks and underwear in one of those stiff brown-paper carrier bags that are the only kind the style-conscious will be seen with these days, and she sat on the cot beside me and put her arm round my shoulder and said sensible and comforting things about how it was only a matter of time before they let me go.

'I know we've been through some bad patches, Steve, but I want you to know that I'm still here for you when you need me.'

I'd been expecting long-suffering exasperation, as that was the standard response our social intercourse had been generating over the past few months. But her visit actually made me feel a lot better. It was almost like going back to the first couple of years of our marriage.

'You'd have made it a lot easier for yourself if you'd phoned the police when you found Karen's body' was the nearest she came to telling me what an idiot I'd been. 'But don't worry. This is England. The police will get at the truth in the end.'

It didn't seem like a good moment to point out that television series about people found guilty of crimes they didn't commit were currently screening on all channels.

When she'd gone, the self-pity that comes with the off-white tiles in a police cell hit me. Private eyes are supposed to be hard-boiled, but the sand was still running through the egg timer in my case. I was still decidedly runny. I stared at my reflection in the vandal-proof stainless-steel lavatory bowl and listened to the tap dripping into the play-house-size sink and wondered why we hadn't been able to make it work. When Beth was like this, I could still be quite fond of her.

What I forgot was that sympathy has the shortest half-life

of any substance known to man. In this case, it lasted less than twenty-four hours.

It must have been something she learned about the gravity of my situation from the desk sergeant on the way in. Beth was much more like her old self the following day.

'I warned you what would happen when you started this private investigator business, Steven. I mean, it's not as though it's a proper job, is it? All this could be very embarrassing for me if you appear in court. You can pick your underwear up from the launderette. A service wash is a pound extra, but I didn't have time to wait.'

The fact that Carol King was just leaving as Beth arrived probably hadn't helped.

5. Carol said she told the police how concerned I'd seemed about Karen's safety when I tried to ring her from the stadium, and she thought they believed her.

6. The chief inspector stopped turning up for the interviews and the sergeant was left to do it on his own.

7. He asked me for the umpteenth time to go over what had happened when I'd got to Karen's flat, but this time he listened as though I might be telling the truth.

8. The woman in the flat next to Karen's remembered seeing two men arriving at the flat with Karen about half an hour before she saw me. (*Source: the police via my lawyer.*)

9. My lawyer told me Dumpy had told the police about her call to Quaynote Securities.

'She's identified Robey and Darren as the ones who took Karen from her maisonette. She even told the police the make of car they were driving. She's a real hard one. She could be charged as an accessory, but she showed no remorse.'

'She's had a lot to put up with,' I said.

Now that Karen was dead and she'd levelled the scores, I don't suppose Dumpy cared what happened to her. It could scarcely be worse than the life she was already living.

10. The police started calling me 'sir' again.

'You might yet be charged with failing to report a suspicious death, but in the meantime you're being released on police bail.'

It was two hours before the arresting officer came back with the paperwork, but that would teach me to make tasteless jokes about the police, wouldn't it?

It didn't spoil the rush I got walking out of the police station into the late-November sunshine. The senses of freedom and a mission accomplished must be among the most intoxicating combinations known to man. I can remember feeling like this only once before. Walking out of school at the end of my O-levels with eight weeks of summer ahead of me and the knowledge that, against all expectations, I'd managed to answer four questions on the geography paper.

Actually, there was no sunshine. There was just the usual watery soup that passes for weather round here in late November, but it felt like sunshine. If the weather carried a list of ingredients in small print like jars of pasta sauce, water would have been at the top (*vide* pasta sauce) but with exhaust fumes and factory emissions in there for flavour and just a smidge of residual bonfire smoke for added piquancy.

I sucked it all down hungrily, anyway, as I walked back to Beth's flat. It would have been nice if she'd been there to greet me, so that I could complete my fantasy of a soldier arriving home at the end of a long war. But she wasn't, so I phoned Tony Wilson at the *Post* instead.

He was almost puppyishly keen to get the story, and childishly anxious that I hadn't given it to anyone else.

'I don't *know* any other journalists, Tony.'

When I'd told him the full tale he started asking me, as journalists do, blindingly obvious questions like how it felt to have cracked such a high-profile case and what I thought having four key players back in the side for the second leg with Ajax would mean for City's chances. I know why they do it. They need to put your words in quotation marks to prove they've spoken to the main man. And it's also useful to be able to point the finger at someone else if the story turns out to be a load of balls.

But I wasn't complaining. The prospect of seeing my words in print and being written up as the hero of the story didn't feel too bad at all.

Then Tom Tomlinson phoned to thank me and to tell me that Jack Cox had authorised a 'consultancy fee' of 5K in recognition of my good work.

I filed away 'consultancy fee' because it sounded like the sort of bullshit that would impress Beth. But 5K! My God, that tiny expression spoke volumes about how far both Tomlinson and I had come over the past couple of weeks. I'd gone from being skint to having a cheque for five thousand quid in the post. Tom Tomlinson seemed to have discovered untapped resources in his language bank. Instead of 'a few bob' he was talking 'K'. He'd be buying an electronic organiser next. So why did it not seem like progress?

It was downhill all the way from there. Beth came home and started to be nice to me again, which is as good as a gale warning for Irish Sea and Humber on the shipping forecast as a barometer of impending calamity.

I told her about the five thousand quid and the publicity I'd be getting in tomorrow's *Post*.

'That's great. I'm really glad, Steve.'

But it was encouraging in the way that mothers are when their kids bring some horrible splodge home from school and they pretend it's better than Rembrandt and blu-tac it to the kitchen wall.

'The publicity should bring in loads more work,' I said.

'You're going on with this private investigator business?'

'Where else could I make this kind of money? And there'll be another round of free publicity for me when the trial comes up.'

'Mmm!' she said.

But her look was that of a woman who'd been enduring a nasty smell from the drains and was now being told by the builders they'd have to be dug up again next week.

'Are you sure about all this publicity, Steve?'

'Why?'

'It might count against you when you go for an interview for a proper job.'

'I've got a proper job. Consultancy fees and everything. Besides, there's no such thing as bad publicity when you're in business.'

'I thought bad publicity is what you've been trying to save the football club from for the past fortnight.'

'Yes, I know, but . . .'

'Anyway, I'm really, really pleased for you, Steve. Now you'll be able to put a deposit down on a flat of your own. You'll need a spare room for an office if you're going to do this full time.'

'There's no rush,' I said.

'Listen, Steve. I didn't like to mention this while they

were keeping you in the police station. But I've met someone else.'

Someone else?

Why did that stop me in my tracks? We're getting a divorce, for God's sake, so another bloke was bound to be on the shopping list when she got round to it, like another packet of amaretti biscuits when you've eaten the last one – no hurry, but they're nice with a cup of coffee now and then.

'You've what?'

'Don't sound so surprised. I met him on that weekend course in the Lake District. He's an accountant.'

Of course he bloody is. And another thing – aren't women supposed to send Dear John letters while their husbands are still away at the war, not hand them over as they walk through the door in their demob suits?

I went to see Mum and Dad because I always want to do something worthy when I'm feeling sorry for myself. It's pure self-interest, really. You join the sympathy club so you'll get something back when they have the share-out at the end of the year.

But on the way to their house I was sidetracked by the ambulance and fire engine and police cars outside the maisonettes, and the crowd who'd come out to gawk.

Whatever had happened must have happened a while ago, because the street kids had mainly lost interest in trying to peer over the heads of the crowd at the bit of striped plastic tape that had been tied between two metal stakes to cordon off the scene, and had started climbing about on the fire engine.

The ambulance was already leaving, although there was no siren or flashing lights.

I realised at roughly the same moment that this was Dumpy's flat, and that my dad was among the onlookers.

'They were both dead,' he said when he saw me. 'You could tell by the way they carried them to the ambulance with their faces covered up.'

He was quite enjoying it, as people who find themselves in a position to be first with bad news usually do.

'It'll have been fumes,' he said. 'From the gas fire. Paper in all the windows to keep out the draught, door fastened. Your flue gets blocked up, you've no chance.'

He gave his verdict as though he'd spent a lifetime in the health and safety department of the gas supplier rather than as a dispatch clerk in a food warehouse.

'Both together in one small room, you see,' said someone next to him, anxious that my father shouldn't hog all the pleasure of the telling.

How did they know all this? It was amazing how information got around. Any journalist arriving on the scene would probably be met with a wall of official silence, but a crowd manages to piece together the full story in moments.

Except I knew they'd got it wrong. I knew now why Ann Humpage had been stuffing paper into the cracks in the windows the last time I was there. This was no accident. She'd taken her revenge on Karen for abandoning her, and in doing so had lost the only friend she had ever had. So now she'd killed herself and her son.

It would be described in tomorrow's papers as a tragedy, but when I tried to put myself in Ann Humpage's place I realised it was nothing of the sort. This quiet, peaceful death must have seemed infinitely preferable to the lives both of them had to look forward to. She probably died happy, in a perverse kind of way.

I didn't say anything. It would all come out at the

inquest. But I bet when they discover what is blocking the flue of that gas fire in the boy's bedroom, allowing the carbon monoxide to build up silently and odourlessly until it filled the room and suffocated them, it would be a screwed-up copy of the freesheet with which she had sealed the windows. Freesheets and Rizlas were the only papers Dumpy could afford.

I walked back to the house with Dad. I'd come across a few amoral bastards during the past two weeks. It was ironic that the insignificant Dumpy had turned out to be the biggest of them all, the one who'd really left her mark on the world. But when you looked at the self-justification each of them had trotted out to me, Dumpy was the only one who had any excuse at all.

Back home, Dad squeezed added value out of the affair by repeating it all to Mum, though his pleasure seemed weaker the second time around, like a reused tea bag. For Mum it was just one more thing to worry about.

'And to think you used to go to school with her.'

'Yes,' I said.

'And with that who-is-it they found murdered.'

'Yes,' I said again.

'You just don't know what's going to happen, do you?' she said. The bad breath of the world's iniquities had wafted a little too close to her for comfort. She'd be mithering for weeks now whether the gas fires in their house were safe.

I didn't feel strong enough to explain the connection between the deaths or my own involvement, though I wondered how she would gloss that to herself when she read about it in the *Post* tomorrow.

'I felt sorry for this one,' she said, referring to Dumpy. 'Not married. And that kiddie she had weren't right in the head. So happen what's happened is all for the best.'

'Yes,' I said.

Dad had settled himself in front of the TV. I took the tea and sandwiches Mum had made, the consumption of which seemed more important to her than my actual presence, and sat beside him on the sofa.

'Fancy coming to the Ajax game tomorrow night?' I said. 'I can get us a couple of tickets.'

'I think I'll just watch it on this,' he said. 'Then you don't have to queue up for your tea at half-time.'

Which was the right answer.

I felt duty-bound to ask him, while my credit at City was still good for free tickets. But the person I really wanted to go to the match with was Carol, because I needed the emotional support of a woman more than ever now that Beth had found somebody else. So his decision to watch the match on TV left me in the best of both worlds – with the righteous glow of having done the right thing, and the satisfaction of doing what I really wanted to.

Carol got us a couple of tickets in the stand, and for the first time in weeks Jimmy Farrell was able to field his strongest side.

It was the former Liverpool manager Bill Shankly who said, 'Football's not a matter of life and death – it's more important than that', and as I watched the players run out I finally understood what he meant. A few evenings earlier, I had risked my life for City beneath these same floodlights. Now I realised that the five-thousand-pound bonus Jack Cox had paid me was not that generous, when every player out there would be earning at least that for this match alone.

Brian Deakin had chosen his victims well. City looked a far better side with Marco and Bartola and Gary Allen and Vince Naylor back in the squad. Naylor began stretching the Ajax defence with his overlapping runs down the right wing, and the bite was back in his tackling now he no longer had a GBH charge hanging over him. Pierre Bartola was as relaxed and immobile as a couch potato in midfield, but with the same control over what was happening in front of him, changing the channels of the City attack at will with a languid flick of his boot. And Marco and Gary Allen upfront looked pacey and sharp and threatened to open up the Ajax defence every time the ball was played to them.

But the goal that would give City the advantage was a long time in coming, midway through the second half. Bartola to Naylor on the right, who takes it to the corner flag. His cross evades the central defenders and falls to Marco on the far post, who nods it back for Gary Allen to scramble it in off a defender's legs.

I would have preferred a volley into the top corner from twenty-five yards, but when you are desperate for a goal in a European cup tie, I'm with everyone else in the stadium on this one. Anything will do. The thunderflash that lifts us all into the air with an explosion of joy goes off no matter how scrappy the goal.

I decide against hugging Carol. A reprise of what happened between us after Gary Allen's goal in the first leg two weeks ago might be embarrassing in front of forty thousand people. Besides, 'away goals count double' has a different meaning tonight. If Ajax score, they go through instead of us. And there's still plenty of time on the referee's watch.

So we drum our fingers on the seat in front and rub our hands to warm them even though they're not cold, and wriggle our toes inside our shoes and indulge in all sorts of other displacement activity as they throw men forward looking for an equaliser. Then the whistling starts all round the stand to persuade the referee the ninety minutes is up, but he adds what seems like ages on for stoppages. So when the final whistle goes, the roar is even louder than it was for the goal.

And the Americans want to widen the goals and raise the crossbar so that it becomes easier to score. Don't they realise that this is such a beautiful game precisely because it *is* so difficult to score and therefore every goal is precious? They've got a lot to learn. There's more to civilisation than a few skyscrapers.

We sat and waited for the crowd to disperse. To leave with the herd would dissipate the extra glow we had as City insiders. But I didn't want to go to the directors' bar. Brian Deakin was still helping the police with their enquiries, and his wife was presumably having to look elsewhere for her complimentary drinks, but there would be plenty of people there to ask me questions I was now tired of answering.

The *Post* was full of the story of Deakin's arrest and my role in his downfall. It also reported that Robey and Darren had been charged with manslaughter. Tony Wilson was even perceptive enough to link the deaths of Dumpy and her son to it all. It was a thorough piece of journalism, but I had spent too long talking to the police about it to want to go over it again, even with Jack Cox.

When the stands had cleared and the only sound was the last straggle of reporters phoning over Jimmy Farrell's after-match quotes from the press box, I said: 'Fancy a drink?'

'If you like,' said Carol. 'But not here.'

She sounded a bit down, as though the reaction that always follows an emotional high was setting in already.

We walked into the city centre. It had been raining,

and even the wet streets wore City scarves, the sodium lamps striping the blacktop with gold. The pubs around the ground were all full, but the gangs of youths surging through the streets singing were just drunk on City's success. I understood now what Jack Cox meant about spending his money to make people happy.

The bar we went into had been an Irish pub the last time I saw it, when every other pub in the city centre was called O'Connell's or McGinty's. It was now one of those post-modernist places with functional furniture and exposed ducting and knowingly naive 1950s design values and a great range of European beers that actually taste of something. There were chalkboards on the walls advertising relentlessly trendy food like artichoke hearts and chargrilled sweet peppers. I'd thought these places were wonderful when the first one arrived, but now there were so many of them I was looking for a reason to dislike them.

Carol gave me one.

We had been fencing with each other over a spritzer and a Budweiser (the Czech real thing), avoiding the knowledge that now the case was finished I had no reason to turn up at her desk, and if this wasn't going to be goodbye, one of us would have to do something about it.

'It's getting late,' she said when she finished her drink.

I looked at my watch. 'We could take a bottle of wine to your place.'

It was like a droplet of water reaching the bottom of a pane of glass. It had to change direction, and I had no idea which way it would go.

She moved closer to me and started fiddling with the metal loop on my jacket zip. (We were standing up because the place was full of people who had been to the match.) She took a deep breath and stretched her mouth into that expression that has the same shape as a smile but somehow you know it isn't, and stared at a spot in the middle of my chest.

'Listen, Steve . . .'

Why do women become the people you always wanted them to be – harlots with a heart of gold – when they are about to give you the big E? Is it because the knowledge that they will not have to deliver takes the risk out of simpering sexily?

'. . . you remember the bloke I was talking to when we went to the opening of Scorer's?'

'Eamon Doyle?'

'Yes . . .'

'But he's a footballer. An ex-footballer. They're either overpaid bastards or they end up running pubs in Heckmondwike. You said so yourself.'

She smiled apologetically. 'Yeah. Well. He runs a pub and he makes a lot of money, actually. It's been a success. They're going to open another place soon.'

'And I'm a success,' I said. 'It's in all the papers.'

She grinned and squeezed my arm. 'Yeah, but he's a better long-term prospect. He doesn't live as dangerously as you.'

'You don't fancy a replay of the other night, then?'

'Tonight's match wasn't a draw, was it?'

Raymond Chandler couldn't write dialogue like Carol's, but when you're the one on the end of the emotional put-down you don't appreciate the style with which it is being delivered.

'I'll see you home,' was all I could find to say.

'I told Eamon I'd go out to Scorer's after the match. I'll get a cab.'

I went outside with her and flagged one down and watched it go.

A moment ago it had been late. Now it seemed very early. The night seemed to stretch ahead for ever.

I decided to go to a club – preferably one where there weren't any footballers – and get blind. I had a cheque for 5K in my pocket. I could afford it.